The Boy on The Hill

By Brent Luke Augustus

2020

1. A short visit

My grandparent's house had once been one of the largest in the area. They used to own a good thirty acres behind them, which my Grandfather sold while my Grandmother was in London one summer. Before that, there were only a handful of families who lived on Applewood Hill.

The sale of the acres had allowed several other properties to be built on one and two acres plots.

After the strategic sale, the area had sprung up in giant houses all over the hillside. Each house built up higher on the rising hill, with forest being taken out to make room for more houses. My grandparent's house was in the middle of the first street on the hill. It once stood out like a shining beacon as we drove into town, usually under cover of night.

"Still, all lit up I see." My mother said with contempt. Grandmother kept an electric candle glowing in every window. According to mother she did it to ensure the large white house stood out from the others. All of the houses were quite nice, but Grandmother took every measure to make sure their house stood out a little more. My mother said my grandparents purchased the hill and built their house there so my grandmother could rule like a queen, sitting in her castle above everyone else. The sale of the acres was like a personal affront to the aging woman, but Grandmother and Grandfather were constantly doing things to aggravate each other.

My Grandmother wasn't the most friendly woman. She had a very specific sense of how people and children should behave, and only she and her children ever measured up to that standard - though you might not know it listening to her talk to any of them as adults. It seemed to me that everyone was a disappointment in her life. Somehow, they all failed to make the impact on the world she always intended them to make. They all fell short at raising their own children in her sight as well.

My older brother Joseph came closest to perfection of any grandchild to that point far, and he delighted in that fact. Straight A's, always knew just what to say, and when to say it. He was allowed to sit at the adult table

1

during holidays and just generally followed her around, kissing up, asking her pointless questions about things and people he couldn't possibly have an actual interest in.

Grandmother took it upon herself to correct the many parenting mistakes being made in her grandchildren's lives. My mother seemed to hate it more than anyone in the family. No one was safe from Grandmother's meddling, yet no one would openly oppose Grandmother the way my mother did. My mother was not hesitant to throw herself on the pyre at any moment if it would ruffle a feather or two of Grandmother's.

Our car rolled to a stop in the long driveway. The driveway was put in with the intent of parking a dozen cars, so Grandmother could entertain hordes of people for her many parties, charity events, and community meetings. She was heavily invested in such things, to the extent that it suited her own agendas and promoted her position in the public spotlight. This weekend was a family event where all family were to attend. I was sure I would have no fun, as there were no cousins my age in the family.

The long driveway was lined with well groomed, flower bearing bushes of all sorts. The yard was carefully maintained and impossibly green. The grass was cut on perfectly cut crisscross diagonals. The entire estate smelled like a basket of fresh cut flowers.

"Joseph! Jeffery!" Grandmother called from the step, waving in a mechanical manner, that barely resembled a greeting. "Dennis. Sharon," Grandmother said with a more formal tone.

"Hello, mother." I had never heard my father refer to her as anything other than mother. Calling her 'Mom' was as out of the question as it was for the grandchildren to call her anything but Grandmother. Perish the thought that even a two-year-old call her gram, granny, gam'ma, or any other variation of her proper title.

"Mom," And my mother refused such formality and always referred to her as 'Mom'. I suspected it was because it got under Grandmother's skin.

"Well don't loiter in the drive, come inside," Grandmother urged as we struggled with our bags. "You know your way to your rooms, you can put your bags and clothes away. Jeffery, there will be no hiding figurines in your room this stay. I would hope we have grown a bit in maturity since

2

last you came." Grandmother and Grandfather collected figurines and carvings during the many travels. I often found the figurines to play with, in distant corners of the huge house. I always aimed for small ones on low shelves, the ones she was sure to not notice. The large ornate ones of value were kept on higher shelves where people were sure to see them and ask about their nature. Anything of importance was kept behind glass, away from the reach of grandchildren. The trouble was I sometimes forgot to return the figurines to their places before she noticed or sent Kim to clean my room.

Kim was a Korean girl who cleaned and cooked for Grandmother. I never understood a word the woman said, and I was pretty sure her name wasn't even Kim, though I never heard her correct anyone. She was always nice enough to me, but she was frequently the reason I got caught doing things I shouldn't.

Walking in the front doors always felt like stepping back into time. The front doors were behind two large black iron gates that stood open during the day but closed over the doors at night. While open during the day, the black iron stood out against the gleaming white exterior of the house.

The entryway and front parlor were covered in ornately trimmed wood from floor to ceiling, and was always so dimly light that your eyes took a minute to adjust before you could make out any detail.

It was a long walk through the front of the house. Our rooms were upstairs at the top of a long dark stairway at the back of the house. It went up to a series of rooms no one ever saw, some of them I had never seen.

When we were a bit younger, Joe and I tried to track down the keys that opened the rooms. We thought that treasures may be kept in those rooms, or perhaps antiques like spinning wheels, looms, and maps that lead to treasure! Still, for all of our efforts over the years, we were never able to get into that part of the house.

There was another part of the house we never entered, and no one had ever wanted to go. Older cousins made us paranoid about the long staircase that went deep down under the house. I spared a cautious glare as I passed the hallway where the staircase descended. The lights to the basement stairs were always off, and cool air flowed up with a damp scent that testified of the dungeon we knew to be below.

We had made a game out of seeing who dared to go furthest down the stairs. We also tried to shove each other all the way to the door to see if they'd get far enough down to not be hurt by the fall. At the bottom of the stairwell, the wall was not made of plaster like the rest of the house, it was cold, smooth stone of various browns and grays. The doorway was a splintery wood with stark contrast to the rest of the refined house - with its lacework curtains and finely polished wood and stone work. The large door was a darkly stained, solid wood.

It was likely where the wine was kept, but we had been told by older cousins that they had uncovered an Indian burial site when building the house. To avoid complications with building code, they had sectioned it off and left the half open graves encased in a stone vault. They then continued to build the house around it. I wasn't sure what to believe, but it gave me the creeps anyway. I tried to talk myself into calmness as we moved by.

"Hi, Granddad," Joe said walking just ahead of me as he passed through the parlor before reaching the rear stairs. Grandfather huffed in vague acknowledgement. He was sitting at his large wood desk, looking at newspaper clippings.

"Hi, Grandpa." I smiled.

"Hey boy." Grandfather winked at me. He was a thin gnarled man who must have been one hundred years old. He looked as if the great depression still had hold of his gaunt physique. Despite Grandmother wearing silks and floral satins, he often milled about in a rich green robe or red flannel button up shirt with suspenders holding up his green polyester pants. Grandfather usually barked replies, or nonsense words at family, friends, and hired help alike, but for some reason, he always spared me a wink or nod as he chased away my cousins and Joe. Sure he included me in his torrent of shouts to get out of the strawberry patches or cherry trees, but he always gave a pause and a sideways smile to let me finish stuffing my mouth full first.

Grandfather had suffered a long hard life, and I had every sympathy for his long-suffering, giving him the benefit of the doubt that below his gruff exterior was a softer side. Still, I wasn't about to hug the old bean pole or anything.

While Joe followed Grandmother around like a puppy, I took to noticing when Grandfather retreated to the carriage house to tinker at his massive long tool bench. I asked about ancient tools hanging on the peg-board.

I picked up on old time slang from Warner Brothers Cartoons which amused Grandfather when I tossed them around. It was probably why he suffered me longer than my more self-centered, vastly more obnoxious cousins. He even saved me from being exploited or beaten up by older cousins on a number of occasions.

Grandfather didn't like people being taken advantage of. He was nothing if not principled. If you could say he had a favorite grandchild, or could stand one of his forty-something grandchildren the most, I liked to think I was that one golden child. I was to Grandfather what Joe was to Grandmother, which suited me just fine.

"I guess I better get to work in the tool shed before you rotten kids start destroying the property," Grandfather said getting up from his desk. I took that as an invitation to come visit him if there was time before bed.

We hefted our bags up the stairs - one stair at a time, resting between pulls. Normally we would get our own rooms, but we had to share this weekend with all the family that was coming into town. We would be lucky if we weren't kicked downstairs to sleep with the other kids in one large room that would be chaperoned like an orphanage dormitory.

When we reached the top of the stairs we dragged our suitcases to a familiar room with flowered wallpaper. We quickly unpacked and stuffed our clothes into the large old dressers in the room, it smelled of cedar chips, masking the smell of century-old wood.

We headed downstairs to say goodnight and heard other cars arrive in the driveway. There was a soft bustle downstairs as relatives brushed by each other. You did not run, yell, or otherwise have fun inside Grandmother's house. Adults were gathering in the dining room around the large ornate claw-footed dining table. They were telling stories about grown-up matters that did not interest any of the kids.

"All of you children are going to bed promptly. Line up in the kitchen for your vitamins," Grandmother barked. We all groaned as we lined up. Grandmother fished a giant bottle, that almost had to be called a jug, from a pantry. She doled out the nasty pills into reluctant hands. The vitamin was a horrid chalky-chocolatey supplement. No one knew what health purpose it served, really, but that it had everything growing children needed. Some of the older kids smiled as they popped them and made a display of chomping down on them. There was no use fighting Grandmother on a good number of things, and the daily vitamin was one of them. My parents would turn me right around to her and force an apology if I resisted. I felt sick as the vitamin hit my tongue.

We were dismissed and I dragged myself back through the house. Joe walked with cousin Jeremy, trying to block me behind them in the hall.

"It works huh?" Jeremy said with a grin.

"It's great!" Joe replied.

"What?" I pried.

"Nothing. Not for kids." They laughed. I noticed Jeremy toss something down the cellar stairwell that looked like a white stone... or a large horrible vitamin. *That didn't make sense. I saw them chewing! How had they pulled that off?* If you got caught trying to hide the vitamin you were in danger of being swatted, or worse yet, the vitamin could melt into a paste, pressed in your cheek and teeth! I still found it best to just chomp down and swallow the gritty shards before it had time to moisten.

I let them run up the stairs and stopped at the window in the parlor. Grandfather's shed light spilled through a crack in the door. I wondered if there was any way to slip out unnoticed...

"In bed," Christine, a teenage cousin, barked. She was a tall, well-built girl who, like her mother, forced her opinion on anyone smaller than her, which was almost everyone - at least among the cousins. Christine's twin, Christopher, was quite the opposite and older than Joseph but nearer my size and weight. "What are you doing? Stealing from Grandmother?" Christine accused, searching my person with her eyes.

"What? No! I was looking out the window." Christine peered at the window sill. Satisfied Grandmother wouldn't keep anything valuable on the window, she raised her eyebrows over her round glasses.

"I don't care what you were doing. Children are to be in bed," she chirped.

"Last I checked you were a child too!" I stuck out my tongue and ran to the stairs before she could come after me.

"Mother!" She darted out of the room. I didn't care, her mother barely remembered which one I was, the few times a year she saw me run past her in the kitchen or on the patio. What would she do?

The rooms upstairs were full of whispers of cousins trying to conspire methods to stay up late and not get caught. I was sometimes jealous they were all so close in age, and had fun telling secrets and stories, and joking around. The girls huddled and talked about boys, the boys boasted tall tales about girls they kissed or exaggerated sports plays they made. I played quietly or tried to inject myself into their games and conversations by standing a careful distance away, and not talking, so as to be included by accident.

Jeremy and Joseph were standing in the dimly lit hall, whispering. They paused when I reached the top of the stairs. I continued on to our dark bedroom shooting them a look that said, *"I know, I know. I'm not invited."*

I climbed into bed and fished in my pocket for a tiny golden elephant with jeweled eyes. I didn't lie to Christine. I hadn't stolen it, I simply borrowed it. I frequently borrowed that same elephant when I visited as well as a small ceramic knight and a tiny porcelain panther. The elephant was often in a new place each time I visited, usually on an end table or corner of a desk down low where I had easy access. A few times it was up high on a shelf where I had no chance of getting it without making a scene. I assumed Grandfather had put it in the window sill where he knew I would find it. He seemed to be the only person who noticed my frequent borrowing and didn't swat me away or land me in trouble.

The soft hall light glimmered in the tiny elephant's ruby eyes. It made his gold coating glimmer and softly glow. I stroked the red enamel blanket that covered his back. As I recognized sleep setting in, I clutched the elephant tight and put a fist under my pillow.

I woke to the sounds of rapid knocking moving up one side of the hall and down the other, "Wake up! Wake up! The sun is up!" Grandmother chimed as she walked the hall. "I'm alive and well today, as Jesus made me this way!" It was a saying Grandmother commonly shared in the morning.

I threw on a robe, tucked the elephant in my pocket, and slipped downstairs before Grandmother had reached my door.

Downstairs smelled of eggs, bacon, breads, and fish. The aromatic signature of trout was a sure sign that uncle Harold had arrived, which would be much to the dismay of Grandmother's sister, Aunt Bessie.

I wasn't sure what Bessie's real name was, but I was sure it couldn't be Bessie. That wasn't a real name. She was younger than Grandmother but certainly looked years older with her thin frame. If Grandmother was prim and reserved, Aunt Bessie was next-in-line for the throne of England. The way she went on about propriety and expectations from everyone in the family, children, and grandchildren alike, she surely had royal blood. She had a much softer tone of voice than Grandmother, but somehow she seemed to look into your soul and know exactly what you were thinking. Perhaps it was her careful selection of words.

The refined Aunt Bessie turned her nose up at the traditional appearance of fish at breakfast, and often refused to go inside the house until she was convinced the scent had fully departed.

Aunt Bessie and Uncle Jacob had their own designated room when they visited, as the idea of sleeping in a bed that someone else, even family, had slept in was abhorrent. That was the main reason she didn't stay in a hotel to avoid the traditional trout breakfast.

I had no real problem with the trout itself, but the smell of it cooking was not the most appetizing of aromas. I wasn't about to put the fish on my plate next to my bacon, but I wasn't going to let it keep me away from food.

Adults were sitting around the long dining table. Kids were gathered around the kitchen table, sitting on benches and chairs. Everyone seemed to be talking at once, while Kim stood at the stove, cranking out eggs and bacon, toasting and glazing breads, swatting at hands darting for pastries on the counter as they walked by. "Grown-ups only!" she scolded Darrin.

"I just want a half a Danish." he pleaded while his sister, Karen, slipped a plate full of scones behind Kim.

"Those are for parents! Kids sit at table!" Kim said wagging a finger at Darrin. I imagined Kim got paid three or four times her usual pay while the family was all in house, and probably thought about going back to Korea by the time we all left. Then again she probably had to pay Grandmother back every time a grandchild made away with an extra dessert or broke a glass, knowing Grandmother.

I quietly took a small plate of eggs and bacon from the counter and slowly faded out the back of the kitchen, through a sitting room where Uncle Tom was sitting with cousin Mark. They were smoking their pipes next to the open window, newspapers all over the lounge. Under the papers were a sea of small decorative pillows, adorned with lace, beads, and crystals. Their velvet material sure held in dust and the faint scent of whatever perfumed water sat out on the claw-footed coffee table. The pillows were hard, horrible for lying on if you were drawing, but did they ever make for a good weapon when wielded properly in a pillow fight! It was amazing, the welts one could leave on an attacker's face when the correct amount of force and back-spin was applied. We often used the long yellow ones for jousting matches or swords. Of course, it was like a muted version of a knight's battle, as you had to be able to hear the footsteps of an adult and to return the pillows to the long lounge or love seat quickly before someone entered the room!

"That's going outside," Uncle Tom shot me a look over his glasses.

"Of course," I said innocently, carefully walking through the room. This was one of the last rooms you wanted to spill food in. The runner carpet from the kitchen to the back door was an elaborate weave Grandmother brought back from England, it almost matched the large one in the middle of the room. The back door was open, but the large black iron gate was closed to keep the dogs from getting in while keeping the air moving. The gate weighed more than I did, even on its squeaky hinges.

"Well hello, Jeffery. Come give your Aunt Bessie a hug." I paused, then set down my plate on a small metal table.

"Hi, Aunt Bessie," I hugged the frail old woman. We had to be getting close to the same weight even though she towered over me. She was

9

wearing a loose, pale pink, knit shirt and white pants. Her glasses must have been framed with pure gold as their tiny frames were almost blinding when the sun hit them just right. A matching tiny gold chain connected each arm of the glasses and looped around her neck to hold them if she took them off, which was rare. She also wore a thin gold chain necklace that held a tear-drop diamond with a gold fastener.

"Have you come to eat on the patio with your Aunt Bessie, you dear boy?" Not wanting to disappoint her or upset some elder custom of which I was unaware, I masked my discomfort.

"Yeah!" I faked a smile.

"There's no fish under those eggs, is there?" She peered at my plate while managing to keep her nose turned up, just in case.

"No ma'am," I smiled.

"That's right, you are the other in the family with the good sense to keep away from such horrid things," she nodded.

"Yeah."

"The word is *yes*, dear," she corrected me, settling back into her chair.

"Yes," I paused with fork in hand, unsure of the proper etiquette for eating scrambled eggs on a patio. I decided to just go slow and careful. I supposed I should eat my bacon with fork, rather than fingers, so as to not upset her.

"Tell me, what adventures have you been having?" She inquired.

"Me? Oh, I don't think I am allowed to have adventures."

"Oh, nonsense!" She leaned forward. "The life of a boy is meant for adventure. I'll bet you play knights of Arthur's Court... or spaceman! My boy's loved to play spaceman, or what do you call them... astronauts!"

"I play Transformers?"

"Oh? That sounds interesting. Tell me, what do you transform into? I always wished to transform into a bird. A cardinal, though red isn't too lady like!" She giggled with her hand over her mouth. I wasn't sure what was so funny, other than the fact that she thought Transformers were people who could turn into animals, which made me laugh along.

"I would turn into Bumble Bee," I smiled.

"Oh! A bumble bee would be a fun one too! Zipping all around, making honey all day." I was amused! I imagined me as a robot car and her in a poorly fitted bee costume! It was hard to not laugh while putting bacon in my mouth.

"Jeffery, I hope that isn't one of my good plates you have outside," Grandmother poked her head out the door. She was wearing a blue shirt with a black cardigan sweater.

"Oh leave the boy alone, Rose. He is the only one of that brood in there who has bothered a whit to greet his great Aunt in her exile!" Bessie huffed.

"You are welcome inside at any time," Grandmother stopped her. "Return that plate the moment you are finished, Jeffery, in the same condition, you found it." She warned.

"Yes, Grandmother," I replied as I ate a little more quickly.

"I will never understand why you insist on that fish fry. It's as though you wish to see me suffer!"

"Oh, come! How many times did we have fish as children? Once a week or better?" Grandmother put her hands on her hips.

"Worse! That is precisely why I shouldn't be exposed by force at my age!" Aunt Bessie leaned back in her chair with exasperation.

"Forced." Grandmother laughed. I quickly shoveled food while the two bantered. I watched the verbal tennis match with amusement. The two were constantly locked in banter. Sometimes it was playful, sometimes it turned into a team match focused on a third party, and sometimes it ended with Aunt Bessie leaving in her shiny town-car, swearing she would not return to the house ever again.

"As if that bears sway. Do you do your own gardening, Rose?" Grandmother reminded me of some kind of bird, the way her head bobbed when she was engaged in arguing. It was quite a thing to see, because Grandmother was always poised and unshakeable, but she let go of that and fought like siblings do as soon as Aunt Bessie came to town.

"What does that have to do with anything?" Aunt Bessie waved her hand around.

"Just because we were forced to do something as children, doesn't mean we must relive circumstance for the sake of nostalgia!" I finished up and carefully slipped between the two.

"Don't run, Jeffery." Grandmother barely looked away from Aunt Bessie to instruct me.

"I won't!" I slowed down and carefully stepped inside.

"Delightful chat, Jeffery!" Aunt Bessie beamed, waving just her fingers at me as I slipped into the house. I was happy to leave the two to hash out the beginning of their weekend long quarrel.

The smell of a full bodied coffee brewing filled the air inside and helped cut the fishy smell. I returned to the kitchen and placed my nearly clean plate on the stack by the sink.

I slipped back upstairs and changed into black pants and an orange shirt. I slid down the stairs on my butt, bouncing as quietly as possible. I slipped through the house and down a hall to a side door.

The door came out to the side of the house where some older girls were sitting by a lilac bush, laughing and talking. I ran through the back yard and behind the carriage house where the fruit trees stood in rows. I climbed into the concrete-lined ditch that controlled the irrigation system for the fruit grove and garden. It ran along a fence where a large wood pile was stacked the length of the ditch system. The ditch had a number of evenly spaced pipes that diverted water across the fruit grove and into the garden rows. While the ditch wasn't flooded, it made a perfect hiding place behind the edge of the woodpile.

I carefully looked around, pulling out the gold elephant from one pant pocket and a GI Joe from the other. I fashioned a tiny shack using small pieces of old roof shank that were in the wood pile and placed the GI Joe inside. He was a rough looking, war-torn, soldier with shaded stubble, dirty fatigues, and sleeves rolled up.

"You're a bit out of place, aren't you?" the soldier said to the elephant.

"Well, you are in my jungle," the elephant replied.

"Aren't you worried about getting that blanket dirty?" the soldier nodded.

"No, not really. I have plenty more of them back at the palace."

"Why is a palace elephant way out here?"

"I took a walk."

"Are you lost?" the soldier stood up.

"I don't think so,"

"I don't see many palace elephants out here."

"I don't see many soldiers in my jungle."

"Your jungle huh? Listen Dumbo, when you are out here, this is no man's land. That goes for palace elephants too. Right now, you are in my front yard," the soldier folded his arms.

"Did you know an elephant can pick up a human and pound trees into the ground like tent stakes with them?"

"Did you know an army soldier can kill an elephant in over one hundred ways, with a pencil?"

"The ultimate weapon would be a soldier riding an elephant then," the elephant hinted cleverly.

"That would be pretty cool! Ok, you can stay," the soldier motioned him over.

"I was about to tell you the same thing," the elephant mused.

Suddenly there were voices coming. I used the elephant to knock down the tiny shack with a crashing sound effect, then shoved the figures into my pockets and sat on the edge of the ditch. Joseph, Jeremy, and Christopher came down the walk and around the corner of the building.

"What are you *doing*?" Joseph huffed.

"Nothing. Just messing around in the ditch," I shrugged. I was at that age where everyone older than me was finished playing with action figures. I still had a year or so left where it could slide, but my brother needed no excuses to tease me or make my life unpleasant. He barely tolerated me playing anything at home, but with an audience, it was his time to shine and show others just how far he could push me down.

"Why?" Joseph investigated.

"The same reason you guys are back here?"

"Whatever worm," Joseph smirked. "Why don't you get out of here?" Jeremy and Christopher smiled behind him.

"Why don't you? I was here first," I blinked.

"Whatever!" Joseph turned around to Jeremy and Christopher. "You got it?"

"He isn't going to tattle or anything?" Jeremy asked, nodding toward me.

"No, he knows if he does he will get a beat down!" Joseph stared at me. I replied by making a mocking face back and mouthing nonsense words.

Christopher pulled out a box of matches while Jeremy was fishing in his pocket. Grandfather was slowly, silently, moving around the corner. He was wearing a green shirt and black pants. His silver hair glinted in the sun. Moving carefully, he held a finger up to his mouth. I tried not to smile while I watched. Jeremy pulled a pack of cigarettes from his pocket and nearly flung it across the yard as Grandfather spoke!

"Are those your mother's?" Grandfather said loudly in the most gruff of voices. Christopher shoved his hands in his pockets, hiding the matches. "I might be old... I'm not blind and dumb! Give me those matches boy, they are likely mine!" Grandfather pulled Christopher's arm up and snapped the matches away from him. "Now, head back to the house, the lot of ya." With shoulders hung low the three older boys were eager to get out of Grandfather's sight as they hurried away. I smiled and followed his slow pace back up the side of the building nearest the fence. He paused to stretch his arms and took notice of one of his rose bushes growing on the fence. "Have you ever seen a Hawaiian rose?" He reached out and carefully touched an orange bud of petals.

"Nope," I strained to see up that height.

"It's this one here. When it finally blooms it will be yellow and orange and pink and red. It's hard to get them to grow here. They don't like the soil, and they don't suffer through a harsh winter easily. I have to keep them bundled up and insulated from the conditions to protect them or they don't make it. Uncover them too early and they get frostbite, too late, and they don't get the warmth of the sun, and bugs and moss start living on them. Other roses are hardier. Some of them like that wild rose down there... You almost can't kill them, they will grow anywhere you put them. They spring up in places you don't wish them to be. Can't get rid of them! They aren't much to look at when they bloom." Grandfather pursed his lips and turned his attention to the bush next to the Hawaiian bud. "These common red roses here, you have to work a bit at them and they are pretty enough, worth the effort for the most part. These Hawaiian's are my favorite, though. They take a lot of work, but when they bloom they sure are worth it." The lesson in botany was mildly interesting. I peered at the forming rose buds and wondered what the bloomed rose would look like. I looked down the row of rose bushes.

"How can you tell this one is the Hawaiian?" I questioned.

"You think I don't know my own roses?" Grandfather questioned me with raised eyebrows.

15

"No, like, how can you tell what kind of rose it is while it's closed up? They all look the same." I studied them closer.

"They might look the same... at my age, with my experience, you can look at them and know which is which early in the season. Before any other signs."

"Hmm," I pondered Grandfather's gift of discerning plants from each other. I suppose one day I might like to garden. Grandfather shuffled away as cars were pulling into the driveway and caterers appeared. The party was getting started. Soon there would be more people than I knew the names of! And more dessert than I could possibly be able to stomach.

2. Short Visits, Long Stays

The patio was lined with tables of food while lines of relatives picked through the buffet. The lawn was full of tables with white tablecloths and folding chairs. The family was broken up into generations. There were, of course, Grandmother and Grandfather's own children, and then all of the nieces and nephews, who were mostly in their twenties and thirties. Then there were all of the niece's and nephew's children. Joseph and I were near the end of all of the children, as my parents married late and started our family even later. I was dead last in the group of children.

Everyone milled about the garden. The total number of people easily broke one-hundred. Uncle Evan and Uncle Tom, my father's brothers, were carrying an upright piano through the house to the back door.

"You boys will tune that thing when you put it back!" Grandmother could be heard from some other room of the house.

"It's going to need to be tuned when I am done playing! Not from the moving!" Uncle Evan called out from behind the piano.

"Lift with your knees!" someone yelled from the dining room table.

"Yeah, thanks for the help!" Uncle Tom replied. I slipped out the door as soon as they were clear.

"Anyone seen Dad?" father asked a group on the back patio, closing the door behind he and his brothers.

"Oh, he's probably avoiding us all in the den or at his tool bench breaking a clock or something," Tom said with a smirk, and locked the wheels on the piano.

"Keep that in the shade," father pointed at the piano. Uncle Tom stood in front of it and played a quick jazz chord scale to see how in tune it was after the move.

"Very nice." Aunt Carol said as she brought him a bench.

"Thanks!" Uncle Tom began playing an old time jazz piece. He got hoots and hollers to the beat, and a few people tried to clap along. The musical performance wasn't an unusual thing to happen at Christmas. This was the first time I had seen them go to this length at the family reunion.

It was a fun tune to bob to. A few of the great grandkids, years younger than me, began to form a dance floor near the piano.

After a few songs, Uncle Evan found a guitar and strummed along with the lyrics to songs they both knew and made up. Sometimes, he changed the lyrics to what he thought were clever kid jokes. It largely bombed, for the most part, but most of the adults found it humorous. I sang along in my head to the ones I knew.

"I know you boys know more classical tunes than that pollution!" Aunt Bessie spoke up, uncovering her ears at the end of the song.

"Oh, I suppose," Uncle Tom began to play Fur Elise, "I don't remember that one!" he joked as he stopped playing.

"Me either!" Uncle Evan added.

"A jazz band isn't a jazz band without a horn section," Father said as he exited the house with a shiny brass saxophone. I had only ever seen him play a handful of times. It was a rare occasion indeed. Even more rare, all of my uncles were getting along well enough to come together in a musical ensemble.

I took to the table of food as they played on and sat near the piano where the notes could be felt in resonance. Nearly all of Grandmother's children and grandchildren were musically inclined, or at minimum, had enough years of lessons thrust upon them to uncover any musical ability. Uncle Russell was not musically inclined in the least, despite the years education in various instruments. Whenever a musical number broke out, he usually grumped sourly and pretended the music hurt his ears, excusing himself with a joke about his stomach suddenly being ill. He could usually then be found in the kitchen soon after.

"Where's your Grandfather?" Grandmother asked Christine.

"I'll find him!" Christine chirped and jumped up, eager to please.

"Have you eaten anything that was once growing in a garden?" mother asked me, poking at a pudding dessert on my plate with her own fork.

"Nope!" I grinned.

"Try to eat *something* green today, ok?" mother warned.

Christine ran from the carriage house to the main house. In a moment, her mother and father briskly walked from the house to the carriage house, looking at no one. I seemed to be the only one paying attention. In a moment her mother, Pamela, came back out and fetched my father. She whispered something to him urgently, and he raced off to the carriage house, leaving her to catch up. Father said something to Uncle Tom as he passed, who played a few notes that waned before he took a look around the crowded lawn and calmly rose, holding up a finger to say, 'one moment,' and then walked to the carriage house calmly.

"What's going on?" I asked my mother. Another hundred people asked each other the same question in a hushed buzz.

"I don't know." Sensing my father's intense mood, she smiled pleasantly. "Stay here, ok?" She walked to the carriage house doorway and came back a moment later. Her pleasant face gave away nothing. She touched my Grandmother on the arm and whispered something to her. Grandmother paused in her conversation and moments later, walked to the carriage house herself. My mother whispered to Aunt Bessy as well, who followed behind Grandmother.

Mother smiled with her hands folded, and loudly said, "Let's get all of the kids together and follow me right back behind all of the tables! I want you to sit in one biiiig, huuuuuge, giant circle, ok? Come on!" She motioned with both hands. "I don't care how old you are, everyone under eighteen. Come on!" She pointed at Joseph. Younger kids ran to the grassy spot behind the table while the older kids dragged their feet, searching for excuses, and told to follow direction by parents.

"Ok! Make sure you aren't touching your neighbor... We're going to play duck, duck, goose, but we're all going to close our eyes, until you are the goose and then you can open them to run around the circle, ok? Dale, you're going to be the goose first." Dale was an older cousin, probably sixteen or so, who was very quiet and usually off reading under a tree or something. He didn't look excited to be taking part in any type of activity.

I was never much for listening to instruction. I was a cheater and kept my eyes cracked and head tilted to the side so I could see. Mother stood back from the circle between the group and the corner of the carriage house. A group of people shuffled from the carriage house and in the back door with urgency. The grown-ups at the tables whispered softly. It was impossible to tell what was going on. Perhaps they had a surprise. A giant cake maybe, or gallons of ice-cream. Why else would my mother be trying to distract the crowd of children? We all played along, but the curiosity was getting to me.

It had been more than ten minutes when rumors started whispering around the circle of kids, like a game of telephone.

"I heard grandpa broke his leg,"

"They have an ambulance,"

"It was Aunt Shirley, she choked on some pop and almost died. I saw it!" I had seen Aunt Shirley choke earlier... But we had all been in the circle, so I wasn't sure how any of us had *heard* any rumors outside of the circle.

My father came over and whispered something to my mother. He looked grim, frantic. He walked briskly back toward the house. Grown-ups whispered to grown-ups, going back and forth between the house and tables. Most of them resided in the house.

While mother talked to one of the grown-up cousins, I slipped around the back of her and ran after my dad. I caught up to him easily enough as he walked around the side of the house. There was, in fact, an ambulance in the driveway. I slipped inside the house and down the hall near the scary stairway to the basement cellar.

When I popped out the hall I could see everything in the front room. Grandfather was strapped to a bed on wheels with a bundle of white blankets and black seat belts latched over him. He was wearing a clear plastic mask with green straps holding it on his face.

Grandfather's eyes danced around the room, trying to fixate on something, anything. He turned his head toward the hall where I crept behind a bookcase. His gaze fell upon me and his eyes stopped dancing around for a moment. He blinked and strained to focus. He wagged a finger at me from under the edge of the blanket. I waved back carefully. He muttered something, paused by a cough, and then he spoke clearly, looking me right in the eye.

"I'm not afraid, Jeffery." It was a strange thing for anyone to say. I peered at him, slightly slack-jawed. The EMT's and grown-ups weren't paying much attention to him, which I found strange. He was obviously in some kind of urgent situation where he ought to be the focus of attention.

Grandfather struggled to keep his gaze on, or near, me. His eyes danced around, not focusing on anything in particular, but they kept settling on me. I shifted against the wall and felt something in my pocket. I lifted out the golden elephant figure. Grandfather didn't strike me as the kind of person to ever be afraid of anything. I tried to work up the courage to run up and put the golden elephant in his hand. Maybe he didn't need consolation, but I still felt like I should.

Before I had the chance to resolve my courage, they pushed him away. As he moved out of the doorway, he winked at me.

I slipped out behind the caravan of people and darted behind the bushes out front, running along the large stone planters they lived in. I must have gotten too close to father as he suddenly noticed I was there, and he turned to catch me.

"Hey, what are you doing?" father asked, as casual as could be.

"I'm tired of playing duck, duck, goose. I want to go with you."

"Well... You need to stay with mom," father settled his large hands on my shoulders.

"Why?" They moved Grandfather to the back of the ambulance. He looked pale in the sunlight. "What's wrong with Grandfather?" I kept my gaze fixed on Grandfather.

"He had a little accident. I'm going to go with them to the hospital, and you will come with your mother." Father's instruction was plain.

"Ok," I replied as it seemed important that I not push the issue.

"Ok," father turned and quickly joined the EMT's in the back of the ambulance. As the doors shut, I saw father's head lower to his hands, fingers combing through his dark hair. I stood and watched as the ambulance pulled away. It seemed to move strangely slow as it got further away down the drive and then disappeared out of sight down the hill.

I stood on the front step for the longest time, as if I might be able to see the ambulance in the city streets below the hill. It felt as if I could just raise a finger and point right to them. I kept my eyes slowly drifting where I thought they would be, just in case they came into view.

I loved the smell of hospitals. It was a strange thing to love, and I never could explain it. They smelled like alcohol wipes and ammonia cleaner, which I loved. Joseph and I sat in chairs covered in fabric I didn't like the texture of. It was rough fabric, and seemed dusty. There was nothing to do while sitting in the lobby but count the ceiling tiles, over and over, for what seemed like hours.

"Was Grandfather awake?" Joseph asked me.

"I don't think so. It was hard to see his eyes. His mask looked like when Luke Skywalker is in the X-wing fighter." I imagined Grandfather in an X-wing fighter ship.

"Do you get what's going on? Probably not, cause you're just a kid," Joseph shook his head in frustration at my powers of observation.

"Shut up. I know what's going on." I pushed Joseph's shoulder.

"No, you don't. You never do." Joseph fixed his shirt sleeve where I had pushed him.

"it was an oxygen mask. That probably means a heart attack," I said flatly, my head resting on the back of the seat, nose to the sky. Joseph returned to resting his chin in his hands, elbows propped on his knees. I didn't exactly know what a heart-attack was, to be honest, but I knew it was something serious; as a person's heart was quite important!

As I was trying to find a faster way to count rows in pairs, my mother came walking up slowly. Joseph jumped up and met her with a hug. I was confused as to why, furrowing my brow. It suddenly set in that something was probably wrong when I saw mother's tear-stained face. Mother motioned for me to join their embrace. I slowly rose to meet them, and we stood in the lobby hugging, not a word spoken. Mother and Joseph shivered in tears, but I choked mine back. I fought hard to keep the sobs in side. No one had said the words that would indicate he was gone, it was understood, but they hadn't been spoken. Until they were spoken... I did not have to give in to the tears, to the heartache I could feel growing inside.

After some time, mother ushered us to the car in the parking garage. I loved parking garages. They always smelled like car exhaust and oil, which reminded me of Grandfather's garage space in the carriage house. I also loved how everything seemed to be amplified and echo. I took a couple of hard stomps just to test the echo. Through a tear stained face, Joseph shot me looks of warning that indicated I was treading on the edge of inappropriate behavior he would deal with himself.

We waited in the car. I stared outside the window, listening to the deep bellowing hum of our car engine. As other cars drove by, it sounded like trains in the night.

I nodded off, leaning against the glass.

"Jeff!" Joseph shoved me. It was dark out my window to the right, but there was a harsh light blinding to my left. "What do you want?"

I looked around, and realized we were at a drive-thru. A white brick building with red accents.

"Cheeseburger and coke? And fries?" I added groggily.

"Sure," mom said, sounding a little stuffy from crying.

We had been offered all kinds of snacks at the hospital but hadn't had anything of substance since the brunch buffet at Grandmother and Grandfather's. The smell of fries brought me fully awake like Pavlov's dog's. When they finally handed the bags through the window, I was feeling hunger pangs.

"I think we'll just eat here, ok?"

"Yeah," Joseph replied. I didn't care where we ate, I just cared that we ate! Mother was never in a hurry to get back to the house when we visited. I couldn't imagine she was in a hurry now.

I wasn't sure who was going to be at the house when we got back, or what it was going to be like. I wasn't sure what to think about anything. This was my first experience with death. I was sad, sure, but I had no idea how to process it. One minute he was telling me about roses, the next he was winking from a rolling bed, and then... gone? It didn't make sense! How did someone go from walking around, busting kids up to no good, working in his shop, to *gone*? I had no reference for understanding this. I thought it best to keep quiet and just see what happened next.

We all ate in silence, except for the radio which was too quiet to make out any of the words. The parking lot light had a yellow cast to it that seemed to be drawing flies to its glow. Against the black backdrop of the sky, every tiny insect lit up and was visible, and the volume of them was unsettling. . . I went on eating my burger.

When we finally pulled into the drive, there were only a few cars. It felt strange getting out of the car and knowing he wasn't there. He had always been there, I couldn't recall the man ever leaving the property. I stared at the darkened carriage house, that would normally have a soft glow of Grandfather's workbench light in the back. Grandfather was never very social, and most of the time he was in a foul mood that resulted in us all avoiding him, but there was a sense of loss - knowing he wasn't inside.

Walking through the door felt strange. The air was different somehow. Mother quietly guided us to the back stairs. Every door in the front halls were closed, dim light spilling under some of them. The dark wood panels looked black as tar. I must not have been used to seeing the front hall with the lights already turned down for bed. In the dining room, Aunt Carol and Aunt Patricia sat straight-backed with tissues in hand, pressed up to their mouths and noses, cheeks tear-stained. As we ascended the stairs, the echoy hall was filled with muffled sounds of crying and low voices. Again, every door was closed with only dim light spilling into the hall from under them. Mother turned on a lamp on the dresser in our room. The house was cold, which seemed strange for the month of May.

We got dressed for bed. "What about our teeth?" I asked mother, in a sleepy daze.

"You can skip tonight," she said as she put my shoes near the door.

"Ok." We had never been allowed to skip before. We were sometimes held up by one parent while the other scrubbed the tiny brush in our mouths. Our heads wobbled in a coma like state, but we never skipped!

"Get in bed," Mother pulled back the sheets. We climbed into the bed and she tucked us in, in silence. Joseph hadn't spoken since the drive-thru.

"Do either of you have questions about what happened to your Grandfather?" mother asked, in a quiet voice. Joseph shook his head and settled deeper into the covers. "Jeffery?"

"He's gone?" I said. It was half question, half statement.

"Yes," she replied, pursing her lips. "In a way. But he is also still here, we just can't see him. Or maybe he's in heaven. I'm not sure how it works." She struggled for the right words.

"Maybe he's at his workbench," I said, comforting myself. He loved to tinker with little projects for endless hours. It was often only after everyone was in bed that you could hear him close up the carriage house and come inside. Sometimes I wondered if he only found projects to work on when we came to visit. He didn't seem to like people, especially kids.

"Maybe he is. He loved his carriage house, that's for sure." Mother stared at the floor, unsure if she could offer us any emotional comfort or understanding. "Maybe that's where he is right now, or watching over his garden."

"The roses," I assumed. I imagined he was watching over them, hands folded behind him, inspecting them closely.

"Yes, the roses, perhaps," mother nodded.

"They need a lot of attention," I yawned.

"Yes, they do," she paused for some time, "Good night." She quietly turned off the lamp and slipped out the door. Joseph turned away from my side of the bed, which was nearest the window. In a moment, I felt the bed bounce and the quiet of our room was broken by deep breathy drawn, wet sounding, sniffle as my brother sobbed into his pillow.

I pictured Grandfather standing over his Hawaiian rose, somehow offering it his continued aid from the other side. Often when we visited, I fell asleep wanting to sneak out to surprise him at his workbench. I drifted off knowing he was out there. It was somewhat the same in this moment. It was like I could feel him out there, but I would never again be able to sneak up on him. The carriage house was dark and physically empty.

It was finally setting in, what his death meant, and what everyone else had come to know immediately. It wasn't that I didn't know what death meant. I just had no reference. Sure, I saw people die on cartoon shows and TV all the time. Other characters stepped over them, and they faded into the next frame without much more thought. Sometimes, people on TV cried, I never understood why, really. I didn't fully get why everyone in the house was crying. It was kind of strange that I didn't even realize I was crying myself. Had the shake of the bed been Joseph or me?

This wasn't like when you got hurt and cried, or became so enraged and frustrated with your parents that you slammed your door and screamed in tears. This was so much more painful than anything I had known. It wasn't triggered by a physical pain like spanking, or a built up teetering tower of frustration like a good fight over cleaning your bedroom. It was simply a thought of the empty carriage house. A cold hard fact of life that millions realized every day. We were born, we grew, we got old, then we got really old, and then we left behind those we loved.

How hard must it be for Grandfather to watch us all, spread throughout his darkened house, unable to console anyone? His crowded house of boring grown-ups talking and kids getting into trouble would be enough to make him retreat to the carriage house for sure!

As I laid in bed, the moonlight cast a bluish hue to the room. The house was rarely so silent while I was still awake. I could hear the soft ticking of the Grandfather clock traveling all the way up the stairwell and into the bedroom. As the roof cooled, the trusses creaked and popped every so often with tiny little sounds that made my eyelids jump back open every few minutes. I heard a different kind of creak, lower in tone and location. It was the hall floor. There seemed to be a soft light glowing in the hall, almost like a distant television. I got up and sneaked to the doorway to see what it was. The hall was slightly lit, maybe from bouncing moon beams I couldn't trace. Someone traveled down the stairs. Out of curiosity, I decided to follow to see who else was awake.

The figure turned the bottom of the stairs and into the den just as I got to the top of the stairs. It was a male figure, and looked like it may have been my father. Surely, he wouldn't mind if I got a drink of water, being the only people awake.

I quietly slipped down the stairs, keeping my feet to the outside of the tread risers so I didn't make any sound. I ran silently through the den and family room. He went out the back door and left it open a crack. I peered out the door. The air was crisp, and the yard was lit up by a large full moon. I scanned the patio for my father and noticed him just going into the carriage house. I looked behind me into the house. It was dark, there was no one awake beside the two of us, so I followed him.

The world was bathed in blue and black under the moonlight. The doorway into the carriage house was dark. It was even more silent inside than out. Inside the front door was a decent sized room, a hundred years ago the room had once been used as a waiting room so the coachmen or drivers could use it to warm up while they waited. There was a door in the sidewall of the room that opened into the garage area, or what had been the barn stall area long ago.

I could see a warm yellow light spilling through the darkness, coming from the rear of the garage area where Grandfather's tool and workbench sat. I crept slowly between the large white town car of Grandmother's and the twin of another make and model that belonged to Aunt Bessie, only hers was a faint pink pearl. My father's figure stood at the tool bench, his robe a dark green like Grandfather's. In fact, it might have been Grandfather's. He stood quietly, slowly running his hand across a project that was laid out, dragging fingers across the details of the wood, and the tools that laid next to it. His head hung low, studying the work.

I stood watching for a while, then accidently bumped into Grandfather's welding cart, knocking the brass blow torch - which hung by two hoses connected to two large green metal tanks with chipping paint. "I couldn't sleep," I announced. He laughed quietly.

"Neither could I," he whispered. "So much work left to be done." His voice sounded strange... like a mix between my father and my Grandfather. I moved forward to peer up onto the workbench at the project there. It was a large block of wood being carved out with tiny bladed tools and hammers. Wood shavings were all over the workbench and floor. "Other people will have to finish it now." I looked up in confusion into the piercing blue eyes of my Grandfather. It was my Grandfather! He reached out and ruffled my hair with a familiar wink. "You'll do fine."

"What?"

"You can finish this," he said walking away, up the loft stairs. I looked at the carving with a studious eye.

"I don't know how to carve! I don't even know what you are carving!"

"You'll do fine!" He called from the top of the stairs.

"Where are you going?!" I called, running to the stairs. The loft ran around the perimeter of the carriage house and had a large area over the waiting room. I ran to the top of the stairs. To my surprise, the loft had expanded into a giant warehouse, high above a vast dark, lit by a strange green light, where welders were busily working. Sprays of sparks and flame shot out frequently with pops and hisses of molten metal being melded together. The men welding were hard-worn men with gaunt faces, sinewy strong arms with thick gloves holding pieces of metal into place. I moved carefully on the walkway, sure in my ability to keep on the walkway, but constantly concerned I was a misstep from stumbling over or through the rail and down into the warehouse.

"Grandpa!" I called out. He was walking down a walkway on the other side of the loft. The walkway on his side was well lit by a blinding light. I scrambled to get around the side and follow him. The light in my eyes kept

28

me from focusing on him, I could only focus on the dark room below where everyone was busily working. I kept pursuing him. Normally, I was much quicker than the old man, but I couldn't keep up no matter how deep into the warehouse we got. The men below seemed to be angry with us, scowling at us and mumbling what were bound to be unkind things. There were suddenly crashes and clangs below my feet. I was sure the men below were throwing tools at us! I jumped, startled at a wrench near my leg, and grabbed a chain hanging down from a pulley. It slid forward as I walked. I grabbed hold of the chain and used it to steady my steps as it traveled down an overhead track.

The warehouse floor was sloping down and getting further away as I walked. Eventually, the sounds of welding and grumbling were faint. The pale green light and glowing red metal were faded glimmers in the darkness below. The light from the distance seemed to be spilling through a larger hole, like the ceiling opened up. The warehouse below was still a dark gloomy place, but the men below seemed to have calmed down.

Suddenly, I realized my Grandfather was no longer on the walkway at all. I couldn't find a pathway he had walked to. He simply wasn't there. I paused, looking around. Down below, I could see my Grandfather's workbench bathed in a warm yellow light. Sitting on top of the workbench was a large oak casket. I slowly descended a ladder into the warehouse. The welders were in the distance behind me, the sounds of their toil echoing in the large spacious room.

I carefully approached the casket. It was a finely crafted thing, with elaborate moldings. I carefully ran my fingers down the surface of the lid's edge. It was finely sanded and stained wood. As I touched the lid, it popped open and slowly raised. There was a dark shadow inside but as it opened further, the warm yellow light spilled in and the sheen of the white satin lining could be seen. It smelled like sawdust, flowers, and spices. I half expected to see my Grandfather jump out at me, but there it stood, empty. I was glad he wasn't inside, but at the same time, it would have been a comfort to have found him. I looked around. The carriage house had shrunk back to size, and the warehouse expanse had disappeared. I stood alone in a familiar place.

3. A Final Farewell

I had never seen my father cry before. He held up remarkably well throughout the funeral service. I rolled my eyes at people I barely knew who told me how much I looked like my Grandfather. I looked nothing like the man!

My father managed to keep a face of gratitude for every condolence offered, a warm hug for the women and a firm handshake for the men. His younger brothers did not fare as well. He was now the pillar upon which the family rested. I kept a sidelong eye on him for a crack in his demeanor.

It was the first funeral I had ever attended. I marveled at the finely carved casket and the blanket of flowers draped over it. Nearly all of them were roses, mixed with a few other flowers I knew from the flower beds around Grandmother and Grandfather's gardens.

I liked the smell of hospitals, but there was something strange about a funeral home I did not care for. It wasn't something I could point out, but the concentrated garden of flowers didn't mask it. It just made it worse.

I tried not to move my eyes up the casket to Grandfather. I could see him in my peripheral vision, I didn't want to look directly at him for more than a quick second. It was strange. There he was, as if asleep, but it wasn't him. He looked as gruff as ever, which maybe played a part in why I looked away so quickly. He had a fresh shave, but still looked as if he had a five-o'clock shadow. It was him, but he wasn't there anymore. He looked as if he might wink at me at any second, yell at my cousins to leave the folded programs alone, tell all my aunts and uncles how they were wasting money on flowers, and how he wasn't paying a dime for any of it. I smirked at the thought. My mother and Aunt Carol shot me scornful looks, questioning what on earth I could possibly find humorous at a moment like this. Once again, he was shooting me a wink behind all of their backs, letting me see the man he kept hidden from the rest. He *was* there. I didn't know the first thing about how death and the afterlife worked, but I liked to think he somehow put the thought in my mind, like his ghost was in my periphery, drawing out images like a cartoonist.

I couldn't pay attention to a word that the preacher said, it was all very scriptorial and over my head. The eulogy was far too grown up, and dry, for child consumption. I sat and stared at the fine moldings that lined the rooms. I imagined cartoon-like mice running around the building in secret tunnels, tiny hidden doors.

Once graveside, after the dedicatory prayer had been offered by the minister, the funeral director handed everyone a rose. They all varied in color. I wondered why the plastic grass was laid on top of real grass for us to stand on... seemed silly, when we could stand on real grass. If they were worried about us crushing the real grass, I couldn't imagine how putting fake grass on top of it and then us standing on that was somehow better for the lawn. I dug at the fake grass with the toe of my shoe.

"Do you even care that he's gone?" Crystal shook her head at me in disgust.

"What?" I asked, confused.

"You don't even cry!" Crystal turned away from me sharply.

"Thank you all for coming," my father's voice quieted the already somber hum of the group. "We have gathered and celebrated Dad's life." My father never referred to Grandfather as *Dad*. "Dad loved to work. When he retired he couldn't stand not working, so he dove into what became his passion, gardening. He got to know each plant variety intimately. He knew exactly when to water each plant, when the seasons were going to affect them, and how. He was tuned into what work needed to be done every day to keep his garden in perfect condition. He wasn't afraid to take an extreme measure to protect a bush, and he was never ashamed to admit when he had no idea what to do, and ask someone who knew more than him. At times, I thought he lost his green thumb and his mind when he would single out a plant and hack away at pruning it. He would nearly knock it down to nothing, and then sure enough next year the plant would be the fullest, most beautiful bush in the row.

He became a master gardener, though he would never be so prideful to call himself that. He always said he was just a novice with some plants in a yard. That was how he raised us. Dad knew what work needed to be done, and would do it, or make us do it. And we would grow from it the next season.

32

We will pay final tribute today by each placing a single rose in the grave after he is laid to rest." That was the moment. The first time I had seen my father shed a tear as the casket slowly lowered into the ground. "We love you, Dad," he managed through a tearful quivering voice. "Your work is done. May you rest in peace."

It took a long time for each family member to pass one by one and place their rose. Most of the cousins - especially the girls - broke into tears the moment they tossed their rose.

"Is it a crying contest?" I asked Joseph, who shot me a scowl.

"Would you shut up?"

"Boys," my mother said very firmly, pulling at the sleeve of my shirt to move along in line. The eyes of the entire family watched as each person took their turn. I felt strange that I was the only one who wasn't crying. Joseph wiped tears on his suit jacket sleeve as he dropped his yellow rose. Was there something wrong with me? Why wasn't I teary? I had cried. I cried the night he died, the next morning I was teary... Every time the carriage house was in my view I choked back the tears a bit. Where were the tears?

This was the last step, in moments he would truly be gone. I had come to terms with that in the days leading up to that moment. I felt whispers as I neared the grave's edge. I wondered what they were saying about me. *Never mind.* I heard Grandfather's voice somewhere in my mind. *Who will protect me from them now?* I questioned in reply. Of course, there was no answer.

I tossed the rose gently and waited a moment. I thought I would feel some kind of finality, but I felt no different. It seemed an important moment to most everyone there, but as I looked in the grave, I returned to the thought *His body might be there, but **he** isn't in there.*

I didn't know exactly where he was... Maybe he was standing next to me, or hovering above like angels did on TV and greeting cards. Maybe he was back home, refusing to go to the funeral. He often refused to join the 'family circus', as he called it. I shuffled on and got back in the car.

As we drove away, I watched workers moving equipment around the grave. A large digger rumbled behind us, black smoke billowing from its pipe.

I sat on mother's lap at the dining room table, which hadn't happened since I was much younger. Kid's just weren't allowed at the dining table once they were old enough to roam without supervision.

"Father Trummel did a wonderful job. Very poetic," Aunt Bessie said.

"Yes," Grandmother said with a deep sigh. There was a long silence. I thought about running off, but no one was playing anywhere in the house, or outside. There was nothing to do but listen to the adults.

"Well," Grandmother said, "the old goat left me alone. I always knew he would, one way or another." Grandmother sank into her chair. "I suppose I always was alone. Raising your kids while he was at board meetings, or at the factory, or out in his garden or work bench." The cavalier tone was upsetting to me. I could sense it didn't sit right with mother either, as her posture tensed.

"Yeah, I don't recall Dad ever making me anything to eat, or helping me with homework," Uncle Evan said.

"No, but he'd sure give you a smack if you didn't do it!" Uncle Tom added.

"Do you know what I remember about Dad?" Uncle Russell jumped in. "He beat me with a garden hose once. I'm sure I did something disappointing... I don't recall what it was. I just remember the beating I got."

"I put a stop to that," Grandmother sipped her tea.

"Yeah, well, aren't we all his disappointments?" Uncle Tom remarked.

"We need not relive the worst parts of the past," Grandmother said, sipping her tea. "There are perhaps too many bad memories to go around."

"Well, maybe he is at least at peace now. If peace is available to him," Uncle Tom smirked.

"Here, here," Others agreed.

"He's probably watching us all right now thinking up a wicked comment to shut us all up before he heads out back outside," Aunt Carol said with a smirk.

"If there is family in here, you can bet he's out there," Grandmother added with a nod.

"I remember Grandfather painted flowers. The purple ones he grew out by the cherry trees. He liked pretty things," I said, somewhat quietly. The room suddenly took notice of me. I was tired of people saying unkind things, and there had been a string of them in the past three days. These were the same people who hours ago nearly threw themselves into his grave, convulsing in sobs? Some of them hung their heads in thought, darting their eyes away from me as quickly as they had turned to see who had spoken.

No one said anything for quite some time. My mother tightened her squeeze around my waist, either to shut me up or because she liked what I had said. I wasn't sure which, but maybe it was both.

As my parents tucked us into bed that night they kept whispering. It was strange that they both were tucking us in. Father rarely, if ever, aided in that task.

"Well, boys," Father said, shutting our bedroom door behind him, "we need to talk." Nothing good ever came after that statement. "Your mother and I have been talking, and with your Grandfather passing, your Grandmother will have a lot on her plate. He was involved in a lot of important things, and she needs people she can trust to help. Things haven't been going the greatest for your mother and me with our careers since we moved to Harold, so we have been talking for some time about moving back here to Woodlawn. We think this would be a good time with good reasons, to do that. So we are going to move in here with your Grandmother for a time while we get set up and find a house and what not. How do you guys feel about that?" Father asked, raising his eyebrows.

Live in Grandmother's house? It was a fine place to visit, like going to a spook alley, but you didn't want to live in the spook alley, you wanted to go home when it was over! Especially knowing there were probably skeletons and ghosts at the end of a stairwell! What was to keep them inside? I wasn't sure the house wasn't haunted before grandpa died, now I was pretty sure he was among the ranks of ghosts, and perhaps leading them!

"Yeah!" Joseph said excitedly. He remembered living in Woodlawn better than I. He still had friends here that he met up with when we came to visit, so naturally, he was on board. I had no friends in Woodlawn. None.

4. New School Structure

Summer was a horrible time to move. School was out of session up North, so there were no friends to say goodbye to or have a send off party. It was easy to cut ties and move. I had been concerned with how my Beta fish was going to fare while traveling, but that was taken care of when a mover left the fishbowl on the porch. It was knocked over by the cat from next door, who quickly made off with him as a snack. I had always hated that cat.

"Such is life." My father offered no comfort as I watched the cat sit on the porch next door, licking its paws of fishbowl water.

Next, on the list of horrid things; I was to attend Oak Ridge Private Elementary. Oak Ridge operated on a year-round schedule because *children should become accustomed to having vacations spread throughout the year and being on a yearly schedule prepares them for the 'real world'.*

The first day of school was a horrible, awkward thing. The white shirt, dark blue pants, and jacket that made up the uniform was itchy and stiff. There was nothing cool about it. At least maybe I could blend into the crowd and go unnoticed if I looked like everyone else.

My stomach had been in a knot the entire morning. I had barely eaten anything. Walking into school, I just wanted to run back to the car, but mother and father were both starting new jobs that day, and mother had not been in any mood for shenanigans.

I kept my eye down cast and shuffled into the school.

"Do you know where you are going?" mother asked Joseph.

"Yeah, Mr. Hartford is down the east hall. We use to go in there for our fifth grade mentor reading thing, in kindergarten," Joseph shrugged as if she should know this.

"Ok. Have a nice day!" She patted Joseph on the back as he darted off before she could do something embarrassing, like kiss him. I wasn't sure how I was going to stave off such catastrophe.

We continued down the hall. I didn't care for the smell of the school. It was nothing like the chemically clean smell of the hospital. There were cleaning products for sure, but it was just nastiness, combined with whatever teachers were doing with air-fresheners to try and mask the horrible smell.

"Well, this is it," mother said, stopping in front of a door.

"Can't I be homeschooled?"

"By whom?"

"You? Grandmother?" I paused and thought about how pleasant that would be. "Never mind,"

"Yeah, that's what I would say too," Mother adjusted my jacket. "Are you too hip to give your mom a kiss?"

"Hip?" I questioned. "No one says 'hip', mom." I rolled my eyes.

"Oh, well then," she gave me a sideways hug. "We'll just have to live with a side hug. You'll do great. This is a wonderful school."

"Yeah," I grimaced in doubt. Mother waved through the tiny window in the door. In a moment, the door cracked open.

"Hello," a woman with piercing blue eyes and a lipstick lined mouth smiled through the door.

"Hi," mother replied, "This is Jeffery."

"Jeffery, very nice to meet you. I'll take it from here." She excused mother, guiding me through the door by patting me on the shoulder. I felt my stomach sink as the door closed. "Class, I would like everyone to meet our newest student, Jeffery Alfrey. His Grandmother is Rose Alfrey." The teacher introduced me and nodded as if to imply that my Grandmother being Rose Alfrey should somehow be noteworthy for the class of eight-year old's. It was, but the wrong kind of note. I noticed the immediate smirks of a handful of students. I had the feeling my desire to fly under the radar had just gone up in flames. She had just marked me, or doomed me rather.

My Grandmother was an important figure in the community, involved in many things and causes. Some of the causes Grandmother was involved in were *The Rose Alfrey Children's Reading Center*, and *The Alfrey Foundation*, which had a set of grants for less than well to do high-school students to get involved with business internships, and grants for college entrance. From what I understood it also meant they would be Grandmother's slave for a year or two, doing all manner of non-business related tasks as she saw fit, all in the name of giving them exposure to a better work ethic. In her mind, these kids were probably going to aspire to be the assistant managers of dry-cleaners someday and she would be instrumental in giving them a boost in that skill-set. It seemed more like an introduction to slavery, to me.

Grandmother's involvement in the community and education had positioned her with a seat on the public-school board as well as the Oak Ridge Administration Council, which is how we got into Oak Ridge so easily during the middle of the term.

These kids were a close knit group and not use to outsiders being dropped into their midst. These were kids who played together, or drank lemon iced teas while their parents were busy with events and tennis lessons at the country club. They bonded over formal Easter egg hunts and played organized games of cards and billiards whilst their parents hobnobbed at galas, benefits, and parties.

Joseph had gone to school here before when I was too young to attend. He was probably high-fiving with his reunited comrades at that very moment while I stood on display as an awkward animal at auction while the spectators turned up their noses at what they saw.

"How is your Grandmother, Jeffery?" she gestured toward a desk on the side of the neat rows, near the front.

"She is well, Ma'am," I replied politely. I sifted in my backpack for a moment and produced a box of birthday invitations I was told to give her. She took it without a word and set it on her desk. My Grandmother thought it would be best to invite everyone to a party, so I could get to know them all. I was pretty sure there was some other social motive. Still I wasn't sure if a party was likely to land me a spot as a popular kid, or get me a string of wedgies.

I moved to the desk the teacher had motioned to.

"Hey, new kid, that's Jacob's desk." I hesitated and looked around. The boy carefully leaning toward me had messy brown hair and nearly black, thick, eyebrows. There were no other open seats. "Jacob is my best friend. You better not sit down." With a long sigh I glanced around. The teacher was waiting for me to sit, I did as the teacher had said, and slowly sat down. "Watch it, new kid." The boy with the dark eyebrows tossed a pencil that spun end over end and struck me in the neck. I flinched and picked up the pencil. I fixed my eyes straight forward on the board.

"Spell words! We are on list sixteen if you recall. Jeffery, this will be a good indicator for us. I have high hopes for you, but from talking with your Grandmother at church, I am to understand that your previous schooling was nowhere near the level we are at. Still, you *are* an Alfrey, so do not disappoint your family name," she smiled. My stomach turned.

"Yes, ma'am," I replied quietly.

"*Yes, ma'am,*" the boy with the dark eyebrows mocked, and then made kissy faces at me while the teacher wrote numbered empty spaces on the board.

"Jacob, Devin, Jeffery, Julia, and Brock, please line up." The teacher called off our names and filled in the numbered blanks on the board. Kids jumped right up and formed a line, their hands held behind their backs. Julia, Devin (the boy with the thick eyebrows), and Brock took a moment to cast smirking glares in my direction as if to not only indicate the impending competition but also to predict the outcome. Luckily for me, this was a subject I did quite well in.

"Jacob, first word... Bearing."

"B-e-a-r-i-n-g," Jacob was a blonde boy with freckles and blue eyes. Leaving Brock, a dark-haired, short boy with a great many more freckles than Jacob, and a constant sour look on his face, but it may have been the freckles.

"Very well. Devin, posture." My stomach turned further. These words were a half year ahead of me. Still, I was confident, if not cautiously so.

"P-o-s-t-u-r-e," he smiled at the back wall. I tried to stare at the clock on the back wall. I felt as if every eye was on me, fingers pointed carefully so as not to be disruptive, all waiting for me to succeed and incur their wrath, or fail and incur their judgment.

"Julia, proximity." *What? Was this woman kidding? I didn't even know how to use that one correctly! Something about measuring something?*

"P-r-o-x..i... m-i-t-y. Proximity." The girl practically sang her response in a sickeningly sweet smile that reminded me of when we saw a play about a redheaded orphan child no one could stand. I was pretty sure I hated that girl. It would depend on what word I was given.

"Jeffery. Your word is Polarize." *What? Polar-ice?*

"Can you use it in a sentence please?" I asked with a gulp. The room all snickered together.

"The two groups of people were polarized." *Oh!*

"P-o-l-a-r-i-z-e-d." I rattled off quicker than I could even keep track of. The letters simply rolled out. One dark haired boy in the back of the room, separated from the rest, lifted his head from lying on his arms and nodded with interest. I had once lost a spelling bee in Kindergarten. My word had been "balloon." With the double "L," I had lost track of how many O's I had given. Not something I wanted to repeat. So, I had worked hard at my delivery for the next several years.

"That is correct," the teacher smiled. The rounds continued on for quite some time. Whenever I was given a word, I asked for usage immediately while collecting the spelling in my head so I could spit it out as fast as possible. Devin and Jacob were trying to do the same thing, but they were having trouble getting the rhythm down. They weren't asking for the word to be used, so they could collect their thoughts. Before long, it was down to just the three of us, Jacob, Devin, and myself.

"R-e-a-c-t-i-v-e-a...t-e-d." Jacob had anger written all over his face, realizing his mistake in his haste. I smirked, which got me a sharp cutting glare from Julia, who was sitting in front of me.

"I'm sorry Jacob, that is incorrect. Jeffery. Your word is Reactivated."

"R-e-a-c-t-i-v-a-t-e-d," I spit out so fast I might as well have just said the word. I didn't need an example for that one.

"Correct," the teacher restrained a small smile. "Devin. Constitution."

"C-o-n-s-t-i-t-u-t-i-o-n," he seemed to fire each letter like a bullet with my name on the tip.

"Correct." If the teacher was mindful of the rivalry that seemed to be growing, and the depth of the anger that was behind Devin's side of it, she must have been loving it.

"Jeffery. Conveyed."

"Can you please use it in a sentence?" I asked while I envisioned the word and got ready to return verbal fire.

"The message was conveyed clearly."

"C-o-n-v-e-y-e-d."

"Well done. Let's give you two something to chew on.

Devin, provoking."

"P-r-o...v-o-k-i-n-g."

"Jeffery, dividing."

"D-i-v-i-d-i-n-g," I spat the word out as if to highlight my lack of hesitation. Devin sneered.

"Devin... Combative."

"C-o-m-b-a-t-a-t-i-v-e."

"I'm sorry, that is incorrect. Jeffery, combative."

"C-o-m-b-a," I paused. If I gave it perfectly, I won and Devin was going to be upset. If I gave it incorrectly, we both got another word... and then I had the chance to let him win. If he won, he would likely rub it in my face just the same. The dark haired boy at the back of the room wore a look of hope and anxiety as if he needed me to defeat Devin on his behalf. I could see him straining for it. "t-i-v-e. Combative." I finished.

Devin glared a hateful glare. I wanted to beam with pride, but I was also fearful of having made a bad choice in beating him. Being competitive and beating Devin, who already had a foothold in the class, would only drive me to exclusion. Being the newest student in the school, I was already an outsider. I kept my gaze lowered, looking anywhere that didn't result in eye contact with the handful of kids who were trying to make it. Why had she put me up there? Was she bent on getting me beaten up? Maybe she didn't like my Grandmother and was taking it out on me.

"Well done, Jeffery. It would seem you are pretty much in line with the class, despite your previous schooling." The teacher said as she put the final tally on the board, next to my name.

I wasn't sure what her comment meant, but I still had the feeling I should somehow be ashamed of my previous school. I did know enough to have figured out a public school and a private school were treated very differently when grown-ups spoke of the two.

Many people in Woodlawn were a gasp when they found out my parents had put us in a public school. Joseph, they couldn't believe wasn't in private school *How was he ever to be challenged in public school?* Bottom line, after rotating through several schools in a matter of only a few years, this day was my worst nightmare.

Until recess, I spent as much of class as possible with my eyes fixed on the board, or down at my desk. The occasional paper football or wad of paper flicked or flew in my direction. I was pretty sure most of them came from Brock or Devin. Julia tried to hold back her giggles, which only spurred them on more.

I was looking forward to recess, to get out of the confines of the classroom. Of course, the playground, while offering a certain freedom, would no doubt bring jail yard hierarchy into play, but at least it wouldn't be sitting at a desk.

When the recess bell ran, everyone leapt from their desks. Kids burst out of the hall door into sprints, rushing to lay claim to their favorite articles of the playground. Girls ran to form groups of hopscotch and jump-rope, others took to the swings, or the monkey bars and large playground structures. I skirted the side wall of the school and surveyed the scene carefully. Jacob, Devin, Brock, Julia (a very blonde girl), and a few others were gathered at the highest point of the playground, a tower platform with a large slide descending. It was pretty clear that Devin was at the top of this pecking order, followed by Jacob and Brock. I wasn't used to girls falling into the playground hierarchy, so I didn't know how to assess Julia and the blonde girl, but they clearly had a role in the ruling of the playground.

The dark-haired boy from the back of the classroom was underneath the playground, sitting in shadow, digging something from the gravel. He pulled several white lumps from the ground and lined them up. Then he began to casually throw them at anyone who ran by, or jumped down too closely to his hideout. The white lumps burst open as they struck people, or fell to the ground in a small cloud of dusty smoke that caused girls to scream and run, and boys to side step and brush it off as they hurried away. I wondered why the dark haired boy wasn't sitting on the outskirts of the commotion, in safety, like I was.

Sure enough, a few minutes later Jacob and Devin took notice of the bombings below their tower and altogether the boys leaped down on each side. The dark haired boy kept his gaze lowered and paid attention to his few remaining white lumps. I wondered what the exchange of words was.

Devin kicked some gravel toward the dark-haired boy, who ignored it. He then casually rose, scooping up his white lumps, and after a few steps, he spun, flinging his white bombs at Devin! He caught his footing in the gravel quickly and darted off into a group of girls. Devin and his friends were caught off guard and scrambled to get traction in the loose stones, nearly falling all over themselves as they went after him. In a blink, the dark-haired boy was gone. He crossed what I assume was an implied boundary onto the playground, where the upper grades were playing. I smirked. *Good for him!* I thought. He obviously didn't care about Devin or the pecking order, or grade separation for that matter. He might be my ally.

"Hey," I turned my attention back towards Devin and friends, just in time to see Brock motioning toward me. They spread apart, like fishermen casting a net, as they walked toward me. I kept looking off at the older kids' playground. Joseph was somewhere over there. While he was often more likely to inflict more damage on me than the average class bully, he was also territorial–as most bullies were–and wouldn't like his prey being messed with. Perhaps I could make it to him.

"Hey, new kid!" Devin said, walking as tall as he could, asking to get the attention of our peers.

"Yep," I said, barely looking his way.

"You made me look like an idiot!" Devin spat.

"I can't make you look like something. I can't help it if I spell better than you." Those were the wrong words. Devin lunged forward at me with outreached hands. I assumed he meant to throttle me, so I did what anyone would have. I ran. I ran toward the older kids' playground and then decided it wasn't in my best interest to do that either. The dark haired boy might be able to escape notice, or perhaps he had earned his right to cross over. If Joseph saw me running toward him and his friends, he would hand me over to Devin personally, but not before tenderizing me for him first!

I decided to take a different route, and I ran into an empty soccer field. I was quite a bit quicker than Devin. Jacob and Brock were far behind. I couldn't contain my smirk and laughter as I turned, running backward to see how much of a lead I had on them.

"You're dead, new kid!" Devin pointed at me to give punctuation, or to ensure I knew he was talking to me. I thought it best to simply keep my mouth closed. I had surely embarrassed him a second time. This time, while he was trying to make an example of me, and on the heels of him being burned by the dark haired boy. It was not a good day for Devin. Then again, maybe it was just not a good day to anger Devin.

The three of them patrolled the edge of the soccer field like junkyard dogs waiting for a rabbit. They pointed and talked, no doubt making plans. I simply walked back and forth between the far soccer goals, keeping a sideways eye on them, but trying to look as if I didn't notice them.

I kept recounting them, making sure I was aware of their positions. They seemed to be slowly working their way toward me. They were nearly at the first soccer goals. I started moving down toward the far side fence which would dump me into the big kid's playground. They weren't likely to start edging into that turf. Maybe I could fade into the background and go unnoticed.

The bell rang, and I was saved. Kids started heading into the school. Devin, Jacob, and Brock stood, waiting. They gathered and kept a fixed eye on me. I kept moving closer to the group of older kids, bringing up the rear of their group from a safe distance. My teacher, Mrs. Potts, blew the whistle long and loud. She managed to make it sound angry. I hoped she didn't notice me in the backfield and was blowing it at Devin and friends. They hurriedly ran back inside.

Once they were out of sight, I headed for another door that entered the same hall, only closer to me. The dark-haired boy was heading for the same door, looking down at something in his hand, and not paying much attention to anyone else.

"Hey," I said as we both reached the door. He paused a few steps away.

"Hey," he looked around quickly and opened the door.

"I'm Jeff," I said as he brushed past me.

"I'm Aaron," he turned to face me for a brief moment and continued on.

"What were those white things you were throwing?"

"Talc bombs. I make them at home and ride my bike back to the school every night to bury them under The Tower," he said, barely glancing at me as we walked.

"Why?" I questioned.

"Because I'd get in trouble for bringing them in my backpack," Aaron said so matter of fact, that I felt dumb for having asked.

"Ok." I had to admire his preparation of his defenses. I was much better suited to hide in the background and wait for trouble to find me before I ran away. Aaron expected it, prepared for it, fought it head on, and then ran away. Still, I would have to say the points of the exchange had gone to him over Devin. "So what's with that Devin guy?" I asked.

"Devin? He's a jerk, they all are. They are like the jerk squad. He's been like the leader of the 'cool' kids since I was in Kindergarten," Aaron paused for a sip from the drinking fountain.

"Is Julia like his girlfriend or something?" I kept an eye down the hallway in case I saw any of Devin's crew.

"No. I don't know... maybe. I don't really pay attention to them." We were getting close to our classroom. "Later." Aaron ran ahead and slipped into the classroom while I lagged behind. I supposed he didn't really want to be seen with me, which I couldn't blame him for.

Once back in the classroom, I moved to my desk, and tried to avoid eye contact with everyone. I somehow managed to lock eyes with a brown-eyed girl with straight brown hair. She had full lips and a broad smile. Her medium brown eyes glinted and her smile was overwhelming when I didn't look away. Her cheeks blushed, I wondered how soft her skin was. As I wondered; I nearly tripped over the row of desks my seat resided on. She turned back toward the board and busied herself. Mrs. Potts was busy trying to set up an overhead projector while kids talked in hushed tones. In a moment, a blonde girl nudged me and slid a note onto my desk with a giggle. The brown-eyed girl kept peeking over her shoulder to meet my gaze and quickly turned around with a giggle and blush. I slid the note into my lap and read it.

"I love you. Do you love me? Check Yes or No." My heart raced. I fished a pencil from my desk when suddenly, the note was snatched from under my arm. It was Brock.

"Dude... you have to circle 'No'. She's been my girlfriend since we were born. Just circle 'No' and you can hang out with us, Ok?" he whispered and handed me back the note and sat up straight in his seat, just as Mrs. Potts stirred toward us.

"Ok, class, quiet down." Mrs. Potts had her projector in working order, and I slid the note into my pocket. I wasn't sure what the lesson on the projector was trying to teach us, as I didn't pay attention to anything but the starry eyes of the brown-eyed girl. I imagined her smile, holding her hand, maybe even, dare to dream, kiss her on that soft blushing cheek! My mind swam. Maybe I didn't need friends. Maybe if I circled 'Yes' I would suddenly be invited into her group of friends. I couldn't think about anything else all day!

 We visited the library to drop off books, which I had none, and then filed into another classroom for music.

"You want to see something?" Aaron said as we cleared the classroom door.

"What?" I asked, not sure I was being spoken to.

"Do you?" he asked in frustration.

"I guess," I shrugged.

"Tell Mrs. Potts you need to use the bathroom."

"What?" I wasn't sure I had heard him correctly.

"Just tell her as soon as you sit down," the boy urged, stepping away from me and hurrying into the room.

"Ok," I said with hesitation. We entered the classroom. As I sat down, Devin was drawing his finger across his throat in a slashing motion, his tongue hanging out of his mouth.

I glanced at Aaron who was drawing on his desk, not on paper, but actually *on* his desk. I raised my hand.

"Yes, Jeffery?" asked Mrs. Potts. Devin snapped to and faced forward.

"May I use the restroom?" I asked.

"Of course. Do you know where the restrooms are?" she asked.

"New kid!" Aaron huffed. "Doesn't even know where the bathroom is. I'll show him." He smirked under his breath as his pencil moved back and forth on the desk.

"You can bring back a damp paper towels to clean your desk of that artwork while you are at it," Mrs. Potts nodded and raised her eyebrows. Aaron dropped his pencil and shoved his chair away from his desk as if to imply he was being put out.

"Come on, *new kid on the block*," he said mockingly, which got a laugh from most of the class. Did he have to call me *that* of all things? I wasn't sure I wanted to follow Aaron anywhere! Maybe I was his stepping stool to another level on the social ladder. Still, the enemy of my enemy was a friend, so I followed him into the hall.
"He's Joey!" I heard someone whisper behind me. "Jordan!" Another whisper came as the door shut behind us.

"We have about five minutes," Aaron pushed a button on his watch.

"Dude! Are you trying to make my life suck?" I questioned him with a passionate tone.

"What?" Aaron shrugged.

"*New kids on the block?*" I huffed.

"Oh...don't worry about that," he hurried down the hall.

"Don't worry about it? Someone called me Joey!" I said quite loudly.

"So, what?" Aaron shrugged it off. "Your name is Jeffery."

"Yeah! They still called me Joey... That's one of the *New Kids*," I argued.

"Oh, is it?" he furrowed his brow. I wasn't sure the point was coming across.

"Where are we going?" I asked.

"Hall five. Fifth-grade hall," Aaron said as if I should know already.

"Why?" I stopped. Joseph was near that hall.

"Come on," he turned the corner. I had no choice but to follow, I wasn't sure I would be able to find the classroom again without him anyway. He ducked into the boy's room. I followed. Inside, he started looking into stalls to make sure no one was around. He put the trash can in front of the door.

"What are you doing?" I inquired, with a bit of concern. My patience was wearing thin for everything, Aaron included.

"Turtle Lair," he said plainly.

"What?" I asked. Aaron tugged a large square metal grate from the wall, just inches off the floor.

"Hurry," Aaron nodded into the black hole in the wall.

"What? In there?" I questioned.

"Yeah, hurry! It goes down, so be careful." Aaron nudged my arm.

"So you can close me up in a boiler or something?" I took a step away.

"We call it *The Turtle Lair*... Like Teenage Mutant Ninja Turtles. It's our hide out." Aaron waved a hand while explaining.

"Who's?"

"Get in! We don't have all day!" He shook the grate.

I gave up and complied with the request, being sealed up in a boiler sounded better than going back to class anyway. I carefully climbed down into the dark small space. There was a strange yellow light in the distance of the dark. I seemed to be standing under the school in an open area, but it didn't sound echoic, so it couldn't have been too large of a space. In a second, Aaron was down behind me, pulling the grate back into place behind him.

"This way," he tugged at my jacket in the dark. We rounded a corner and suddenly we were in some kind of hallway under the school. There were old metal pipes running in bundles along the wall. The wall was made of some kind of old shiny tile with a layer of dust on them. The ground was a dark gray concrete. Behind us, I could see several large pipes going into the darkness, probably the toilet drains. It was like being in some kind of sewer. It smelled like the dungeon stairs at grandma's house. There were strange groaning noises. They were likely mechanical, but still creeped me out!

"The Turtle Lair," I said quietly. I got it.

"There are only a few of us who know about it. We come here at lunch, just before recess starts, so no one notices. Sometimes you can get back in during first recess, or last recess. Don't come here alone, not at first anyway. You have to get in and get out fast so no one sees you," Aaron explained.

"How did you find this?" I asked looking around.

"Jason."

"Who?" I asked.

"Oh, he's our leader," he said matter-of-factly.

"Leader?"

"Yeah, he's a grade ahead of us. He is like a karate master, and has a green belt and stuff. Sometimes, he teaches us things down here. He's like splinter."

"So you guys are the Ninja Turtles?" I asked.

"Pretty much. Mutant outcasts. learning karate in the sewer," Aaron nodded.

"Ok," I was still taking it all in.

"Anyway, I'm pretty sure Jason will let you in because you know about *The Layer*. Either that or he will kick your butt."

"What?" I asked in shock. Another person who might want to kill me? Great!

"I don't know. He's kinda crazy. But you are *so* one of us. Once he sees how much Devin hates you... Rival gang." Aaron said making a fist.

"Do you know that brown-eyed girl who fits at the front of my row?" I wrapped my fingers around the note in my pocket.

"Kendra."

"Yeah...she wrote me this note," I pulled it out.

"Let me see," Aaron pushed a button on his watch and it glowed. The tiny light might have actually made it more difficult to read the letter. "Whoa, heavy! What are you going to circle?" He handed it back.

"She's a babe... I don't know. I don't want to piss off Brock." I folded the note back up.

"Brock? Oh, right. He likes her," Aaron nodded.

"He said they have been dating since they were born." I put the note away.

"She hates Brock! I don't know. I guess if you don't care if Brock hates you, circle *Yes*," Aaron patted my shoulder.

"Yeah... I think he already hates me," I said, thinking deeply. Aaron's watch beeped.

"Time to go," He was a very interesting kid, for sure. He quickly went back to the dark corner, and I tried to keep up. He listened at the grate. He carefully opened the metal shutter, letting light spill in. He peered through the grate for a time, and then whispered to me. "Be ready, and climb up fast. The trash can is still at the door, so no one has opened the door." Now it all made sense. Aaron was like some kind of genius, or... Ninja. I decided I might have to steal the trash can idea around Grandmother's house.

In a flash, the grate was pushed out and Aaron was through the hole. As I scrambled to get up and out, I wondered how many other kids had used this hideout over the decades. Maybe it was something passed down for a century of outcasts, a rite of passage and protection. Or maybe it was a total accident and was used for venting some kind of gas everyone else knew was going to kill anyone who crawled down there. Then again, maybe no one else was willing to crawl on the bathroom floor to use it... Until Aaron.

5. Ninja Turtle Power

The entire class sat quietly, waiting. I assumed if the class did not meet Mrs. Pott's exact expectation, they would not be excused with the bell. I carefully straightened my pencil box and notebooks, making sure everything had a proper home. I placed everything with something on top, or something overlapping every corner, so I would be able to tell if anyone had disturbed anything.

"A place for everything," Mrs. Potts said behind me, in a pleased tone.

"And everything in its place," I finished, which drew a smile on the woman's stone face. I knew the adage well from Grandmother. Mother hated the notion. As much as she liked a clean house, she thought things needed a natural order more than a man-made one. Planned chaos... She said something like *If you try to organize the chaos, you aren't enjoying the details.* I supposed it made some kind of sense, like not being able to see a forest for all the trees. She used to say Grandfather was too busy gardening to smell the roses. I didn't know how that was possible, but it seemed to make some kind of sense anyway.

"I have high hopes for you, Mr. Alfrey," she said as she turned.

"Yes, ma'am," I nodded instinctively. She smiled as she kept walking up and down each row, inspecting each child.

The school felt like a strange extension of Grandmother's house. I might as well have just been in another wing of her house, just off the study. It had a similar air of what was proper protocol, and expected from everyone. It was like I expected her to walk in at any moment and instruct me in some way I was falling short in, perhaps for using a word she found to be common, or disrespectful. It also felt like perhaps Grandfather might walk into the room and mill about in Mrs. Pott's desk at any moment, then grumble and walk out. I could almost see it before my eyes, surely it was only in my imagination it happened. Still, I smirked and nearly let out a quiet giggle. I hadn't decided on any course of action with Kendra's note, so it stayed in my pocket. The bell rang, but no one moved.

"Class excused," Mrs. Potts said, setting to erase the blackboard. Devin and his friends seemed to have shifted their focus away from revenge for the moment and didn't even cast me a sideways glance as they left, much to my chagrin and relief. Everyone else drained from the class quickly enough, but I was content to filtering out last, to make sure Devin was gone. I also didn't think I could face Kendra at the moment. I noticed Aaron was also milling toward the back of the group.

"What bus do you ride?" Aaron asked, pulling his backpack straps tight.

"Ummm fourteen? I think," I thought hard.

"Really? That's my bus. Follow me," Aaron said as we exited the room. Mrs. Potts gave us a small smile. Instead of heading to the right toward the outside doors, we turned left and headed upstream in the sea of kids who were all hurrying to get out. I was pretty sure that was safer than heading into the playground side of the school.

"Jason is on our bus," Aaron informed me. "Where do you live?"

"Grandstate hill?" I was pretty sure that was what everyone called it.

"Duh. I mean like where on the hill?" Aaron said in a frustrated tone.

"Oh, it's like kind of toward the front of the hill."

"The old estates? The originals?" Aaron asked over his shoulder.

"Yeah, I guess," I shrugged.

"That's what we call them. The originals...most of the people who live in them have been there for a hundred years, at least. The bus stops at each street. I can get off with you and then walk home to my street. The Turtles will probably meet at four PM today, so I can come by and see if you can come play so your parents will let you go." Aaron seemed to have a plan for everything.

"Yeah, that sounds good," I was hesitant, but the prospect of playing would be a welcomed change from quietly drawing, or reading at Grandmother's. Still, I didn't know this kid or his friends from a hole in the ground.

As we walked out the front doors we approached a kid resting against the wall.

"Jason. This is ... Jeffery, right?" Aaron urged. The kid against the wall, who had a nearly shaved head, looked me up and down. He took his glasses off. He looked a little rougher than most of the other students. Not pressed and trimmed. Something about him was out of sorts. I couldn't explain the feeling. He was a year or two older than we were, and like most boys a couple of years older than me, looked like he could flatten me without trying. "He is a turtle, or he could be." Aaron added as we moved toward the bus line.

"You?" Jason challenged.

"Yeah, I think so," I said with unease.

"Why?" He raised his head, holding it up high and looking down at me. It looked quite uncomfortable, I wasn't sure why he would do such a thing.

"Devin & Brock singled him out right away, they hate him," Aaron offered. "He's stealing Kendra from Brock too."

"Really?" Jason smiled.

"Yeah, I don't know what I did, really," I sucked my lips in.

"Any enemy of Devin's... is a friend of mine," he didn't sound so sure.

"Jeffery even lives on the hill," Aaron continued his pitch.

"Great! We are getting ready for a battle in the park," Jason popped his knuckles.

"A battle?" I blinked.

"Yeah, with the Cougars. I'm meeting with the leader of the Cougars someday soon. So we don't have long to train. Have you taken Karate?" Jason questioned me.

"Nope," I shook my head.

"That's ok, I can teach you what you need to know," he smiled, self-importantly as we got on the bus. Joseph glared at me as if to tell me I better not acknowledge him openly in public.

This was my inaugural bus ride. I had no clue where to sit, or what to do. Did I wear a seat belt? Were the seats assigned? The bus driver was a gnarled old man, Mr. Speaker, who didn't look as though he felt well. I was somewhat familiar with Mr. Speaker growing up. He lived in the house across the street from Grandmother's, where he must have been as long as Grandfather and Grandmother. Mr. Speaker attempted to rule the neighborhood with an iron fist, barking orders he expected to be carried out by children playing in front of his house. Some of them must have owed him or were under threat from their parents as they stopped in place to do as they were told. Most children would simply laugh and roll their eyes, boasting about how he wasn't in charge of them. I got the feeling most kids were simply riding close to his lawn simply to get a rise out of the old man. I was half sure he was demonically possessed.

"If everyone will please sit down, we can get a move on!" he growled.

"On the right. Always sit on the right," Aaron nudged me.

"Which right?" I asked, puzzled.

"What do you mean? You only have one right," Aaron pushed my backpack.

"If I'm facing the back of the bus, my right will be my left once I sit down and face the front," I smirked.

"When you sit down, you should be on the right," Jason gave me a glare as if I should have known that.

"Hey, what was with you giving chocolate milk to underclassmen today!" A large boy in the seat in front of me shouted across the aisle at a boy sitting with Joseph. Joseph was on the left side of the bus. I shrugged.

"Shut up. I have to give chocolate milk to anyone who comes through the line, it doesn't matter what grade they are."

"That's crap. You move the chocolate milk crate to the back, or up top, cover it up with skim milk so they don't see it, and then you pull chocolate milk out of the back for 5th and 6th grade only!" He pointed at the other kid.

"That's ridiculous!"

"They haven't done one thing to deserve chocolate milk! How many years of wedgies and fights have they been through? Like two? We're the 5th and 6th grade!"

"Did you get chocolate milk?" Aaron asked me.

"Nope," I shrugged.

"Yeah, me either," Aaron frowned.

"I get chocolate milk," Jason smiled quietly.

"Yeah but you're a leader," Aaron waved him off. I was inclined to agree with the boy defending giving chocolate milk to younger kids, mostly because I was one... that affected me immediately! True, in a couple of years, I would be in a position of power to control the chocolate milk. Even if I wasn't, I would be getting it by default of my grade. I could see this playground/school bus drama from both sides. It was getting heated. Other kids were taking sides. Some from the left side agreed chocolate milk should be limited, but disagreed which grade. Joseph seemed to agree with the 5th graders and was making some kind of vocal argument I couldn't make out in the commotion.

"When have you ever not had chocolate milk, Gib!" Aaron shouted, leaning over me and pointing at the older boy from the left side of the bus, who started the argument.

"Shut it! This doesn't involve you!" The boy snapped back.

"It kinda does, actually!" Aaron sat down, content with his two cents being cast. Kids all over the bus were shouting now, over various arguments that may or may not have anything to do with chocolate milk.

"You knew I was going to wear my pink headband!" A girl behind me yelled.

"I don't care, it looks better this way!"

"But you promised!"

"I had my fingers crossed!"

"The bus is always like this?" I asked Aaron. I was beginning to understand why the bus was divided, left and right. It was a safety mechanism. The left side really did seem to hate the right side, and the right hated the left. They all seemed to barely tolerate anyone who wasn't in the seat with them to boot! There was so much division, grades, upper and lower classmen, Cougars and Turtles, sides of the bus. My brain hurt just trying to process and remember where I fit in, or where I was told I fit in.

"Shut up! Shut up!" Mr. Speaker finally screamed into the microphone. The arguments quieted down but continued on again gradually increasing in volume and intensity as the bus bounced down the road. The commotion went on for many blocks as the bus wound through the streets climbing the back side of the hill. I was grateful when things started to look familiar again and quiet down as each stop let out another group of bustling kids. The strange thing was, it seemed as soon as they were out of the bus, and most of the groups went from bitter rivals to laughing and joking as they went their own way. Still, others continued on and even became more violent as they left the bus. Once they were out of the bus, Mr. Speaker didn't seem to care much what happened to them.

Devin and Julia got off the bus a good two streets before my stop. Joseph and a friend were long gone by the time Jason, Aaron, and I got off the bus at our stop.

"So, what's the deal with the Cougars?" I asked as we walked toward Grandmother's.

"Cougars and Turtles have never gotten along," Jason expounded. "Cougars are mostly from The Orchard Estates." The Orchard estates made up the back half of the hill. Once upon a time, before I was born, it was all orchard land, owned by Grandmother and Grandfather, except for a few houses on the opposite side of the street from them. What had once been a serene landscape became several smaller houses. Those *smaller houses* were still bigger than what we had been living in until now.

Jason continued, "Turtles are the other group, the group who don't think they're better than everyone else." I had noticed Grandmother and her associates talked about The Orchards as a group of sub-class people of lesser means and privilege, who begged for acceptance, yet also thought they were better than the Original Estates because they lived in a newer, better quality of home, as they saw it. Less being more, the new style was better on principle alone than the old fashioned, as they saw it.

"Turtles do not allow anyone who wants to be friends with, or wants to actually *be* a Cougar," Aaron added. Aaron and Jason both nodded, to emphasize the importance of this.

"Mutants?" I inserted my interpretation.

"That's right," Jason pointed at me.

"So, are all Turtles Originals then?"

"No. Turtles don't think they are better than everyone, we accept anyone who is like us." I wasn't sure that exclusive catch was different, but it did feel nice to have like-minded brothers after a morning of intense awkwardness.

"Alright, let me run inside and talk to my mom and see if I can play. Orchard park, right?" I asked.

"Yeah," Aaron blinked and nodded.

"You're an Alfrey? Jeffery Alfrey?" Jason questioned. "That's funny. I knew you guys were moving in, I just didn't know it was *you*... Cool," Jason seemed surprised and maybe a little hesitant about letting me associate with them, almost as if *Cool* had a question mark after it. I was used to the hesitation whenever other kids came over to Grandmother's.

"We'll see you there," Jason said as I walked away. I thought I heard him asking Aaron something about whether or not he was sure about me, but I couldn't make it out.

I made my way inside. Inside, the smells of freshly chopped ingredients signaled that the evening meal preparation was just getting started. Joseph was in a room whispering and giggling with the boy from the bus, their backpacks open, papers scattered on the floor. I filtered through the house looking for my mother, finally finding her in the study.

"Hey," I greeted.

"Hey!" she smiled. "How was the first day?"

"It was good," I shrugged, eager to ease her unrest about transitioning us into the school, me in particular. Joseph wasn't a concern as this would be an easy slide over for him.

"Yeah? Did you make lots of friends? Do you like your teacher? It's Mrs. Potts, right?" mother lowered her glasses.

"Yeah, I guess. Actually, some of my friends are going to play at the park in a bit." I rubbed my eye, and thought about the note in my pocket. Maybe I needed a minute before I ran off to the park.

"Sure, yeah! Do you have any homework yet?" mother asked.

"Some reading is all," I replied.

"Well, get all of that done and then you are free to hang out. I want to hear a full report!" She pointed at me with her glasses.

"It was school. Not sure what else there is to say," I backed away.

"Ok... well keep me posted. There are all kinds of possibilities in a new school," she urged. Wanting to please her, I didn't roll my eyes, or tell her all out Devin and others.

"I won a spell off in class." I knew she would like that.

"Yeah?" She said wide eyed. "You are a great speller!"

"Yeah," I stifled a small smile.

"Ok, well go get your reading done and you can play with your friends. I have a city council planning thing tonight," she patted the papers in front of her.

"Where's dad?" I asked, rocking on the heels of my shoes.

"He's at the office. He'll be home before I leave. Don't do that with your shoes!" She waved a hand at me.

My father's company had let him transfer to the local office, which was where he had started his career. It seemed everyone was resuming business as usual, except for me, I was lost in a new place.

I slowly walked out, my backpack in tow, sat on one of the swings on the back porch and fished my book out. I tried to focus on the words on the page, but the only words I could seem to focus on were, *"Do you love me? Yes, or no?"*

After some time, I decided I was done reading. Kim let me sneak a few crackers and a taste of some kind of sauce from the kitchen before I headed out.

I felt a slight nervousness walking to the park to meet my new friends. I was familiar with the large park. We had played there a number of times when we visited Grandmother. The park served as a separation zone between the two neighborhoods of the hill—The Original Hill, and The Orchards. Many of the original fruit trees still dotted the pristine park, serving as monuments as though it justified leveling acres of producing trees to build houses, so long as homage was paid to what had once existed. I often wondered what happened to the fruit. Perhaps it was sold at market, or simply thrown away as it fell to the ground, over ripened. I couldn't imagine any of the residence bringing it into their homes. If something wasn't store bought, or grown in your own yard by your gardener, it was just too common and substandard.

I had many an occasion to observe the foul mood of Grandfather and his distaste for what had happened to what had once been his great orchard. He had cultivated the orchard from seedlings, and turned the orchard into an enterprise that kept several stands across the city busy with the produce. I recalled a few of those stands, even a few years prior to his death. It all but dwindled down to just one street corner stand that now got its fruit from a mass produce wholesaler. It soured Grandfather greatly if the topic of the orchards came up at all.

I would frequently seek out whatever fruit was in season and eat myself sick. Grandfather would always notice and with a pleased smile and what boast a bit about what was left of what he had once created. He would tell me about the orchard that had once stood there. I could hear his words as I surveyed the hallowed park. *"Rows of them... as far as they eye can see... People would flock from all sorts of other counties to buy our fruit. This orchard produced so much that we had to sell it to a dozen different stands just to get rid of it all. Sometimes we had to give it away. We gave bushels to homeless groups and churches. When apples came on too strong and too many, we'd make huge drums of the best cider you've ever had! It was quite a sight, Jeffery. It's a damn shame."*

The sense of loss was greater than I was prepared for. It was the first time I had reflected on much of anything with the perspective of losing Grandfather.

"Over here!" I heard Aaron calling from the far end of the park, to my left. The far end was less landscaped and butted against a ridge where the old canal ran. The canal had once been a valuable resource, providing irrigated water to the orchard, as well as the original estates. It had remained a valuable resource for maintaining the lush landscape, and the sharing of rights to said water was a constant power struggle or source of contention among the largest estates.

The water flowed through under-street aquifers and branched into sections of the forward portion of the hill. A series of twelve 'gates' controlled the flows, with three master 'head gates' controlling the canal.

On many occasion, I had been privy to fights about who was to use the water for what and when. The Orchard folk were content to benefitting from the uphill runoff or using city water delivered via automated sprinkler systems. The sprinklers didn't soak as deep as the controlled flooding of the irrigation system, and didn't give quite the same benefit of deep lush vegetation. The city water came at a much higher cost than the canal, but there was very little effort involved. Plus, no one ever fought over water from their own tap.

I made my way to the far end of the park. Around the side of a row of bushes were Jason, Aaron, and a few other boys. They were doing something with large sticks and poles.

"Hey," I said, carefully observing. I was waiting for this to be some kind of trap, carefully planned by Devin, or Joseph even.

"Jeffery, this is Nicholas and James," Aaron motioned to the other boys.

"Hey," I waved. James was a strikingly blonde boy with thin-framed glasses, who seemed to be fashioning a spear.

"So, what are you doing?" I inquired.

"Preparations," Jason said, pointing a long stick at me and then spinning it in some kind of choreographed manner.

"For what?" I asked, confused.

"Battle!" James grinned.

"Battle?" I raised at least one eyebrow.

"Yep. Next week the Cougars and the Turtles will fight it out in the park," Aaron said, rocking on his heels and bouncing his eyebrows up and down.

"Ok." I wasn't sure if they were serious, or how serious.

"It's a turf thing," Jason explained. "The Orchard is common ground, but they want it to themselves because they think they are so much better than everyone," he waved his stick around as if to emphasize his point. "We are taking it back for everyone, the way it was intended." He slammed the end of his long stick on the ground in front of him.

"Actually, it was never intended to be a park at all. It was supposed to be an orchard," I corrected. They looked at me like I was speaking another language. "It used to be my Grandfather's orchard," I explained.

"Exactly!" Jason pointed at me. "He never meant for it to be their park," he went on, as if he knew Grandfather. "so, they could say who gets to play in it, or who gets to play on the playground, or play soccer in the field. It used to be trees and stuff, we had a fort! They told on us, and it got taken apart and hauled off in pieces."

"So we built another one," Aaron added.

"Yeah, and they took that one apart too! Now we hang out here at the canal bridge," Jason pointed. The bridge was little more than a bunch of two-by-four boards laying across some large boards. The whole thing looked like it might crash into the canal at any moment. "So, it's coming down to a final battle for ownership of The Orchard!" Jason growled.

I didn't necessarily agree with the reasons, but it was easy to get caught up in the movement. The idea of Devin and his friends ruling The Orchard flared an anger inside of me. I would join the throng of battle, not only because it was personal against Devin, but also to get a little revenge for my Grandfather's orchard. The park was built and there was nothing I could do about that, but I could have a say in how the park was run, and not ruled.

"Are you in?" Jason asked.

"Yeah!" I was excited for the first time in weeks, maybe even months.

"Good!" Jason shouted. "Turtle Power!"

"Turtle Power!" Everyone shouted back.

"Turtle Po-wer!" I was a little behind them and not quite as loud. "Ok, what do I do?"

"This is a staff." Jason held his stick up.

"Yeah, like Leonardo," James added.

"Yes. You have to study the foundations of battle, each style: Leonardo, Michelangelo, Donatello, Raphael. Why are the turtles so strong?" Jason asked.

"Their mutant muscles? Slow and steady? Powerful bite?" I searched for an answer. "I don't know," I gave up.

"Steady," Jason explained. Walking slowly as he did. "A turtle's greatest asset is his shell. He spends years building it. He has all he needs. He can even breath under water. A turtle can survive on what he has built, and out-wait any adversary, as long as he needs to. Have you ever been bitten by a turtle?"

"No," I smirked.

"They wait in their shell, patiently..." Jason whispered. "Their attacker will claw and claw at the shell and never leave a mark. As soon as the attacker gets too close to the opening, the only spot the turtle is weak, that is when he strikes forward and bites with everything he's got!" Jason jumped and struck at the air with his staff. "A turtle can bite with hundreds of pounds of pressure. It can crush flesh and bone. It only needs to injure its attacker in one small area to win because it is so painful. We are turtles, we are protected, we are patient, and when we strike, we cause pain, and we win." It was easy to get caught up in the passion of our leader. "Let's train." He tossed me a long stick, and he took a short one.

"You have the advantage because you have the longer stick, right?"

"Yeah, I guess?" I said cautiously.

"Come for me," Jason beckoned. I carefully balanced myself and swung the stick, which was promptly blocked and he delivered a swift reply blow striking my arm. The blow stung, a lot. I kept the wince to myself.

"Not bad." What seemed like a surgical, ninja-like strike was in fact one clumsy child attacking another clumsier child.

"Why didn't you block me?" He asked, like a sage master.

"Because you had knocked my staff away?" I reasoned.

"No, because you weren't waiting for me to hit you. The turtle waits." I had no idea what he was talking about anymore, but I nodded as if I had just learned a great truth. My goal was simply to not get hit again, or if I did, minimize the sting.

We drilled again. This time, as he knocked my staff away, I spun it back in front of me and managed to keep a bout of stick to stick blows going for what seemed like minutes. The other boys watched and 'ooed'. They went back and forth, egging us on, siding with whoever seemed to be *winning* at the moment, based on nothing more than the expert assessment of cartoon watching nerds.

"Good!" Jason complemented finally not taking another blow. The other boys were nodding amongst themselves. I nodded along, self-satisfied that I hadn't suffered a beating.

"Let's get working on a cache to hide the weapons," Jason said to Aaron and me. "James and Nicholas, keep working on weapons," he ordered.

"I have more smoke bombs," Aaron opened his backpack to reveal a good dozen or more of the talc powder filled napkin bombs. "I need like five of them, though."

We set to work, joking and playing. I missed friends back home, but this was pretty close to what I would have been doing with them. It eased my stress. It was amazing how many jokes could be made about bodily sounds, but nine-year-old boys would always find one more while we worked.

"We need to store the weapons. Someplace safe... I think *The Shack*." Jason proposed, gathering up bundles of sticks, now made into contraband.

"Yeah!" Nick agreed with a smile.

"What's the shack?" I asked. I thought I knew every place on the hill.

"Follow us." They each carried smaller weapons like wooden daggers and spikes of sorts in their backpacks, and the longer staffs through their backpack straps. Jason and Aaron both had two staff poles, making a large X on their back. Their shadows truly looked like Ninja Turtles as they walked.

"This is my spear," Aaron pulled one of the staffs off his back to show me the semi-sharpened end. The last eight inches or so were carved with decorative symbols inside a spiral that twisted along the staff.

"Cool," I said inspecting the handy work.

"I've had it for a couple of years. No one dares go near it," he smiled, pressing his thumb on the almost sharp tip, as though it would pierce his skin. "I hide it in the woods, so the Cougars don't find it, or so my parents don't take it away. I had a flame flower once, and my dad took it away," he frowned.

We walked the length of The Orchard to the end of the hill, across the main road where it dropped off quite sharply to the city below. The hillside was covered with thick tree cover and amazingly tall grass.

"The shack is in there," Aaron pointed to the trees. I didn't see anything. One by one they casually glanced around to make sure no one saw us cross the road that ran on the border of the hill. Everyone casually sat on the guardrail and kicked stones for a moment, surveying the road and windows of the houses. Jason was finally satisfied that no one was watching.

"The path goes through the grass. It's hard to find. Don't step off the path, or it's pretty much a long fall down the hill," Jason instructed as he found the path by dividing the grass with his staff. He wasn't kidding. The thick grass and weeds fall right back in behind each of us. We carefully and quickly followed Jason downhill and out of sight from the road above, cutting a diagonal on the hill. We were like elephants in a savanna. Soon, we were out of the thick brush and into the dense trees. The tree-lined portion of the hill was much more difficult footing with twisted roots and rocks all over, but at least you could use the trunks to stabilize yourself. It was like stepping into another world. Suddenly, you couldn't hear any city sounds below the hill. No cars, no kids yelling and playing, and you couldn't even see a building through the canopy of leaves.

"We should build a fort in here!" I smiled.

"No. These woods are off limits," Jason shook his head. Everyone seemed to be keeping an eye out, like prey watching for the hunter.

"Why?" I pondered, looking around as we carefully moved on.

"Bob," Nick said.

"Bob?" I asked.

"Bob," Aaron said plainly. "Bob is a hobo who lives in these woods. He's an old Vietnam vet. He lived in the jungle in Vietnam, now he lives in the woods here. He will pretty much kill and eat anything that he can find.

"He probably knows we are here already," Jason lowered his voice. "There is a shack. Over there," he pointed with his staff. "That's where he lives."

"He's killed, people. He eats them too," James said with wide eyes.

"Shut up," I dismissed.

"No, it's true!" Nick continued. "Carter Harper went missing two years back. It was Bob." Jason stopped behind a big tree that blocked the view of the shack.

"He knows all kinds of ways to kill people and get rid of them," Jason said, peeking around the tree base. "Things he learned in Vietnam. There's no way they can catch him without the bodies, and they will never find those," The hair stood up on the back of my neck as if I were being watched. I peeked around the tree.

"That's why the weapons will be safe here," Jason said with a smile. "Because the Cougars will never come here." He winked. Jason and Aaron started sorting the weapons into like piles at the base of the tree.

"He knows we hide from the cougars in the edge of the woods," Jason explained as he worked, "so he allows it, but if you go any closer than this, he has traps set up all over out here. He can make you disappear before your parents even realize you haven't shown up for dinner."

"Crap!" I jumped back behind the tree.

"What?" Everyone went on guard!

"I saw him! He's right out there, to the left of the shack, up the hill! Dark green jacket." I pointed to where I was sure I had seen the figure.

"Let's bail," Jason shoved the last daggers from Nick's backpack at the pile. "He won't let us be here long, and now that you've spotted him, he will hide."

Jason didn't wait for anyone else, he simply bolted for the trail. I followed in tow, watching over my shoulder. As we cut through the grass, I glanced at the tree with the weapons cache to see a dark figure hunched over, holding a dagger, testing the sharp point against his thumb. His blue eyes like glowing crystals in the dark forest shadow were a chilling site. His face seemed broad, his features concealed by a mask of some kind. I never wanted to go back to these woods again!

"He's there! He's at the weapons!" I whispered as we all sat on the tall grass at the top of the hill, below the guard rail in what we felt was safety.

"It's ok. He understands a warrior's need," Jason assured us all. "He will let me go back for them. I'll take my hiking pack and get them all before the battle." Jason was still holding his long staff. I kept a close eye on the edge of the woods, waiting for those blue eyes to peer out at us. I shuttered as we watched.

6. The Order

The next few days were pretty much like the first day of school. I sat with my eyes fixed straight ahead, sometimes leaning on my hand to block my line of sight to Devin, Brock, and the others. My shoulder was starting to get tired of the awkward posture.

It was interesting how the mingled factions of students were segregated into little two, three, four friend groups, and all seemed to seek the approval of Devin, Jacob, Brock, Julia, and the blonde girl, Cammie. It really was like their own little kingdom where they had a number of servants at court who were just dying to please them!

I was thankful for every bit of busy work we got, it was a reason to keep my head down and try to ignore their taunts. They seemed to have a general disdain for anyone who wasn't in their top tier, but being the newest and weakest to the herd, it was a given that I would be the main target. The fact that I had the attention of the brown haired girl only made things worse. I hadn't even responded to the letter, and still I was subject to the fury that came from Brock being offended that I had somehow stolen his girlfriend.

I wanted to respond, but I was afraid that after the day she gave it to me, they had gotten to her, or worse yet, it had all been a clever joke designed by Brock and Devin! Even if there was no malicious intent, I couldn't find the guts to check 'Yes' and send it back her way. Oh, I had tried! But luckily, pencil erased.

At recess, I wasn't about to join Aaron under the playground. I was quite content to sit on the wall and wait for his escape. It was obvious that he threw his bombs every day for his own amusement, but also to keep it fixed in the minds of other students that he existed, and whether or not they liked him, they would have to acknowledge his presence and even tolerate it. It was interesting, if I even set foot on the gravel, I would be shoved by any number of students, making sure Devin and his friends saw it. Yet Aaron was ignored for the most part, while he was in their midst, attacking them no less! When he ran out of bombs he casually strolled toward me.

"Want to go to the other playground?" Aaron asked.

"We... aren't allowed over there. Are we?" I shook my head.

"It's fine. There are a few who can visit the other side, just don't get in the way of anyone," Aaron cautioned.

We casually strolled over. "So have you ever had a girlfriend?" Aaron asked.

"Kinda, Chantel, at my old school. We kissed a couple of times." I shrugged.

"Radical!" He said, admiringly. "I don't think I like anyone in our class. There is this girl who has white hair in Mr. Clark's class. She's kind of why I visit the other playground. I'll try to find her so you can see, but you can't steal her!" He shot me a glance.

"I won't!" I held up my hands in defense. I knew if there was one sure fire way to destroy a friendship early on, it was to say anything about liking the other guy's girl. I had seen many friendships end over that kind of thing in my many days of elementary education. I had also made an enemy or two simply by talking to a girl I thought was cute, or now by simply even being alive where a girl might see me and think I was cute!

"So you're having a birthday party?" I had almost forgotten about the invites. I hadn't noticed them being handed out.

"Oh yeah, I guess. My parents are making me because my grandma wants to have all of the mother's over for tea while we do something lame," I rolled my eyes.

"Sucky. There she is! On that slide." He was right, her hair was nearly white in the sun. She was probably inches taller than us, and the word beautiful came to mind. She was obviously one of the popular upper-grade girls, as she seemed to be frequently approached by just about every boy and girl on the upper playground, all seeking her attention with a comment, or joke, or attempt to get her to engage in whatever game they were about. She smiled politely and waved off the attempts, content to hang out with a brown haired girl, who no one seemed to pay attention to. The brown-haired girl idled by, waiting for their conversation to resume.

When the she turned toward me and Aaron for a moment, I got a good look at her. She was beautiful! I had never been so overcome with the desire to talk to a girl. Her light eyes stood out from her dark hair like a black cat's might.

"Her name is Jessica. I'm going to marry her." Aaron could have her. I was struck by her wallflower friend. Surely being two grades ahead of us implied they were both vastly out of our league! We both attempted to find other places to look but kept sneaking peeks at the two.

"I'm marrying her friend," I whispered.

"What?" Aaron asked.

"Marry Jessica. I am going to marry that girl she's talking to."

"Oh, Megan? She's not blonde," Aaron shook his head.

"No, she isn't," I pointed out the obvious nature of the statement. "Do you know her?"

"Our dad's work together. I get to talk to her sometimes at his work things."

"Does Megan come to?"

"No, Megan's dad doesn't work with them. Sometimes she's over at Jessica's house, though." I was entranced. I could practically feel Grandfather's bony elbow nudging me to go talk to her. There was no way in this world that was ever going to happen!

"Do you want to take a picture? It will last longer," Aaron joked. Perhaps I had been staring. "Follow me." Aaron headed toward the pair, with hands in pockets. I had this overwhelming sense of impending danger, yet I followed in Aaron's every footstep in the gravel. Regardless of being an outcast in our classroom, he walked with purpose, regardless of which side of the playground he was on. I wished I knew his secret, but at least I felt less like I was going to be attacked on this playground unless Joseph saw me.

"Hey, Jessica," he shrugged as he walked by her. She paused for a second.

"Hey," she said plainly. *Say hi to the friend.* The idea came from nowhere but sounded like my Grandfather whispering from among the playground commotion.

"Hey, Megan," she looked at me in surprise, her lips parting as if she were going to reply, exposing a hint of braces, but couldn't find the words. I quickly looked away and back to Aaron's footsteps.

"You talked to the friend," Aaron sounded shocked. "I don't know if that was brilliant or brilliantly stupid," Aaron smiled.

"What's brilliantly stupid?" I asked, kicking gravel out of the ankle of my shoe.

"That, what you just did. I mean, it's fine. You can do whatever you want, but if they come after you over here, I can't help you out."

"I don't need to be helped," I shrugged.

"Yeah, that's what you say right now," Aaron challenged me.

"I don't," I furrowed my brow.

"Yeah, ok," he said sarcastically. "Guess we'll find out." His quick pace slowed as an old kid with a face full of freckles and a mullet stepped in front of me.

"Did you just talk to Jessica?"

"No," I shrugged.

"Bull! I just saw you!" He stuck his finger in my chest.

"I didn't say anything to Jessica. I swear."

"You better not, worm," he shoved my shoulder to drive his point. I got the feeling he was not even close to being someone Jessica and Megan would ever talk to. He was just out of place and angry. He was likely a future version of us with a mullet. "Well?" he demanded.

"Well, what?" I asked in confusion, giving him a look that summed up my feelings about what an idiot I obviously thought he was. His reply was almost more intelligent than I had expected but was no less shocking when his fist made contact with my face. In my daze, flat on my back in the gravel, I took note of several voices "ooing" and laughing. The older boy smirked and spit down at me as he walked away. The sound of gravel crunching under his shoes seemed to drown out everyone else.

"Whoa," Aaron mused, not offering me a hand up. He shifted his feet, unsure of how long to be seen with me, beaten down on the playground floor. I wasn't sure how long I wanted to be seen! I forced myself up quickly and stumbled toward the field. Aaron was somewhere behind me, trying to look casual and unassociated. "Are you ok?" Aaron asked. We were finally far enough away to be in close proximity.

"Yeah," I shook my head.

"Sorry, I couldn't jump in. It's kind of pointless when we are on their side. No point in both of us getting our butts kicked, ya know?" Aaron patted me on the shoulder.

"Yeah, I know." I couldn't blame him. I was the new kid, and we barely knew each other. I couldn't very well expect him to have my back, even if I was the newest member of their club.

"Have you ever been in a fight before?" Aaron asked.

"Yeah. My old school had lots of fights" I rubbed my aching face.

"You can't tell on him... that's not how it works here." Aaron said, walking backward for a moment.

"I don't even know who he is. Can't really tell on him," I said, blinking and sliding my jaw from side to side.

"I'm just saying, sometimes you just have to take a beating from the upper class if you want to go on living. Ya know?" Aaron waved his hand, gesturing that it wasn't a big deal.

"It's bull crap," I carefully touched the throbbing mark on my cheek. It would bruise, but he really hadn't put a lot of force into it. I had been hit harder, by smaller people.

"Well, you did talk to an older girl," Aaron winked.

"So? I said hi."

"So? That's crossing the line in two ways. She's an older kid, and she's a popular kid. Put in a couple of years and maybe you can earn that, but you are far too new to the hill to go around talking. You should have just not spoke," Aaron shrugged.

"Not spoke to who? Her or him?" I joked.

"Both!" Aaron shouted. I knew his advice was good. He knew a lot more about surviving this school than I did! I could only hope to get to the point he was at by the time we moved across the fence into the middle school and high school.

"I never even said anything to Devin and that dude hates me," I said, trying to reason it all out.

"That's just how it is," Aaron shook his head.

"So I just...what? Get my butt kicked by Devin, by that guy, that girl, anyone who wants to kick it, for a couple more years?" I asked in a huff.

"Probably," Aaron nodded, pursing his lips.

"And then what? If I shut up are they going to leave me alone?"

"Probably not," he shook his head.

"So, I might as well talk to whoever I want and say whatever I want if I am going to get my butt kicked anyway, right?" I stopped walking.

"I dunno, man. I spent two years as the new kid. Everyone already had their best friends by the time I showed up. Brock is the only other new kid I have seen since I got here, and he went right into the top like they were just waiting for him to show up and be one of them. You're either one of them or you aren't." He put his hand on my shoulder. "And you aren't."

"It's bull crap," I knocked his hand away. "My family has been here longer than any of them!"

"You're my friend man, my only friend in our class, but we have to be smart."

"So how did you do it? You fight back and go wherever you want?" I asked anxiously.

"I fight other people at my level, I never go after the top, or anyone near the top. That is suicide," Aaron was explaining, when James came running up.

"It's going down today!" He huffed and puffed, out of breath.

"What?" Aaron questioned.

"The battle, the rumble... it's happening in The Orchard today at like four or five. Jason and Devin just talked it over in The Tower." James stammered.

"Without us?" I protested.

"I guess," James shrugged. "We have like no time to get things ready!"

"It's fine. Jason knows what he is doing," Aaron assured. I was not as confident in our leader, as I rubbed my sore cheek. I wasn't exactly ready to take one on the other cheek.

I spent the afternoon tapping my foot nervously and trying to avoid eye contact with Devin and his friends. I tried to wish the clock to tick away the minutes left in the school day with wishful thinking, but it wasn't working. I picked up a word here and there among other kids, in their occasional whispers. Words like, "in the face," "Jeffery's butt." They rang through the soft murmur of kids doing math story problems like a church bell on a snowy morning.

I lingered as long as possible while Devin practically bounced out of the room, beaming with excitement - likely the excitement of getting to trounce me into The Orchard grass later. I had already suffered a surprise pummeling, I really had no interest in receiving a more formal extended version.

The bus was normal enough, full of disruption and argument. Jason and Aaron were talking about a video game. I was far too tense for casual conversation. I was trying to figure out a way to not show up to The Orchard. I felt compelled by a sense of duty to back up my new friends, even if Aaron hadn't been able to come to my aid. This was different, this was peer against peer on equal footing. This was an opportunity to show them I had their backs in the thick of it, to shore up our friendship. Even if I was more of a liability than an aid, I would be there. The very thought of standing in The Orchard, in rank and file, was enough to cause me some serious threat of diarrhea, but I would be there for my friends. I would show them.

My nervousness quelled only slightly when we got to Devin's street. The bus stopped and opened the door. No one moved. Devin and his friends sat still, casting looks toward the back of the bus, and I felt like directly at me.

"No changing stops," Mr. Speaker ordered them. "Follow the order." He tapped at the clipboard of names he kept on the dash, his makeshift desk. Devin and his friends rose. He stared directly at me with a knowing smirk.

"Later," Devin nodded at me, no doubt to signify he would personally be looking for me at The Orchard.

I began running through scenarios in my head of how I could beat him. Any weapon I had would really only have one shot at him before he would be on top of me. If having an older brother taught me anything, it was how to take a beating, not how to defend myself!

I had one chance to not miss, and then hope I could drum my fists at him quick enough to get the upper hand and get back to safety. Maybe I could use a staff pole and trip him. Maybe I just dove right for his feet and knocked him off, balance before he even got to me, and then I could run.

78

"See you at The Orchard at 4:30," Aaron patted my shoulder as the bus started slowing down.

"Yeah," I nodded, my foot bouncing rapidly against the floor as I stared out the window.

"You're getting the weapons?" Aaron asked Jason.

"Don't worry. I have a secret weapon." He winked at Aaron and smiled widely. I held out hope for his optimism.

Another moment, and the bus stopped at our street. Joseph and his friends were off like a shot. I wasn't sure he actually remembered I got off at the same stop. By now, Jason should be half way to collect the weapons.

I wondered what the secret weapon was. Perhaps some kind of pepper bomb, like Aaron's powder bombs. Maybe I could steal the huge can of pepper from Grandmother's butler pantry, make some tissue bombs, and impress the other Turtles. It would make a good defense for sure. I finally had some kind of hope at being able to defend myself! My own secret weapon!

I practically ran home, passing Joseph with ease. I slipped into the butler's pantry and directly into the bathroom before anyone even saw I was home. I set to work filling tissues with a good handful of pepper each. I quietly sifted through the cupboard and medicine cabinet until I found dental floss. Then, I tied each of them shut. I had enough pepper to make four of them without using up all of the pepper. We should be moving into a new house by the time anyone needed to refill the pepper shakers, so I would be long gone before anyone asked questions!

I carefully hid the pepper tin under the sink, behind some stacked toilet paper and cleaning products. I slipped the pepper bombs into the pockets of my jacket, careful not to tear them open. I carefully slipped out of the bathroom and laid my jacket and backpack down next to the fireplace in the parlor where they would go undisturbed for some time. I went out back and behind the carriage house, glancing around as I turned the corner. I took the opportunity to practice a few karate moves I hoped would help me, practicing how to make a sweeping kick, intended to knock someone's feet out from under them. Then, I quickly scrambled from a crouch and jumped on top of the grass where my victim would lay.

79

I felt quite confident. We were going to win this thing! We were going to rule The Orchard, and when word spread that I had defeated Devin, Aaron and I would ascend The Tower, and rule the playground as well.

I darted out of the house and headed to the park. I held the pepper bombs carefully in each hand, buried in my jacket pockets. The other turtles were all waiting on our end, near our hideout by the canal. The cougars were all standing on the playground talking and joking around.

"Hey, guys," I said trying to sound bold and confident, rather than the bundle of nerves I was inside.

"Hey," Jason nodded. "Ready?"

"Yeah I guess," I shrugged. "Where are the weapons?"

"Gone. Hobo Bob must have taken them."

"What are we gonna do?" I asked with concern, clutching my pepper bombs in my pockets.

"It's ok, we don't need them."

"Maybe *you* don't," I exclaimed. Easy for the karate master to shrug off, he didn't have an entire gang looking for a chance to stomp him into the dirt. I started trying to think of ways out of this. I could fake my mom calling me home. No way would I hear that from here.

"Let's go," the Cougars had left the playground and were walking our way. The turtles started walking. James and Nick beamed with glee. Aaron seemed much more cautious. Suddenly, both groups started running at full pace across The Orchard, including myself! I was immediately swept up in the action, with my heart pumping, I bolted into battle with my new brothers.

Devin picked me out and started running out ahead of his group, on a direct collision course with me. Just as we were nearing each other, I pulled my hand back to throw a pepper bomb when my feet suddenly stopped, and I flew face forward into the dirt with amazing impact. My ears rang, and I was unable to tell what direct was up. While recovering from the daze I suddenly became aware of, sharp pains that I quickly

80

decided were either punches or kicks being delivered from above. I tucked into a ball, being weighed down by the force of someone on top of me. After a moment the weight lifted. I kept my face tucked between my arms. The sound of muffled laughter surrounded me.

"Good job," Devin said, laughing. I peeked up to see Devin and Jason high-fiving each other. I had been betrayed. Rage welled up inside but was drown out by the desire to avoid a further beating. Out of the options, "Fight or Flight," "Flight" won out. Still, how did I get away with being jumped on from all sides? Maybe I could get a piece of revenge and make my get away. I still had a pepper bomb held tightly in my fist. I could smell it in the air, the tissue was already breaking apart. I had one chance to make my escape.

"As agreed," Jason said, pointing down at me. Aaron shifted and looked anywhere but at me. James and Nick were practically bouncing with excitement.

"So, what now?" Nick asked.

"You can come on the playground," Devin said, matter of factly. I summoned all the courage and rage I could. I imagined Devin's face, his stupid devil eyebrows as he laughed. I jumped up and threw my pepper bomb at his face as hard as I could. It broke open leaving my hand broadcasting a spray of the fine powder into the air, and I ran away from it in a burst of speed.

Everyone coughed and waved, swatting at the cloud. They quickly overcame their shock and lit after me. I had a good lead on them! I ran toward the main road that bordered the park. I couldn't keep up this pace all the way back to Grandmother's, these guys were all on the Soccer team, and they would catch me any moment! I turned up my sprint and headed for the guard rail. I aimed to be right in the trees near the weapons. Maybe Hobo Bob would be there. Adults had to stop kids from fighting, it was some kind of grown-up law.

"Stop him!" Jason screamed. "He's going for the weapons!"

"Get back here!" Devin yelled.

Jason was gaining on me faster than anyone else, he was a grade ahead of us after all. I got to the guard rail first and cleared it with ease. I headed straight into the tree line, near what I thought was the path. I suddenly lost my footing and began a steep downhill slide toward the trees. I skidded and bumped and rolled through the tall grass, right into a bush just inside the tree line. I quickly jumped up to my feet and stumbled into the trees. I headed in the direction of the weapons cache. I dodged trees, bouncing from trunk to trunk, dancing across the thick roots with ease.

I reached the large tree with the weapons and quickly grabbed two large staffs, stomping the others repeatedly in a frenzy, crushing and cracking them into pieces. The last eight inches of Aaron's spear was sticking up, and I picked it up and put it in my jacket.

Satisfied with the damage, I headed deeper into the woods, trying to stay as far uphill as I could, away from the shack. My side ached and burned with every breath like a tightening rope across my ribs. I found a tree with several nice branches forking from the base and like a monkey, I quickly scaled myself a nice height up the massive trunk, and hid behind the trunk and leaves. If there was something I excelled at, it was climbing. I could scale trees, house rain gutters, doorways, fences. You name it, I could climb it.

I heard the cries of my attackers moving through the grass and to the tree line. I stayed hidden.

"He's already been there!" Someone yelled.

"He destroyed the weapons!" I was pretty sure that one had been Jason.

"I thought you said he would be a wuss!" Devin accused.

"He is!" Jason shouted back.

"You're dead!" Someone shouted, presumably at me.

"You might as well move into these woods looser!"

"The second you come out, we'll be waiting!"

Their voices were retreating from the woods. They would no doubt be waiting on top of the hill, watching the guard rail like junkyard dogs pacing a fence line. I could move downhill and walk along the bottom of the hill and come back up the front, right to our street. They probably wouldn't be that far down.

I sank into the draw of the branch where it met the trunk and breathed a sigh of relief for a moment. I was suddenly aware of the taste of blood in my mouth. It was hard to tell if it had come from my nose or lip, as both were obviously aching now. I carefully touched both, yep they hurt just as bad as I thought they would. Also, I had peed myself, which seemed like I should have noticed that before the blood. What else could go wrong? How could the day get any worse?

After sometime, I carefully and silently climbed down. I crept through the trees, looking for the easiest way to the bottom of the hill. The trees seemed to be thinner, in a diagonal to the bottom.

I heard distant laughter of the newly united group. I clenched my teeth in rage and tightened my fist on the staffs I was carrying - glancing uphill toward their direction. I quietly mocked them, making a face. While my eyes were off the path, I tumbled forward, flailing with the staffs to stop my fall. My efforts were in vain as I landed again face first into the dirt. I felt the trickle of warm blood down my lip. I spit the thick salty warm spit back to the ground and raised myself up.

On the ground in front of me were large dark boots, and dark green pants, covered in mud spots. Piercing blue eyes stared down at me behind a camouflage rag mask.

"Hello there," a deep rough voice said, curiously. I almost wished I had waited to pee myself.

"Hi?" I managed to squeak out through my surprise. Strangely, I wasn't exactly afraid, more surprised.

"Having a little trouble with your friends?" the man asked.

"Yeah, well, they aren't really my friends," I shrugged, slowly getting to my feet. He held my arm and made sure I was steady enough to stand on my own before letting go.

"I gathered," the man nodded.

"Are you... Hobo Bob?" I asked carefully, not wanting to offend him.

"I've been called a lot of things. You can call me something else if you'd like."

"Like what?" I tilted my head.

"Whatever you want."

"Are you going to kill me?" I asked in general curiosity.

"Am I what?" He took a step back.

"Going to kill me?"

"Why would I want to kill you?" he asked, tilting his head in confusion. "Do I look like someone who kills children?" he laughed holding his arms out to his sides. "Don't answer that, of course, I do." He lowered the camo mask from his face, revealing a mass of wild facial hair. The dark dirty hair was almost the color of his sun-baked, dirt-stained face, making his lips and eye pop even more so. "I know a lot of people like to judge me... if the guys who told you I eat kids are the same guys who did that," he motioned to my face, "I don't know if I would believe much of what they are telling you."

"They said you went crazy after the Vietnam war and live in the trees and eat birds and rats and kill anyone who comes in here," I said quite casually.

"Ok... that's kind of a lot at once, there. Let's just leave it at I don't harm people, ok? I'm sworn to protect," he nodded.

"Like Optimus Prime."

"Like who now?" He was clearly not familiar with the work of the Transformers.

"Optimus Prime, leader of the Auto-bots. Sworn to protect the human race from the Decepticons," I stated, as if he should know what I was talking about, from that description.

"Sure," he nodded along.

"Ok," I must have still looked pretty stunned... which I was, for multiple reasons. The primary of which was not the hulking camo-clad figure before me.

"Well, I'm not a big fan of walking much uphill, I can take you to the tree-line, though," he motioned. I shook my head.

"You're welcome to wait out your friends in the woods if you'd like," he half stated, half questioned. "They aren't much for coming into these woods. I don't suppose they will give you much trouble," he tried to reassure me.

"I can just walk to the bottom of the hill and go around the long way," I reasoned.

"Oh, through the condo's and such... yeah that's a good idea too," he waved me onward. We carefully descended the hill.

"So you live in that fort?" I nodded back where we had come from.

"Yeah, it's a nice little place. No one disturbs me much. I don't get many visitors, but the rent is cheap," Bob joked.

"I'll visit. If you don't mind me playing in the woods?"

"I don't mind. I'll bet your friends won't follow you into the trees. I'm not around too much, but they don't need to know that. It's safer if they think I'm always watching for them," Bob winked.

"Good idea," I agreed. "If they chase me into the woods can I knock on your door or hide behind your shack."

"Sure. I don't have much of a door, just a board really. You feel free to hide inside if I'm not home." He stopped at the edge of the woods. "Well, this is about as far as I am going tonight," he said, gazing down the street.

85

"People don't really like me much and being seen together, well it's kinda hard to explain. You gonna be ok from here?" Bob asked.

"Yeah," I nodded. He turned without a word and tromped back into the woods toward his shed turned home, muttering something about hating *rotten kids*.

I began the long, slow walk home down the street lined with condos and townhomes. It was a young neighborhood with plenty of high-end cars and young professionals, eager to put their marks on the world and earn their spot on the hill ten or twenty years from now. A couple of such young men came walking down the sidewalk, their pressed shirts crisp and clean, their hair precisely placed and held firm, their dark sunglasses making it hard to tell if they were looking at me. One of them smirked a laugh to himself and nudged the other as he approached his shiny black sports car.

"You ok, kid?" one of them laughed.

"Yeah," I shrugged, limping on.

"Little school yard fight?" another guy inquired.

"Yeah," I replied.

"It's good for ya! It'll turn you into something," he laughed getting into his car. He rolled down the window, "Go home and watch the Karate Kid a few times!" The car roared off, with the two laughing and joking. Not that I expected anything else from anyone. At least they asked if I was ok. I wet my hand in the sprinkler of a condo lawn and used it to wet and wipe the blood off of my face.

7. Welcome Home...

I dragged into the house, hoping no one would notice. I needed to get to the bathroom and assess the damage before I was ready for anyone to call me out on my appearance. The last thing I wanted was for Joseph to notice my disheveled nature and incontinence. I run a line down the entry and into the hall, to the closest guess bath. Kim caught sight of me from another room and said something to someone. My hand was just about on the bathroom door knob when my Grandmother spoke.

"Jeffery!"

"Ma'am," I replied, only turning slightly, my less beaten side toward her.

"Come here," she commanded in a tone, put out she even had to say it. I should have already been heading toward her.

"I really need to ... go," I resisted, quietly trailing off.

"Jeffery," she growled. I slowly turned and shuffled toward her, down the long hall, keeping my head turned away. I pretended to be looking at the ornate shelves of trinkets from around the world. When I had gotten close enough, she reached out and snapped my face forward by the chin, causing me to wince. "What in the world have you done?" she demanded.

"I tripped. Playing in The Orchard and the Canal."

"Tripped," she said flatly.

"Yeah," I locked in eye contact. I didn't lie... not exactly anyway. I didn't know what came from the beating and what came from my series of falls in the woods.

"Come with me," she took my hand and dragged me to the larger bathroom near the parlor. She opened the large wardrobe style cupboard and set a metal first aid kit down on the marble sink top with a click. I had been subjected to the box's ancient medicines after thorn scrapes and other injuries over the years. Everything in that box was painful!

She opened a glass bottle and spilled harsh stinking contents onto a white gauze cloth. She was not gentle at all as dabbing and wiping my cuts and scratches. I clinched my jaw.

"Did this happen after school?" she inquired.

"Yes," I said plainly.

"I hope you aren't proud of this," she scolded. "People are going to brag that they did this to you. Don't dignify them by even engaging in their game. I don't care who did this, it didn't happen. Do you understand that?" she asked. I nodded. She increased her grip on my chin to keep my head from moving and continued her nursing.

"When I was your age my family moved a lot. A lot of other girls teased me, pulled my hair and dress. I never fought back. I always turned the other cheek and was twice as nice to them. That is how you win. You be the bigger person and you gain power of them by being above them." I had no idea what she was talking about. I didn't fight back! I had run away! Wasn't that the same thing? Girls didn't understand.

"Yes, ma'am." I agreed for sake of not wanting her to continue on.

"Go work on your schooling," she practically pushed me from the bathroom with a swat. I shuffled off and dug my spelling and math workbooks from my backpack and sat on a chair at the large dark lacquered dining room table. I almost leaned on my hand before getting a sharply painful reminder that my cheek was scuffed. It must have been the salt from my hand that made it sting for several minutes.

I tried to focus on reading, but couldn't get the dread of school the next day out of my head. I tended to agree with Grandmother, that I shouldn't even acknowledge that anything had happened. I was going to have to face them all the entire day. How could I ignore that fact while they all sat and snickered, as they no doubt would - as they told and retold the story in whispers behind my back. I played scenarios in my head.

"I kicked your butt, dude!"

"No, you didn't. My brother did this... My Grandmother's horse did this... it ran me into trees... I vowed to never strike another human. I took a

vow of peace." They all resulted in the same ending, Devin punching me in the face. I didn't *ever* want to get punched in the face again! Or kicked. Or wet myself for that matter.

Suddenly I heard voices speaking quickly, with urgency. My mother entered the dining room.

"What in the world happened?" she stopped in the doorway with a forlorn look.

"What happened isn't as important as how he responds to it." Grandmother followed her in.

"Thank you, Rose. I think I have it from here," my mother said, rolling her eyes out of Grandmother's sight.

"If he goes into that school trying to bully them, he's going to make more trouble and lose more friends," Grandmother advised.

"Thank you, Rose. I'll take him upstairs now." Mother was obviously keeping her true opinion to herself. Which was fine as far as I was concerned, it kept mother from scolding me for the time being.

"I am on the board of that school, as you know. So how he responds is a reflection of this family," Grandmother nodded, and stared over the top of her glasses.

"Rose," my mother glared.

"Well listen to me, going on about things you already know full well." Grandmother turned slowly and left. "What do I know anyway? I only raised a brood of boys while managing to help run several businesses and a household, as well as public committees. I might only have valuable insight, but other people know better than I. Did you know that Kim?" Grandmother continued on down the hallway.

Mother rolled her eyes as Grandmother's voice faded, more slowly than it should have for someone who was walking away. Mother lead me upstairs to my room.

"What happened?" mother questioned.

89

"Nothing," I shrugged.

"Do I look like your Grandmother? What happened?" she demanded.

"Those guys I was playing with... we had a battle in the park, and I don't know what happened, but a couple of them took it kinda seriously." I casually explained away.

"Kind of serious? Your friends did this?" she glared at me.

"I don't know," I was not about to try to explain the politics involved.

"What is going on?" she said full of concern.

"They aren't really my friends," I said staring out the window.

"Well, why did you go to The Orchard with them for a *battle* if they aren't your friends? Are you trying to drive your Grandmother insane? Or drive me insane with her interjection?" Mother put her hand on her forehead in frustration.

"I don't know. I was trying to make friends."

"Well, you stick with your own friends and leave those guys alone," mother said with such assured grasp of how things worked, but she clearly didn't have a clue.

"I don't even have friends," I shook my head.

"Well, obviously they aren't the guys to hang out with then. What about your friends you play with when we would come visit? Are any of them in your class?" mother asked.

"That is Joseph," I said with a bit of insult taken. "I don't have friends here." I couldn't believe she didn't know this.

"Well, surely some of the guys you play with. You have safety in numbers, if you are alone they will pick on you, but if you are with other boys they will leave you alone. So just stay with other boys..." mother smiled, as if she had just solved a cross-word I had been working.

"There are no other boys. I don't play with anyone when we visit. I just hang out in the garden and watch," *Grandfather in the shop*. Was this how the rest of the statement went?

"Well, hang out with some of the girls in your class," she raised eyebrows.

"Are you kidding me!?" I replied with all the indignation I could muster.

"I am just trying to help you stay away from trouble. Finding friends is the best way to do that," she threw her hands up.

"You aren't listening! I have no friends! I can't change that! I'm alone here!" I threw myself on the bed and buried my aching face against the cool pillow. The pain wasn't as bad as the conversation, and that was saying something.

"I have no time for this," she said, shaking her head and walking away. "Joseph, can't you walk your brother home?" she asked Joseph as she walked down the hall. He had been hiding in the hall, listening.

"No. It's his problem, not mine!" Joseph protested.

"Joseph!" My mother shot back at him.

"No! It's not my fault he doesn't have friends!" Joseph continued.

I threw a pillow at the door, knocking it closed with a loud bump. The golden elephant's ruby chip eyes gleamed out from under the pillow. I clutched it in my fist and stared at the old fashioned wallpaper in the fading sunlight.

 When I emerged from the bedroom, it was nearly dark outside. I wasn't sure if it was morning or night as I stumbled down the stairs. I rubbed the sleep from my eyes and smelled some kind of beef dinner that convinced me it was evening of the same day. I made my way through the parlor the scent of Grandfather's cigars wafted in the air. Someone must have raided his humidor.

How many times had I stood behind Grandfather as he read the paper and darted my face into thick ribbons of the rich smoke as he puffed his cigars? I rarely even inhaled, as it made me choke and cough, usually to

Grandfather's amusement. I studied the curls of smoke as they slowly drifted, seeing how close I could get to them and still focus my eyes before breaking through them like a fighter pilot cutting through clouds in the sky.

I stood motionless, looking at Grandfather's empty chair. With a heavy sigh, I continued on. I could hear my father on the phone in the study, and my mother was standing next to him.

"Ok, so if the class action lawsuit goes through, what kind of timetable are we talking about?" Father asked the person on the other end of the phone, hovering over papers.

"How do we even know this is legal? We don't even have the money to get involved," mother shook her head.

"Dear, five hundred now could mean five million a year from now," Father said to mother, covering the phone with his hand.

"I don't like this..." My mother glanced and saw me in the hall. She moved and shut the door. I was tempted to listen at the door, but it sounded like boring grown up stuff. I moved on.

Joseph and Christopher, a cousin Joseph's age, were laying belly boost at the top of the scary stairs to the cellar, carefully folding paper airplanes. There were several such small paper airplane models, of various technique, laying in a growing pile at the bottom of the stairs. Joseph gently sailed his next plane down the staircase. He encouraged it 'go, go, go', as it glided.

"Yes!" Joseph cried as it struck the far wall, only skimming the side wall for a moment.

"What are you guys doing?" I asked, mostly in hopes of inclusion, as I could plainly see what they were doing.

"Not getting our butts kicked on a playground," Christopher laughed. Joseph high-fived him.

"No, get my airplane," Joseph instructed me, as he started folding another piece of paper.

"No way! I'm not going down there!" I shook my head.

"Because Grandfather is down there?" Christopher said assumptively.

"What?" I asked.

"Grandfather. It was in the will. He wanted to be buried here on the hill, but they wouldn't allow it in The Orchard, so the next option was here in the house."

"Shut up," I shook my head in disbelief.

"I'm serious," he said looking up from drawing a shark face on his airplane. Joseph nodded in agreement.

"They don't let people do that." I was pretty sure anyway... "I was at the funeral!" I challenged.

"No, they won't let you be buried in your yard, in case they need to put in a phone line or something. The funeral was all for show. You can be buried in your own cellar. It's just that most people don't have a cellar, they have a basement which has walls and a floor and stuff, so it doesn't work. I'm serious, come on, I'll show you" he started down the stairs. No one ever went down the stairs! He paused and turned. Joseph got up and followed him, and turned to look at me.

"Well? Come on," they continued on down to the old wooden door. The door was original to the small house Grandmother and Grandfather had originally built the home sixty years before, when they farmed the whole hill. The cellar had been used for storing cans of food they grew, and later was used to run plumbing and other things as they added onto the now massive house. My father said they had actually knocked down the entire house except for the floor and built the entire house around that existing cellar.

The door was several long wide boards, latched together by a board top and bottom, on giant metal hinges that must have been a hundred years old. The door knob had chipped white enamel and attached to a huge black metal box that required an ancient key that hung on a rusty nail on the door frame. The entire stairwell was contrary to every other aspect of the house! Everything else was decorative woods and inlay, carefully worked stone and metal ornaments, plush fabrics, sprays of design and pattern everywhere. But not the stairwell, It was as old and gnarled as Grandfather had been, and just about as welcoming.

I eased down a couple of steps. The air immediately changed as I knew it would. It was far colder and held a dank quality. I had only ever approached the door a handful of times. I was sure they were lying, yet for some reason I was creeping down the stairs. They seemed completely casual about unlocking the door and walking inside. Surely it wouldn't hurt to peek inside and prove them wrong. The stairwell was lit by a single lightbulb overhead in the middle of the stairs that created a dark shadow in the doorway. I peered inside, inching my way to the doorway, straining my eyes to see in the dark. It was so dimly lit inside I would almost have described it as being a brown light if that was possible.

I looked to each side of the doorway and didn't see either Christopher or Joseph. Massive wooden shelves stood from floor to ceiling, in long rows. They extended into the dark until I couldn't see the far wall. The shelves were loaded with canned goods, and bottles of vegetables and such. Giant barrels lined the wall, filled with who knew what, and stored for some unknown reason that only made sense to people who 'remembered the second great war'.

I heard Christopher and Joseph talking and messing around a few rows down. I glance back up the stairs and carefully walked inside. I moved past the first shelf and peered to see if Joseph was down there. I thought I saw him when suddenly I heard him by the door.

"Say '*hi*' to Grandfather, you wimp," Joseph smirked and shut the door. I froze in place in the darkness. I couldn't even see the door once it had shut, so it was pointless to run for it. It was just as well. At least I knew where he was, and he couldn't bother me further if there was a door between us. My stomach grumbled, but the nervousness I usually felt had faded. Perhaps I was just done caring and worrying for the day.

I sighed and took a jar of peaches off the shelf and sat in an old wooden rocking chair. I managed to get the large golden ring off the jar and pop the top. Kim often brought the jars of peaches or pears up for a treat for us. I lifted the jar and drank a good portion of the sweet syrupy juice off the top and then slurped up a peach slice. I sank into the old wooden chair and looked around. This wasn't too much different than the layer Aaron had shown me under the school. I might just start hiding down there on a regular basis. I considered the possibilities as I rocked slowly.

After some time, I began to wonder how I was going to get out. Surely they missed me for dinner. Then again, they might be happy that the trouble-maker, shame of the family, wasn't dining with them. Joseph would likely tell them I was in my room! I struggled to keep my eyes open. The room seemed to fade in and out. Suddenly I snapped my eyes open as a dark figure came down the row of shelves.

"Stealing my peaches?" the gruff voice sounded amused. It was unmistakably Grandfather!

"I," I didn't know what to say!

"That's ok. You've had a rough enough day, I would wager. Don't let it get you down. I lost plenty of fights, walked away from plenty too. Stand up for yourself, speak with authority." Speak with authority might as well have been put on Grandfather's headstone. It was practically a trademarked statement. "You don't need to hide in a cellar eating peaches your whole life." He reached for the peaches. As I looked down at the peaches I wasn't sure if I jumped because I was startled when I felt Grandfather's hand touch mine, or if I had been dreaming and leaped awake, but as I scanned the cellar, I was sitting alone. The door popped open as Kim carried a box toward me, suddenly she gasped and dropped the box. Whatever was in the box made a horrible crash, and she bit off an oath in her native tongue, with a dark glower toward me.

"What you doing?!" she demanded in her thick accent.

"Joseph and Christopher locked me in here," I said bashfully.

"Why you listen to them always the time? Huh? They bad boys!" She motioned me out of the room. I staggered up the stairs.

8. Avoidance

The next day, as I walked into school, I felt every eye in the hall center on me. It seemed everyone I passed was whispering something to the person next to them and laughing. My stomach burned with nervousness as I walked into my classroom. It felt like walking into the lion's den, like as soon as I got through the doorway I would be slammed in the face by unforeseen enemies. Luckily, Devin and his goons weren't there at all.

I made my way to my desk and sat down, letting go of a tight breath. I fished a book from my desk and opened it to a random page. I scanned back and forth, only appearing to read, but really trying to listen for my name floating around the room as more kids came in. Finally, Devin came in, with others right behind him.

"Wow!" Devin laughed. "Jeffery, what happened?" he joked. I didn't look up from my book.

"Take your seats, boys," Mrs. Potts instructed from her desk, glancing over the rim of her glasses at me.

"You look like you fell down a hill, after getting your butt kicked," Devin whispered in a low voice as he moved to his desk.

"Yeah, it only took like ten of you," I whispered back.

"What was that?" Devin paused and fixed his gaze on me. I didn't move. I turned my head slightly to the next page, away from Devin. Class continued much like that until first recess. I, of course, waited for everyone else to leave first, but I forced myself out of my desk.

"Come along Jeffery." Mrs. Potts motioned.

"I don't feel well. Can I stay in the room with my head down?"

"Patton never won a war by laying his head down on a desk Mr. Alfrey," she raised her eyebrows. I supposed it was obvious from looking at my face, what had happened. "I have no interest in seeing you have your hat handed to you on the playground, nor do I intend to let you hide away from life's unpleasantness." She said folding her hands.

I assumed having one's hat handed to them was old speak for getting your butt kicked and stomped into the ground by a dozen guys. I hung my head and dragged out the door. I had no refuge, nowhere to go. I couldn't skid over to the older playground, it was surely off limits - more than ever. I couldn't head for the field, as the playground was in between us. I exited the outer door and skimmed as far down the wall toward the older playground as I could without drawing too much notice from either side. Their forces had nearly doubled now that they had the Turtles. They could easily stake out the entire playground.

I hugged the wall just beyond where the last of the girls were playing hop-scotch. I hated leaning on the cold brick wall in the shade of the building, I would have much rather been ten feet toward the playground where the sun was warming, but I couldn't risk it. The shade made it harder for those in the sunlight to see me.

After several minutes I hoped I had avoided their notice and bought some sort of safety. I kept an eye out for any movement that seemed to be coming toward me, but I began playing with the rock on the ground with the toe of my shoe. I started playing a miniature game of soccer between my two feet, floating back and forth on the wall, but trying to keep in the same place, so as not to get too far to one side or the other. I must have gotten too comfortable and let my guard down because eventually I looked up to find Devin, Jacob, Brock, Aaron, and Jason all closing in from a widely cast net. Like a pack of wolves singling out a sheep.

I hefted a sigh at the realization of being caught, like a melon collie fish. James and Nick seemed to be creating a barrier between us, standing another twenty feet behind everyone. I wondered if they realized they weren't part of this little gang they were so eager to trade my friendship for, surely that was why they hung back, they were still the lowest rung of the ladder, of course the ladder was settling on top of me, so even the lowest rung was a better place to be.

"What?" I asked.

"Whatchya doin?" Devin chirped in his friendliest tone. I glance to Mrs. Potts who had her back turned, talking to some of the girls in the class, near the hopscotch area. She clearly knew what had happened to me, and who had done it. Why on earth would she turn her back on me? Did she want a student to be killed on her watch? That couldn't look good on a resume!

"It says here a child was killed by a pack of children in your class? Tell us about that?"

"Well, he was this loner kid, and everyone hated him. He was new to the school, ya know?"

"Ah, say no more."

"Nothing," I managed to roll my eyes while keeping them downcast. Devin picked up the rock. "That's my rock," I sighed. Devin squinted at me, tossing the rock up and catching it.

"What did you say?" Devin shot me a hateful stare.

"I said, that's my rock," I felt the pit of my stomach quiver. *What was I doing?*

"So take it," he tossed it again. I glanced around, leaning on the wall, but trying to be ready to dart back to the classroom if an opening in their net became available, or if the bell rang to signal the end of recess. All I needed was something to take their attention off of me for a moment!

"Fine. Have the rock," I shrugged.

"I will! Because this is *my* playground, just like The Orchard is mine. So you better never set foot on either one." He shoved my shoulder. I put my hands in my pockets, in hope I had left a pepper bomb in the jacket, but no such luck. I felt something else in my pocket though, I pulled out a peanut. Devin swatted it out of my hand and crushed it with his foot.

"Oh... sorry *peanut*!" Devin smirked. They all chuckled. "That's your new name! Peanut," Devin pointed his finger an inch from my chest. They all laughed, repeating the name *peanut*, in their most mocking tones.

I sighed. *Really? Peanut? This is going to be a thing? Peanut...*

"Aaron," Devin called, "kick peanut's butt," Devin instructed, folding his arms. Aaron twisted a bit, looking around for teachers and then stepped forward at an awkward pace. I locked eyes with him as if to communicate both: *why are you doing this, and to go ahead and do whatever he felt he must do*. His look said he had to do this. For some reason, I didn't understand, but I accepted. Also for a reason I didn't understand.

Aaron caught me off guard by kicking fast and hard, catching me partly in the buttocks and part upper thigh. They all laughed as I tried to catch my balance.

"Careful, *peanut!*" Devin shoved me in the other direction. The bell rang. "See ya at lunch, Peanut." Devin shoved me again as he walked off. They all followed him away. I hung back with a now familiar pit in my stomach. This new kid-in-school business was going just great.

9. Under the Table

After school, I managed to sink into a seat on the bus, away from all Turtles and Cougars. Mr. Speaker seemed to understand my plight, and though he had a smirk for me, he ignored my placement in seating. He was likely just happy to have someone being quiet and not causing a problem he had to deal with. What happened off the bus was none of his concern.

As the bus made a stop ahead of mine, I kept an eye on Devin and Jason while keeping my head down.

"Where's *peanut?*" they joked. "Maybe he walked home!" I sank back into my seat, the first I felt any kind of comfortable all day. I watched them as the bus drove off.

I got off the bus at my stop and quickly found a rock to start kicking. Joseph and his friends were already a good distance ahead of me. I was in no hurry. I had spent enough time locked in the basement for the week.

As the bus's rumble faded into the distance I heard the faint patter of running feet. As I turned to see Devin, Jacob, and Jason rounding the corner, they slowed down to a walk. I kept my eyes forward and figured it would be better to be safely locked in the basement than to be found alone by Devin. I didn't want to appear scared, running to my big brother, so I tried to keep my steps a simple and brisk and keep the distance between us.

I stared hard at the back of Joseph's head, trying to will him to turn around. I tried to glance behind me by lowering my head to where I could see behind me. It seemed they were gaining ground. In just a moment, a large rock struck the ground next to me, followed by another overhead. I kept my head low, trying not to get struck anywhere it might hurt too much. The laughs and giggles were closing in as were the rocks. Suddenly, the laughs fell silent as a large rock sailed over my head from the opposite direction, accompanied by a loud shout.

"Hey!" Joseph picked up another rock and tossed it back and forth in his hands. "Maybe on your playground, but not on my street! Now get back to

100

the right side of The Orchard butt-heads!" he commanded. They glared with indignation and murmuring to each other, they slowly backed away.

Satisfied with defending our side of the hill, Joseph and his friends turned and continued on without a word to me. I doubted he was being protective of me, though he did have some sense of family. Perhaps if anyone were to throw rocks at me, he felt it should be him. Or maybe, he just didn't like people north of The Orchard attacking anyone in our neighborhood. Whatever the motives, I was grateful! I nearly wanted to hug him, which I wasn't about to act on, but it was a moment!

Grandmother's house was bustling with activity. She was on the boards of several organizations, and most of them were political in some way. She was hosting some kind of discussion in the house that night. I weaved through people I had never seen before, arranging food in the kitchen, folding papers in the dining room, pouring through folders of papers in the sitting room.

There was bound to be some kind of snack to be found in this hustle. I plotted my course into the kitchen, next to the china cupboards, and darted under the table to wait for backs to be turned. I took my backpack off at my usual place near the fireplace.

"Uh!" Kim shot out of nowhere. "No backpack! You put in your room! Upstairs! Kids upstairs! Your Grandmother orders!" She shooed me away. I went, with a glance over my shoulder.

It took me only a moment to put my things in my room and scurry back downstairs. I crept through every side hall I could, and darted into bedrooms and closets. I waited longer than was necessary for the coast to clear before advancing toward my destination, the dining room.

Grandmother, aunts, and house staff alike were all too busy bustling about to notice me concealed behind curtains, chairs, and doors. I finally made it to a linen closet in the hallway between the kitchen and dining room. I waited while footsteps hurried back and forth. The linens were the first thing to be setup in the dining room, no matter the occasion, so I felt safe. Still, I hid under the bottom shelf and pulled a tablecloth over me. I reached up a cloaked hand and carefully opened the door a crack to see out into the hall. I waited. Eventually, I heard voices getting distant. I got myself ready to make my careful escape to a dining table. I could see the long table at the end of the room through the crack. The table was already loaded with trays of finger foods all sitting atop a golden tablecloth that draped clear to the floor. It would be the perfect hideout!

I listened to make sure no one was around. Just as I was about to dart out from under the tablecloth, the door to the closet slammed shut! I sought the back of the closet and made myself small. The air got scarce as my heart raced. When I was pretty sure it was over one-hundred degrees, I made an airway with my hand, parting the tablecloth from the corner of the closet. Cooler air poured into the hot, heavy fabric borough, buying me some time. When I was sure there were no footsteps around, I peeked my head out of the table clothes and listened at the door. It was quiet.

I carefully cracked the door to the closet again and listened. No one was nearby. I quickly slipped out and darted toward the table. As I scurried to the table, I tried to take note of what was located in what spots of the table. The tablecloth concealed me like a rabbit sinking into a snowbank. I watched the feet scuffling around the house and began carefully timing, reaching out from under the table. I felt edges of trays for food in reach, carefully slipping them down and under the table. I found amazing flavors of meats and cheese concoctions on tiny breads and crackers. Some of them I did not care for, and they ended up in a pile near one of the feet of the table's large center pedestal. I managed to find the trays with desserts. I kept slipping chocolate mousse bites and tiny cherry cheesecakes.

"Well if you ask me, he gets every bit of what he deserves, that child," Grandma was ranting to someone. "He is a hellion, that Jeffery. He certainly doesn't get it from our side of the family," she continued. I grinned and tried to not laugh.

"Surely not," a female voice agreed. "It's that hippie mother of his." I didn't know what my mother's hips had to do with it, but if they were calling her fat, they were asking for it!

"Too right. If she or my son took the strap to that boy once in a while he might amount to something of worth. At this rate, he will be a bartender while Joseph is passing the BAR exam!" Grandmother joked.

I wasn't sure what any of that meant, but I could tell by the tone of laughter I had been insulted. I *did* know she was implying I needed a good spanking, and I wasn't so fond of that idea! She had many ideas about how Joseph and I ought to be parented, and she was never shy about sharing them with anyone willing to listen. I hoped I had better things to talk about when I was old.

"My son's wife is about as weak and liberal as they come. You would think that would only assert my son as being stronger, rather than reducing him to her level. . . Birds of a feather I suppose."

"They often *do* flock together," the two laughed again. I assumed it was Joanne, one of Grandmother's dearest friends. She seemed to always be sitting casually while something was going on, a drink in her hand and a knowing glare. It was interesting how grown-ups still seemed to follow playground rules, the less popular person following around the more popular, eager to laugh at their jokes and feign interest in anything the leader may fancy.

"Let me tell you, that Tracy he dated he dated in high school, she was a girl with a backbone and future," Grandmother continued, but in a much more pleasant tone, suddenly. "She went on to become a physician, *and* she teaches at Northwestern. I met her children at Morely's last fall. Those children are a delight! Well-mannered, ambitious, respectful, and eager to please. Then, there are *my* grandchildren. . . No, no dear, that doesn't match the centerpieces!" She hurried off, yelling at some poor soul. I made sure Joanne had followed her. *And then there are MY Grandchildren, who are idiots and behave badly!*

I thought a moment before I promptly started pulling silverware under the table, licking them, and returning them to the table top. Strangely unsatisfied, I also started pulling cookies off a plate, licking the tops of them, and shoving them back on the plate, upside down, so they would be identifiable when I watched people pick them up. Pleased with myself and my sweet tooth, I slipped back out from under the table and strolled down the hall, through the dining room.

"The Association is modifying the hill's code to allow them to build more lots at the end of The Orchard, near the canal." Grandmother tossed a piece of paper on the table while she ranted. "If they think they can do that under my nose and expect me to remain quiet, they have another thing coming! I have had enough of these bottom dwellers who have no business living on this hill. They come in and try to make something of themselves, carving out these tiny townhomes, as if *they* belong here! As if living in some cramped home they forced onto the hill is going to make them something.

Peter Caulder bought the Avery estate and plans to build a house behind it. Behind the existing house! Who knows what kind of trash he means to sell that plot to! Better yet, maybe he will *rent* it out!" She spat the words like filth from her tongue. "What are you doing, Jeffery?" Grandmother questioned.

"Nothing," I smiled sweetly.

"Run along," she said with mild suspicion. I pulled a couple of G.I. Joe's from my pocket and headed for the rear stairway to play.

Quite a while later there was a buzz from downstairs as Grandmother's get together got underway.

"They keep building and stealing houses!" Grandmother said firmly.

"You don't own this hill," a thin framed man shouted.

"No, I don't, do I?" she said with a bite. Even I knew her reply emphasized that she once had. "*We* own the hill. Collectively *we* can decide to protect what this community has long stood for, what the people of this city have long looked up to, or we can simply sell our legacy short and let it fall into ruin, and tenementism." It sounded as though civilization as we knew it would collapse based on this neighborhood meeting. I doubted if any of it was that important, but there were a great deal of important adult things I didn't grasp. I wove my way carefully in between the rows of chairs, grouped together by families and partnering power players of the hill association. I edged up to my mother's chair. She didn't get much of a say, but she was simply invited because she was expected to fall in line as an Alfrey. They were to all present a united front per Grandmother's orders. I knew better. My mother loved nothing more than getting under Grandmother's skin.

"Citizen's do still have the right to do as they wish with the land they own, do they not?" My mother questioned. "I'm just curious what law would someone be breaking by making their gardens into a plot for a home? Or what law is it that says only a person of a certain creed and bank account may live in a certain home?"

104

"Sharon," Grandmother attacked her with cold blue eyes, but her tone was very bland and dismissive. "Maybe you don't see the merits because you haven't invested the majority of your life building something... so it may be hard for you to understand the devastating effect a community can suffer from bowing to the whims of chaos and entitlement. This is exactly why persons who are recent to the hill should have limited to no say in how we proceed." My mother's jaw nearly dropped. She clearly wasn't ready for Grandmother to be so pointed, but Grandmother sounded as though she had been waiting for mother to say something so she could attack her. "It's difficult for this free love generation to understand building a legacy worth protecting," Grandmother continued.

"They are all too eager to welcome every gypsy vagrant to home ownership and call them brother, while the silverware is stolen out from under their noses. . . They would probably just give them the silver if they even realized they had any. They would in the name of equality and activism destroy a community this city has looked to for leadership. They want to lead the charges as we did for women's rights. They want to bask in social security without having suffered and worked through depression. They want to live on a hill for all to see how wonderful they are, without doing anything of note." Several people laughed and clapped. My mother sank into her chair and folded her arms with a dark glowering mood. If my mother knew how to get under Grandmother's skin, my Grandmother knew how to dig right back without much pause.

"I licked the silverware and cookies," I whispered. My mother shot me a questioning look. I raised my eyebrows with mischievousness glint. Mother covered her mouth to stifle her laugh.
"What? When?" mother asked.

"While they were getting ready. She made some joke about me and Joseph being in a bar," I tried to recall what she had said better, but that was as good as I could get.

"Good boy," mother pulled me close. My father raised an eyebrow at the two of us, wondering what I was even doing there.

"How surprised will she be when we buy one of those lots?" My mother whispered the threat to my father. He waved it off. *Residents of the Hill? Like,* Official *residents?* The idea sounded horrible! As traumatizing as this new school experience had been so far, I would happily start a new again in some poor corner of the city just to be away from The Hill! Besides, there was no way we could afford to live on the front of the hill, we would have to be in The Orchards! Near Devin! That could not be allowed to happen. I kept telling myself that Grandmother would never allow any of that to happen.

The meeting went on, and on. After I was told to go to bed, I went into stealth mode and started sneaking about from table to corner, hiding around corners and what not. I went unnoticed, collecting a cache of desserts on a plate under a draped table, like a carefully devious squirrel.

"I have been in talks with a few friends who are well-placed legal counsel to some important people. They are just as tired of the city, state, and federal involvement, and the erosion our country is suffering." My father's voice commanded a group, it was only slightly different than the voice he used when we misbehaved. "They have taken it upon themselves to start a class action suit against the federal government for civil rights infringement. For overstepping those liberties, habitually. The result will be a reformation of how government works, a return to operating the federal government the way our forefathers intended. Of course to make sure they follow through, there will also be a punitive action tied to the suit." I caught the general tone of what he was saying, but there were several sounds made by crowd that indicated they didn't understand or didn't agree.

"You're talking about suing the government?" A man with thick glasses asked.

"*They* are, yes," Father explained.

"That's ridiculous. We can't count on some nut jobs suing the government to help us," a redheaded woman shook her head.

"Someone must have said that about severing ties from Great Britain," my father shrugged. "I'm not saying they are coming to the aid of us on The Hill specifically. But if they succeed in their suit, it will mean changes. It will give power back to city and state."

"Well, in the meantime let us all not count eggs not yet in our baskets, let us all get to work and make an effort to save The Hill before these hipsters take away everything," Grandmother seemed in a hurry to wrap up.

"Thank you for coming tonight. This meeting will adjourn until next month. Feel free to converse and organize efforts as needs be. We will keep the refreshments out until 10:25." Grandmother tapped a tiny gavel on the table. That was her way of telling people they better leave by 10:30. People started milling about and talking loudly. Several people headed right for my father.

"Tell me more about this suit. I assume this is a class action?" the man with the thick glasses asked.

"It is class action, yes. That is the best way to show the federal courts people are serious," Father explained, emphasizing with hand gestures.

"What is the basis of the suit?" Another man asked.

"Well, it's basically that by the federal government making laws like eminent domain or federal education, they're taking away the rights of the states even states take away civil rights, like gun laws, that infringe on the constitution and amendments," Father went on.

"So, if it's class action, it is open for people to join?" someone asked.

"Yeah, they have a filing fee. I think it is like one hundred per application, but they are taking care of all the legal costs, and their percentage of the settlement will be three percent of the total."

"I'd like to talk to someone more about the suit," the man in the glasses shook his head.

"Sure, Becky is my contact. We are organizing a meeting in a few weeks."

"Ok, good." More people filtered over, and the talking points just kept going in a loop. Eventually, I slipped through the crowd, with what was left of my desserts, and went up to bed.

Maybe if Father sued the government, we really would end up living on The Hill. Shoot, if we sued the government, maybe we could buy The Hill!

"Are you Devin's parents?" My body guard asked.

"Yes?" Devin's mother asked, clutching to his Father.

107

She had the same eyebrows as Devin.

"You have 30 seconds to get out of the house, we are going to bull-doze it," the body guard high fived me.

"I don't understand," his father shook his head.

"Oh, it's easy, your son is a jerk, so I bought your house, and I'm wrecking it. Then, I will set it on fire," I said, high-fiving my body guard again.

"You can't do this!" Devin ran through the door.

My body guard sensed his attack and punched Devin in the face.

"I'm mega rich. My family owns this hill," I waved him away.

He cried as his parents carried him away.

I let the fantasy carry me off to sleep.

10. The Spear is Returned

I sat alone during lunch, at the end of the table, near girls from a grade below me. There was plenty of pointing and laughing in my general direction. There were a good dozen people at the other table who all shared a common interest at my expense. A few morsels of food items were hurled through the air toward me, but I didn't lift my eyes. I was simply waiting them out. Other kids would leave as they finished eating, I was pacing my bites. It was getting down to just a handful of kids left.

The lunch room always smelled like a pool for some reason. How many cleaning chemicals did one lunchroom need? I kept my head down, but I gazed around the room now and then. Mostly, I looked down at the fake wood grain of the lunch table and the orange fiberglass bench seats, where other students had tried to scratch their names with forks or other contraband. A teacher passed by me and nodded toward my plate, to indicate I should hurry up. She ventured down the next table toward my adversarial classmates.

"Let's go boys," she instructed.

"We're aren't done yet," Brock raised his eyebrows.

"Yes, you are," she scooted them along, and they complied with a great deal of groaning.

"I guess we'll just have to wait outside!" Jacob spoke loudly over his shoulder. I wasn't about to leave the lunchroom a moment before I was made to. I watched them all shuffle out. Everyone looked over their shoulders, back at me. I relaxed a bit with a door between us.

Finally, when there was nothing left on my tray, I slipped a math sheet from my pocket and reworked problems. I thought I was being pretty sleuth by avoiding them, but one look at my face and every teacher, and student, knew I had been in a scuff. Knowing glances passed between teachers and staff as they straightened chairs and wiped down tables with the last of the kids exiting. They were nice enough to leave me alone and not force me to leave.

Finally, the bell rang. I dropped my tray off on the large stainless steel counter and casually made my way to the hall. I was pleased with my success in wasting my entire lunch. I didn't care about the rest of the days of the week, month or year, I had a success for this day! Now all I had to do was spend recess in the bathroom and make it to the bus! I could only focus on one victory at a time. I would try the same tactic again tomorrow, and if it didn't work, I would invent a reason I had to go back into the school. I would fake a trip to the bathroom, or a sick stomach that needed the attention of the school nurse. I would make myself vomit if I had to!

I exited back into the hall of the school and quickly wove through students trickling into the hall from outside as I made my way to my classroom. I was nearly the first kid to sit down in the room. I actually wondered how someone had beaten me there. I put my math sheet back into the folder I had taken it from and kept pulling out and returning books to my desk, as if I were looking for something. My new strategy was simply waste time by looking busy and never making eye contact with anyone. All I had to do was out wait every block of the day where the Cougars could be plotting against me. It was quite a healthy way to live!

An hour or so later, during spelling, a small sea of tiny spit wads and folded triangle paper footballs were amassing on the floor around my desk. Once in a while, someone's aim lucked out and got me in the side of the face, or down my shirt. A dozen kids tried to hide their giggles every time someone succeeded. Even kids I didn't know the names of started taking the opportunity to fling something in my direction, simply because they wanted to make Devin and Brock or Julia laugh. I simply kept my eyes fixed on the board, or downcast at my work.

"And that is the law of apostrophe," Mrs. Potts concluded a sermon. "Does anyone have any questions?" The day was almost done. I wasn't sure if I needed to be the first one out of the room, or the last one. If I were first, I could hit the bus before anyone else *If* I didn't get caught in the hall by Devin. If I were last to leave the class, I risked being caught by surprise on the way to the bus. I was starting to realize I was damned no matter what I did.

"The bell will ring soon, Jeffery. You can spend that time picking up that mess," Mrs. Potts nodded downward.

"I didn't...," I shook my head, and an immediate twenty pair of ears perked up, eager to see what I would say.
"What was that?" Mrs. Potts waited.

"Nothing." Maybe I could still be first out of the room. I started picking them up quickly on hands and knees. The cold wet spit wads made my skin crawl and rage boil inside! I flicked them into the palm of my hand with a large paper football. It was better than squeezing them one by one, but I could not stand to have more than a few in the palm of my hand at a time. I grimaced with each trip to the trash can. My rage was building inside with every smug look I noted, mostly from Devin. The face that made my blood boil was Aaron, though. His expression was simply relief that I was taking the brunt instead of him. For the first time in who knew how long, he wasn't the focus, he was a part of the crowd. I was dying to smack that look off his face with my community dampened hand. I made eye contact with him every time I swept spit wads from my hand into the trash.

I kept a close eye on the clock and timed when the bell would ring. I slowly move around the last few paper footballs under my desk. When the second hand was on the nine, I rose with my backpack in hand and headed to the trashcan. I stood, slowly dropping the papers in. The second the bell rang I moved to the door. I burst into the hall like a horse out of the gate. I was halfway down the hall before I even heard another classroom door open, or saw another kid. I was in the clear! I glanced over my shoulder, making sure anyone from my class was far behind me. I slowed down, so as not to get in trouble for running. My heart raced, but I smiled with self-assurance that I would make it through this horrible day, untouched.

It was a breeze making it onto the bus. I sat as far forward, and as close to Mr. Speaker's line of sight as possible. I was sitting in younger grade territory, but I knew Devin and Jacob wouldn't ever sit this far forward, and Jason and Aaron wouldn't dare risk losing a seat next to their new buddies, unless told to. My stomach still flipped when I saw them getting on the bus, laughing and joking around as the line of kids filtered to their seats. Younger kids were sitting all around me, but no one in the seat with me. I stared into my backpack, pretending to fish for something. I knew Devin and Jacob were close, with Jason and Aaron right behind them.

Devin pretended to stumble into my seat with a loud "Oops!" He landed a well-played punch in my ribs. I was prepared and tensed every muscle before he had even gotten parallel to my seat, so it didn't hurt much. He smirked as he moved on. Jacob laughed a stupid laugh that sounded a lot like a donkey. Jason stomped his foot to see if I would flinch. Aaron didn't even look at me. *Good. Screw you, Aaron,* I thought to myself in a harsh jaded tone. *Who needs friends?* I rested easier with them behind me. I imagined in my head a situation where Aaron and I were alone just long enough for me to sucker punch him in the face. I was sure I could take him. All things being equal, I had more rage and motive on my side than he had karate training in The Orchard. He might be socially rehabilitating, but I had not yet been broken down.

My anger and betrayal were fresh and vivid.

I spent the whole bus ride home formulating a plan in my head. I knew they would all be in The Orchard gloating, just waiting to see if I would dare leave our street. They would likely not count on me venturing outside at all. I fully planned on taking them by surprise, I just didn't know what the attack would be yet. They laughed as each one made sure their backpack hit me on their way off the bus. I tried to keep an eye on them as the bus drove down the road. They didn't seem to be coming after me on my street today, they seemed to be headed to The Orchard.

I let Joseph and his friends get off the bus first, and then I carefully waited near the corner, pretending to tie my shoe. After the bus left, and Joseph was a safe distance away, I darted across the main street and over the stone wall that acted as the guard rail. I stayed ducked down and waited, watching down the road. Once I was sure there was no one watching, I started working my way up the road, toward the end of the hill where I wasn't welcome.

I popped my head up to check my location. I could see The Orchard and make out the group of kids playing. I darted down the grassy incline and into the tangle of woods. I danced my way through the thick mess of brush and across the network of roots. Finding the spot where the weapons had been was a breeze. I glanced around to see if there were any signs of Bob. I listened carefully but heard nothing. I started searching through the debris of makeshift weapons. I knew immediately when I found the piece of the one I was looking for. I tucked it into my jacket.

"Phase one. Check," I smiled to myself.

"I have to ask. What exactly is phase two?" a gruff voice came from behind me. There was a moment of surprise where I leaped, but I quickly resolved that it must be Bob. I turned to find his tall frame leaning against a tree trunk, arms folded, face veiled with camo. His blue eyes pierced the dark shade of the leafy canopy.

"Hey," I adjusted my backpack straps.

"You appear to be healing well."

"Yeah," I shrugged with a smirk, that hurt my face muscles. I tried to not let on. "Can you teach me how to do that?"

"How to do what, exactly?" Bob questioned.

"That sneaking up on people thing. All quiet and stuff?" I waved my finger all over the woods, at where ever it was he had come from.

"Stalking is easy," Bob walked on roots toward me as if he were dancing. "You simply have to get something between you and the thing you are stalking. Move up quickly without a lot of movement, with careful, quick, light steps so you don't make noise. It's quick, but also slow enough you aren't running. It takes practice."

"Yeah, practice. Can I practice?" I beamed.

"I'm confused," he shook his head. "What do you mean?"

"Like here in the woods?" I jumped onto a large root.

"Now?" he asked in shock.

"Yeah!" I jumped over a large root and rock, toward him.

"Well," he didn't quite seem use to people being around him, or talking to him for more than a moment. "Why not?" Bob shrugged. "Most people aren't very interested in staying in these woods for very long. I'm sure you aren't supposed to be in here."

"Well, I'm pretty sure you aren't supposed to be here either," I winked.

"You do have me on that one," Bob drew in a long breath. "If anyone sees me, I disappear, Ok?"

"Ok," I nodded.

"... and I mean disappear. You won't see me again. It's about time for me to move on anyway. I don't need a village coming in here with pitchforks all because you got beat up and wanted to hide in the woods," Bob tried to explain, but I wasn't following him. Grown-ups were no good at explaining anything to kids.

"Ok," I shrugged. "Right after you show me how to stalk!" He dashed a good ten yards away, putting several trees between us. He propped himself against a tree, sideways from me. I slowly moved behind a tree and then darted to another, further behind his view. I imagined I was some kind of cat trying to sneak up on a bird. I used the weapon fragment and pretended it was my knife.

"Good. Now, close the distance between us and see if you can stay quiet." I watched him, but I watched my feet and where they were going next, placing them as quietly as I could. I danced from root to root, and tried to stay off sticks. "When you get close to me your urge will be to slow down, but if you slow down, that is when I will notice you," Bob explained.

I nodded and kept my pace even, then, once I was close, I quickly ran up behind him.

"If you notice me," Bob was continuing as I ran up and tapped him on the shoulder with the stick, that he promptly grabbed. "Not bad," he shrugged. Something in the way he moved and spoke reminded me of someone else, but I couldn't put my finger on it.

"Not as good as you, but maybe someday?" I asked.

"Maybe," he winked. We both quickly turned to look up the hill at the sound of boys yelling and playing. I crouched down and started slinking behind a tree. "Fading away?" Bob asked.

"What?" I asked. He slowly walked backward behind trees.

114

"That's a fade away, retreating to blend into the landscape. You are a natural, boy."

"Were you a natural at this stuff?" I questioned.

"I've spent a long time practicing. I was responsible for a special unit. We were sent in to take care of situations and protect people."

"Optimus Prime." I kind of frowned, nodding knowingly.

"What?" Bob tilted his head.

"Optimus Prime, the leader of the Auto-Bots. He is highly specialized. They resolve situations and protect people. He's the leader," I explained.

"Oh," he shrugged with a nod. "I suppose like that then. You know, you might be going about this the wrong way. Most people don't try to sneak up on a pack of their troubles, they would be more interested in how to avoid it."

"Yeah, well... I have unfinished business," I patted the weapon fragment I had tapped him with.

"Keep your head. Don't do anything that's going to make things worse for you."

"I won't. They can't get much worse at the moment anyway," I shrugged.

"Oh, things can always get worse. I live in a forest," Bob tilted his head toward me. "I use a coffee can for a toilet."

"Well, a few months ago, we lived in our own house, in a school I liked, and I had friends. Now, my Grandfather is dead, we live with my Grandmother, and I'm hiding in the woods while a bunch of guys who hate me play in the park my Grandfather use to grow apples in. I'm not sure how much worse things can get right now," I detailed as I sat down on a root.

"Not one for sitting back and letting things slide?"

"Oh, I don't want to go fight a dozen guys. I'm not crazy," I shook my head. "Just Aaron."

"Why just Aaron?" Bob raised his eyebrows.

"Well... I don't know, he was supposed to be my friend. I mean we were the same, and then he just jumped in with those guys to be cool."

"Ah, betrayal," Bob nodded. "So, what is Phase Two?"

"Sneak up to The Orchard. See if it gets down to just Aaron. Maybe Aaron and James, or Nick," I smiled. "I better hurry, Grandmother will be looking for me to do chores before supper." I scrambled across roots, "I'll see you later Optimus!" I waved.

"I'll be watching Phase Two. Try not to do something you regret."

I wasn't overly confident this wasn't a horrible idea, but I felt compelled to go through with it. I gripped the spearhead tightly inside my jacket and worked my way up the hill.

My nerves crept up on me by the time I reached the top. My stomach was alive with butterflies as I crossed the road. I tried to survey The Orchard from afar. It was not a dense forest... There really wasn't much to keep between me and everyone else. Maybe I could blend in with the bathroom and playground equipment, though. If all else failed... I could run home! I was confident I could outrun anyone as long as I had a few feet of lead way.

I slipped behind a tall long hedge on the opposite side of the street and casually strolled across a few drives and yards until I managed to get the bathrooms between us. I crept up the side of the building. The cool rough stone blocks of the wall snagged tiny fibers of my jacket as I slid along it. My heart was racing. It was now or never. I either turned back or took the last step around the corner. I peeked around the corner carefully. There were a few play toys between us. They were all on the ground on the other side of the large playground toy. I slipped up the toy using the slide and paused at the top to listen. They didn't seem to notice the slight noise.

"No way! Jessica is not hotter than Mandy!" Devin argued.

"Check again man! She so is!" Jacob replied. I crept along the high bridge, directly over them.

"Maybe, but not hotter than Sarah Burns in Mrs. Lark's class." I peered over the edge and looked for Aaron. I wasn't totally sure of my next move, but I had to act quickly. Maybe being up high wasn't the best idea, I may be treed like a cat.

"Got him!" I was suddenly blindsided by Jason and knocked to the plastic coated metal floor of the bridge. My breath escaped me, and I laid motionless.

"Get him!" I heard shouting from below.

"Hey!" I heard an adult shout from afar, quickly followed by the scramble of the boys below. Jason leaped over the side rail of the bridge and joined them grabbing their bikes. I stood up and met Aaron with a cold stare. I fetched the spear from my jacket, luckily the spear hadn't impaled me when I fell! I threw it like a dart, aimed at his front bike tire. I hoped to cause a wreck. I had no such luck. It struck him in the shoulder.

"You can have it back!" I yelled. He skidded to a stop. He looked at it for a moment and glanced back at me before tilting his bike over to pick it up, then righted his bike and took off.

I dragged myself up with a huff of frustration. I dusted off my jacket and scuffed my feet against the ground to shake out my residual anger, then headed toward the far end of The Orchard toward their old hideout. I thought about going back to the woods, but I didn't want to see anyone, especially someone who had been watching what just happened. There was no way the old hobo would cross the neighborhood, and any resident or gardener who had been watching us probably waved it off and went back to what they were doing.

I stomped through the tall grass near the hideout. I had been *in* their little group for a fraction of a moment, yet I felt some attachment, or ownership to the hideout. I was now the last Turtle. I had been traded away, and the hideout was likewise cast off for an upgrade to the playground. We were perfect for each other, destined to hang out on the outside perimeter.

I plopped myself down on the structure of boards laid across the canal. I dangled a stick into the moving water, causing a ripple that I traced back and forth. I wondered if they would come back to the playground. Even if they did, it was unlikely they would come back to the old turtle hideout, I would surely hear them long before they got there.

I don't know how long I sat staring into the water. Eventually, I figured it must be safe, and nearing dinner time, I released my grip and let go of the stick, watching it quickly drift down the canal and out of sight. I relaxed and let my head fall back, staring at the sky, mouth open. Again, I forced myself back up, and with heavy steps, I headed home, thoroughly defeated.

11. The Last Turtle

The next few days were like living in another reality. I was invisible to everyone, no one seemed to notice I was in school at all. Being totally ignored may have been a negative for some, but it was a vast improvement over the rough treatment I had been suffering through. I thought it best to not push my luck, so I did my best to stay clear of The Cougars. The lunch ladies were nice enough to continue to let me sit far away from my class and shuffle about long after the lunch room had cleared.

"You can make yourself useful," a thin lunch lady nodded toward a spray bottle and towel rag. I shrugged and set to wiping off tables and chairs, I was used to doing such chores. The irony was that if my Grandmother found out I was cleaning tables at the school, she would throw a fit; insisting that her grandchild not be reduced to cleaning up tables in a school she donated so much money to, and yet this was exactly the kind of thing she and my parents forced me to do at her house.

In afternoon recess, I slipped down the halls to the upper-grade bathrooms. The trash can wasn't against the door, so I figured it was safe below. I carefully moved the vent cover and listened. Satisfied that there was no one in the crawl space, I lowered myself into the hole. I was still quiet and careful, like a cat creeping on snow. I followed the pipe in the dark until I found the dim light and fished the golden elephant out of my pocket. I had swiped it on my way out the door, like I did some mornings. Normally, I would have been afraid it would be at risk of it falling out of my pocket in a scuffle and being stolen or taken from my desk or pocket, but my ignorance from The Cougars had its own liberty.

I made my elephant dance down the pipe, his metallic feet making tiny clinking sounds against the metal surface. I pulled a mini-Transformer out of my pocket and had them meet on the pipe. They journeyed with me as I explored the underground lair. I supposed at some point I would have to find better friends, but for now, I was content with the variety that wouldn't, or couldn't, stab me in the back.

I saw a vent up near the ceiling that was spilling light into the dark. There was an air duct laying on the dirt floor, softly blowing cool air. I could hear voices. It must have been somewhere teachers or other staff were, because the voices I heard were adult. I froze in place as I noticed the figure of a slender man in the distance. He slowly walked around the corner without noticing me. I carefully crept passed the vent and down to the corner. There was some sort of fence gate blocking off the passage. On the other side, there was a work bench and a rack of tools lit by a yellow light bulb. - which was what gave the strange space its dim yellow glow.

I saw no sign of the man. I crept forward, sticking to the darkest side of the passage, hiding in the shadows. I looked down the pipe-lined hallway with all sort of mechanics: boiler, blowers, water heaters, air vents, and plumbing galore. I inched up to the chain link fencing and peered through at the workbench. It was littered with nuts and bolts, screwdrivers, and a small chrome looking glass of some kind. It was too small to be an actual telescope.

I stretched my hand through the fence to see if I could get a hold of it the looking-glass. I tipped it toward me with my fingertips. My heart stopped as it tipped over and fell off the bench and to the ground, making a surprisingly loud sound for such a small object. I quickly jerked my hand back, scraping it on rough metal, and dashed back around the corner. I peered over and around pipes to see if anyone came to inspect the sound. Of course no one came, no sounds of feet, nothing but the gentle blowing of the ventilation. I headed back down the passage and suddenly became very aware of the footprints I was leaving on the dusty dirt floor. I was somewhere near where I had seen the slender man. I stopped and squinted in the dim light for the trail that wasn't my own, but I couldn't find it. I followed mine back to the corner, where the light was better. My footprints were the only ones to be found. I suddenly felt a chill, like I was being watched.

I darted back down the dark passage I had come from, looking over my shoulder into the dark the whole way. The dark isolation seemed better than the dim yellow light. At least I couldn't see much back there. I heard the muffled chime of the bell in the hallways above, signifying recess was over. I scrambled back to the opening of the vent and carefully listened to see if anyone was in the bathroom. There were students filtering out or the restroom and back to class.

I slowly exhaled a big breath and waited. I kept one eye fixed down the dark passage toward the tiny bit of yellow light that spilled onto the dirt floor from around the corner. It was a couple hundred feet if anyone or anything came around the corner I had more than enough time to stuff myself through the vent. There was a possibility that someone would be waiting for me to climb through the vent. I could count my heartbeat pounding in my ears. I was pretty sure the bathroom was now quiet as the door closed. I listened for a moment more before reaching up to the vent.

For just a moment, I was sure I saw the slender figure sitting in the dark, just out of reach from the yellow light behind where I had been. I strained my eyes to make out any detail, but I wasn't *that* interested in knowing anything further. My anxiety overwhelmed my curiosity, and I scrambled up the vent and onto the bathroom floor, shoving the vent back in place with a stamp of my foot. I climbed up and dusted off the knees of my pants, creating clouds of brown dust that quickly descended to the floor. I slunk back into the hall and tried to blend in with commotion on my way back to class, holding the gold elephant tightly in my pocket. I kept looking over my shoulder to the bathroom, sure a slender man would soon exit. Luckily, no one came out of the bathroom.

12. Getting to Know Optimus

After school, I took my usual casual pace behind Joe and company. I continued past Grandmother's estate and continued on toward the far side of The Orchard. I danced over the canal stream and slipped through the wide bars in the fence that bordered the neighborhood. I disappeared into the tall grass and moved along the hillside.

When I was younger, and the canal stream bed was dry, we took skateboards and rolled up and down the canal above the neighborhood. There was a concrete structure in the hillside that had once been some kind of storage below a house. We named it The Haunted Cellar, because kids are quite good at naming things in a very logic oriented manner. My mother had warned us that any abandoned structure was sure to be a place where devil worshipers gathered to perform secret rituals. Not knowing what any of that actually meant, I was pretty much unafraid - which was likely not my mother's goal in such warnings.

I was willing to bet everyone left it alone, or didn't even know it existed. Even Joseph hadn't brought it up in years. I had never been with anyone who dared go more than the first couple of feet into the pitch black darkness beyond the doorway of the place. Maybe I would brave it and turn The Haunted Cellar into my new hide-out.

Once you got further above the neighborhood from The Haunted Cellar, the hillside was too steep and too rough even for the orchards that had once covered the landscape. It was also too close to the busy main road that bordered above the neighborhood to the north for anyone to want to build houses near it. It was as alone as the woods on the other side of the hill.

I hadn't been in that part of the neighborhood in a good year or more. Looking down into the neighborhood of estates, there were new houses closer than I had remembered. I could make out the figures of boys my age playing on bikes in the street, but no one was close enough to really see me against the tree and grass lined background. I was above the Cougars end of the neighborhood, so they were likely the ones who were in the street playing.

I crept closely from tree to tree, practicing my new stalking skills. Like a military recon mission, I was closely watching them. I kept heading along the hillside, which climbed and went further away from them. I might be able to get far enough that I could start coming back toward them in the tall grass where the road ended. I might actually be able to hear them at that point. I crept quietly and quickly, making sure to step where the least amount of plant life grew, so I didn't make noise or create motion. I was confident, a practiced pro. I watched as the group of my enemies biked away from the ridgeline. I crept down the incline into the field at the back of the hill.

At this end of the hill, it wasn't wide enough for anyone to have interest in building anything, and it was all sloped to boot. Even Grandfather had never put trees this far back. There was an old car in the tall grass that had been there for quite some time. Grandfather had something to do with it, but it was probably before I was born. I had heard something once about it belonging to a friend of his that needed to store it and never picked it back up. Now it was just a decaying shell, waiting for someone to do something with it.

I crept close to the car and opened the heavy door. The car had been a pale beige yellow and white once upon a time, now spotted with splashes of bright orange rust along the lines of the body panels. The windows had been broken out long ago and the glass was mostly on the ground, or floor of the car after years of intrepid kids playing in and around the thing.

Rocks littered the floor boards, and the vinyl seats were cracked and weathered, the materials rotting away.

I used a stick to sift the rocks around looking for anything of interest. I was always finding things down in seats of people's cars and couches, things they had forgotten were missing. Money, knives, sunglasses, cassette tapes, credit cards... I had a secret collection in the bottom of a baseball card case. I was busy seeing what other people had missed deep in the crease of the back seat when something caught my attention outside the car.

I suddenly noticed there were no birds chirping near. I was quite sure there had been birds chirping since I got off the bus. I poked my head up and quickly ducked back down, just in time to miss a rock that came through the window. There were several people outside the car. I picked up rocks from the floor boards and blindly started hurling them in random directions outside, trying to go off the memory of where I thought boys would be standing. Their rocks seemed to all come in the same window and miss me, but not by much. Soon I heard their voices whispering from all sides of the car and their rocks started to become more accurate.

I jumped up and out through the side window and took off running toward the tall grass in the direction I figured I heard the least voices from. I was quickly knocked flat. All of my breath escaped me as my chest crashed into the ground followed by the jarring ringing in my ears as my face hit the compact dirt.

"Right here!" I heard someone yell as I drew a ragged breath. I didn't know what was going on, but I was being dragged on my knees. I quickly got my wits back and started to struggle as I realized I was being hauled toward the car. Suddenly, I was shoved, so hard I was near flight, and then I was hauled by several people at once. My breath was taken again as I crashed into another hard surface. Then, darkness and deafening quiet. I heard laughter like a distant muffled echo. *What was going on? Where was I?* I shook my head rapidly and flailed in the dark. I quickly came to realize that I was in the trunk of the old car.

Suddenly, there were deafening booming sounds, crushing the dark quiet of the trunk, which rocked and vibrated with each boom. I discovered it was the sound of boys jumping and stomping on the trunk lid. I could make out their words and laughter clear enough. "How do you like it in there? Huh?"

"Spying on us?!" said one of the boys.

"Take that!" others retorted.

"Yeah, screw you, Jeffery!"

"What a wussy name!"

"No, his name is *peanut!*" I knew that voice was Devin's.

"Poor peanut!"

"Run!" Suddenly the noises changed from snide mocking to panic, as boys bumped and bounced off the car. The sounds of commotion moved away quickly, voices trailing off into the distance. I was alone in the darkness.

I twisted myself around to face the trunk latch and fished around in the dark with my fingers, trying to find a mechanism that would free me. I searched in vain. I growled in aggravation! I couldn't believe they had gotten the drop on me so easily. I guess I needed a few more lessons. I could also use lessons on opening trunks from the inside. Suddenly, the trunk popped open. The bright light of day was nearly blinding, but I could make out the face of Optimus. A hulking figure with an outline blurred by the bright sun.

"Sorry, is this one taken?" he grumbled jokingly, gruff deep robot voice trying to be inconspicuous.

"No. You can have it," I smirked as I climbed out.

"You should be a little more careful." He reached under the trunk lid with a knife and did something, then shut the trunk lid. The trunk popped right back open, disabled. He turned and headed for the steep ridge and the canal. I glanced around and didn't see anyone else, so I followed him through the tall grass.

"Where are you going?" I asked.

"Home," he sighed.

"I thought you lived in the woods, down there."

"Wherever you go, you're home. I have multiple homes," he spoke softly as he ducked into the tall grass of the ridge.

"Cool."

"Yeah, it kind of is. Lots of freedom that way. I come and go. Switch places when I get bored," he nodded.

"Awesome! When I get tired of sharing a room with my brother I find another room to sleep in."

"Yeah, that is a nice option."

"Dude, I wish I lived in the woods. I would build my own tree house mansion. Like Swiss Family Robinson!" I tried to be quiet, but was probably not doing a good job of it.

"Well, the problem with living in the woods is you don't own it. Someone else owns it, the city, or someone else who just hasn't done anything with it yet. So, you have to be careful, so they don't know you are there." He explained as we reached the canal.

"Oh, everyone knows you live here," I nodded.

"What's that?" his brows raised.

"Well, all the kids anyway. You are like a legend," I informed him.

"Really? Well, how about that," he paused, pondering this new information.

"Yeah. You're famous."

"Now, how is it that I am famous, but you're the first one to actually talk to me?" he continued moving.

"I dunno. I guess the rest of them are just too scared." I shrugged.

"Yeah, that is true of some. I remember when I was a younger, we had this big area to take care of. I had to mow it with one of those mowers without the engine, just blades."

"Oh yeah, Grandfather has one of those. Or had one..."

"Well, I had to cut the grass twice a week. Two times every week, all spring, summer, and fall. There was this one fence that ran by the drive and I was always in a hurry to get the mowing done so I could go fishing, or get to the swimming hole, or something... I never noticed this little sprout, all summer one year, it just crept up next to the fence. I walked feet away from that thing, we passed it in the car all the time... That fall the fence line got buried in leaves and then snow. You know what? All that grass clipping and leaves turned into fertilizer and that next spring the

126

first time I went out to clean up with my mother... that sprout I hadn't noticed took right off and became a legitimate sapling tree. Right out in the open. I had just gotten so use to overlooking it, I couldn't see it."

"So wait, a tree grew up in your yard and you didn't even notice?" I furrowed my brow. How could that be?

"Sometimes a thing can be right under your nose. You can spend all day looking for something that's in your pocket."

"Huh," I pondered how odd the concept was, but he was right. "Where's your family now?" I asked.

"What's that?" He half turned his head as we carefully stepped through the tangle of bushes and roots that grew around the canal.

"Your family. You grew up in a house with a yard..." I deduced.

"Well... life sometimes happens differently than you hope." He shook his head.

"How so?" I knew I shouldn't pry, but if he didn't like inquisitive kids, he could just tell me shut up, like everyone else did.

"Well, don't you have a dream? Something you want to grow up and be or do?"

"Yeah. I want to help people. Like a spy or detective or something. Someone who can make a difference and save people. Like a Transformer!" I smiled.

"Well, that is a great thing... I'm sure you will do it too. But you might not get to choose how you do it. You might not be a spy, you might work in a kitchen. That doesn't mean you can't still make a difference, though."

"Yeah... I guess." I tried to follow his explanation.

"Well, I had a whole different life planned. It never involved this place. I just came to be here."

"You mean earth?! I jumped up and raised a sword-like stick to the sky."

127

"Yes, this earth," he winked. "I've been alone a long time."

"Well, I have your back Optimus!" I grinned. "You saved me, so I have to repay the debt. It's the honorable thing to do." I nodded.

"Well, that is very nice of you. Being that I am a bit of a celebrity down near The Orchard... maybe you shouldn't mention me to other people, though?"

"You mean humans?" I grinned.

"Yes, humans," Optimus grumbled. "Horrible things humans."

"Except for me!" I jumped from one tree stump to a rock and spun with my stick sword to find Optimus... Bob... gone. "Hey! Where are you?" I peeked around and heard voices just below. I hid near the ditch-line just like Bob must be doing.

"Optimus?" I whispered. "Bob?" I scanned the trees but couldn't make him out. I nodded and smiled. It really was a master of the woods. I carefully crept down the canal edge toward home, watching for anyone who might notice me.

13. Playing Near the Shack

I abhorred shopping for pants. Joseph always somehow managed to talk his way into something stylish while I was forced to shop in the husky section, and end up with whatever boxy, stiff legged things my mother could find in my size. I didn't even understand why I was shopping in the husky section. I didn't *think* I met the physical qualification of a *husky* child, but I reasoned that I must have been edging on the husky side, because that was where we shopped for me. It would be a good twenty-five years before my mother would explain that the *husky* line she was shopping for were a heavier material in the knees and were less likely to rip and wear-out prematurely. I was abnormally hard on the knees of pants, in part to activities like diving down wooded hills and being thrown into gravel filled trunks of abandoned cars and such. So I went on being a seventy-five pound weakling with a mild body dysmorphic disorder. I even started self-imposed diets and workouts, trying to trim myself out of the *husky* pants. But there they were, a new pair of *husky's*, neatly folded on my lap in the car. I simply hoped no one at school found out and locked away another thing to make fun of me for.

"When we get home, you boys should ride bikes or skateboard until dinner. It's supposed to get a little colder the next couple days." Mother informed us as we pulled up the hill.

My Grandmother and mother alike forced me to go play outside every day. They urged me off Grandmother's property toward the park, or to ride my bike around. Anything that would somehow force me to *resolve my little tiff with the neighborhood boy.* There was little use in arguing with them, and I certainly didn't mind getting away from Grandmother's house.

I got good at navigating driveways and tucking behind hedges when I saw The Cougars out on patrol. I couldn't go any of the places kids were supposed to play, so I found new places where none of us were supposed to go. The one place I knew they wouldn't go for sure was into the woods near Bob's shack. When you were driving down the main road, if you knew where to look, you could spot just a glimpse of it tucked away in the trees. It was easier as fall started to set in and the green foliage started to die down.

129

"See, mom! That's the hobo shack, Hobo-Bob lives in!" Joseph excitedly pointed out. I cringed.

"There is not a hobo living in the woods," My mother rolled her eyes.

"There is!" Joseph insisted. I stayed quiet. "One day getting off the bus we saw him in there."

"You probably saw someone's gardener dumping grass clippings in the woods."

"No, mom. It was Hobo-Bob." I was pretty sure they had in fact seen him, but no one was brave enough to go in there, except for me of course.

"Well, all the more reason to stay away from the woods!" she mocked. "You boys don't need to be near the main street anyway. Mrs. Dixon saw you boys hanging around after the bus left the other day and complained. She said you were setting nails in cracks in the road for cars to run over."

"No, we didn't!" Joseph protested. "We were catching snails and putting them in the Miller's garden," Joseph explained.

"What? Why on earth?" Mother questioned.

"She's always coming out and telling us not to ride our bikes in front of her house, like she owns the hill or something," Joseph shrugged off the question.

"You sound like your Grandmother." Mother muttered. "Well, you guys just stay away from the main road, and the woods," mother warned as we jumped from the barely parked car. Joseph took off like a shot, down toward The Orchard. I headed up the road, toward the woods.

I sneaked up a row of lilac bushes on our side of the road and sprinted across the main road, sliding into the cover of the woods, and vanishing in a flash! No one ever saw me going into the woods as far as I knew. I darted through the woods until I was sure I was deep enough that no one would notice me.

I found a stick that could work as a hiking stick, or help me keep balance as I crossed the roots. I could also double it as a gun, a machine gun perhaps. Yes, a machine gun disguised as a hiking stick! Bob was sure to like that. I hadn't seen him yet.

"Bob?" I whispered loudly as I neared the shack. I tapped on the edge of the weathered roof with my stick. "Bob?" I called out a bit louder. No reply.

Somedays, I didn't find Bob. Maybe he was napping or hunting or something. He was probably pretending to be gone so I would leave him alone. Grown-ups did that kind of thing to kids a lot. I still played around in the woods, even on days there was no sign of him. It was still safer than being near The Orchard.

I moved back into the woods and took out a small notebook from my pocket. I sat on a stump and drew a circuit board on the page. I was working on something highly classified. I looked around. It was quiet. The only real sound was the cool breeze. I was a lone soldier, air-dropped into a remote forest in Russia, seeking an outpost that held secret nuclear research. The circuit board I was working on had been damaged when I was air dropped into the woods. It would help me gain entrance to the facility, and deactivate nuclear weapons and research the Russian's were working on. First I had to navigate the strange landscape. The trees were different than American trees in some strange soviet way. They were more rigid, unwelcoming. The light seemed colder in Russia, more bluish, the colors less vivid. There seemed to be less wildlife.

If I were to be caught in the USSR I would have to fight to the death. I knew somewhere close, there was a patrol of Russian soldiers who would *love* to get a hold of me, but I couldn't let that happen. I knew there were legends about the woods being haunted. I was familiar with the folklore that told of the hulking monsters and terrifying phantoms that were famed to be living in these woods. Sometimes, I wasn't totally sure they were just stories.

I checked my map and then made sure I had one of my dust bombs handy. The dust bomb was so much quieter than a grenade and allowed you to rush up on your victim and take him down without alerting anyone else. I moved on.

Suddenly, I saw it, a tiny shack in the middle of the woods. It was so brilliantly secluded that it would have been off limits to American spies and Russians alike. I quickly moved in range of the building and began my recon work, surveying it from every side. I quickly moved up to the door and fixed my circuit board into the security box on the side of the building. It only took a moment to break the security, and with a quiet beep sound, I knew I was in.

"And what are we doing today?" came a deep, familiar, robotic voice.

"Prime! You scared the crap out of me!"

"Sorry... Human. I do not get scared. Or crap. Because I am a robot." The large figure was hard to make out against the bright sky up-hill.

"This is the Russian nuclear defensive lab. They have nuclear secrets here," I explained to him.

"Of course. Why do you think I came?" Prime shrugged.

"Turn small so we can get in, and get the data, and get out of here."

"Sure," Prime shrunk down in a flurry of movements and folding, parts inside of parts.

"Let's go," we moved in.

"What are we looking for, exactly?" Prime asked.

"It could be anything. It could be a disk or a cassette tape. I heard these Russian spies can put three-hundred words on the back of a penny and hide it in their pockets."

"I have seven billion records in my databank," Prime nodded.

"If we can find the data you can record it into your databanks and they will never know we were here!" I exclaimed quietly.

"Great idea. I think I found it. Hidden in this magazine," Prime picked up a magazine.

"I can't read Russian," I furrowed my brow, looking it over.

"Exactly." Prime nodded.

"That's it! Record it by flipping through the pages super fast, so we can get out of here!" I held up the magazine and flipped through it quickly, like shuffling a deck of cards.

"Done." Prime gave me a thumbs up.

"Let's get out!" We made for the door. Just then, silent bullets flew through the air. "They found us! They are shooting at us with silencers!" I pressed my back against a wall.

"Silencers! Those maniacs! We'll shoot back and make a run for it." Prime held up his blaster. I held up my machine gun, and I got out my dust bomb.

"I've got a distraction!" I smiled. I threw the bomb on the ground outside and we dashed away from the smoke, dodging the whisper of quiet bullets that streaked through the air with soft whistles. We headed deeper into the forest.

"I'm pretty sure they were outside the trees, they wouldn't dare go in here," I said relaxing and skipping over tree roots. "The woods are haunted.

"Of course they are," Prime winked. "I'm low on oil." Prime stopped and rested on a large rock. I stopped too, catching my breath.

"Prime?" I asked.

"Yes, human?" he huffed.

"Are you real?"

"What do you mean? I am robotic." Prime shrugged.

"No. I mean...is Bob real?"

"Ah, the human, Bob. Well, I see him out here a lot," Prime stated in a matter of fact way.

"My mom doesn't think so. She says the woods aren't haunted, and there isn't anyone living here. But I see you here all the time." I wore the confusion on my face. "She says whether or not you are real, the woods aren't safe. She's never been to the park when Devin and Jason are there. The Orchard isn't safe!" I pointed my stick uphill, toward The Orchard.

"I've always liked the safety of the woods," Prime rested his head on the tree. "The world is a harsh place, full of people who are like wolves, waiting to attack. The woods... I have all the friends I need all around me. They protect me, give me shelter, give me warning. I always liked these woods." Bob patted the tree. There used to be more of them. It seems like every year there are a little bit less. One day, the world will consume them, and they will be gone."

"What will you do then?" I asked with concern.

"I don't know? Find new woods I suppose. It's too sad to think about really. So I just enjoy it today, while I can," he nodded. My watch beeped.

"I have to go," I jumped up. "It's ham night. Oh! I almost forgot!" I reached into my jacket and pulled out a can of chunked ham that came in a white paper wrapped with red devils on it. I tossed it to Bob.

"Thanks! But robots don't eat," he winked and tucked it into his own jacket.

"Later!" I smiled and ran off.

14. Getting off the Bus

School was the usual for the next week or two. There was constant torture peppered with bouts of being ignored. Brock frequently found opportunities to pass me by in class and flick me in the neck or ear with the sharp end of his pencil and whispering the word, "peanut." I believed it had been two days solid where I didn't speak even once the entire school day. On the third day during art class, that changed.

"Peanut." I heard the taunt from the table next to me. I kept my eyes on my paper. "Peanut's mom is a whore."

I pursed my lips. An arm reached over my shoulder and started drawing on my paper. A stick figure with a skirt followed by the word H-O-R-E. Brock leaned in close to my ear and repeated. "Whore."

"Shut up!" I shoved him away. I glanced around the room, there didn't seem to be a teacher anywhere in sight, but I knew one must be close. Several kids took notice and were eagerly awaiting Brock's response. He smiled and stepped back toward me. I stood up straight, eye to eye, as Optimus Prime would do. Just then, the classroom door opened and a teacher with files came in. Brock patted me on the shoulder.

"You're dead," he whispered and sat down. Of course, the whole thing went unnoticed.

The entire bus ride was a repeat of art class.

"Peanut..." I heard being chanted by several voices behind me, including Jason and Aaron. "I heard Peanut's family had to move here because they were so poor they got kicked out."

"I heard peanut's mom is a janitor at the school, she comes in after everyone leaves and cleans."

"Yeah, I heard peanut is a janitor. That's why peanut cleans the lunch tables because they can't afford to pay for school."

"If Peanut wasn't an Alfrey, there's no way he would even go to school with us."

I was thankful and terrified of the bus slowing down to its stop. I could hear the excitement of the boys behind me as they lifted their backpacks. I heard rhythmic pounding behind me getting closer. I refused to turn and look. Suddenly the question of what the pounding noises were, became clear as everyone who passed me, even some kids I didn't know, dragged their backpacks over the seat backs - swinging them into my head as each one passed. Each laughed as they exited the bus.

I choked on my rage and frustration as the bus slowly continued on to our stop. Why had I gone back on their radar? Why was today different? I jumped up as soon as the doors came open and burst passed everyone. I was off the bus and halfway down the street before the Cougars had a chance to turn the corner of our street. I kept up the pace all the way home. My feet made slapping noises as I slowed to the front steps. I casually breezed inside, the smell of some kind of fish being cooked filled the air. I slipped through rooms and to the back stairs without notice from anyone.

I nearly stomped up the stairs, but refrained, concerned Grandmother would come scold me for treading to heavily. I slammed myself on my bed, shoved my face into my pillow and burst into tears of frustration. I buried my head under my pillow, making what I hoped was a sound proof barrier. I was sure this unfair situation was going to go on for years, probably through college and into adulthood. I would end up with some job where Devin was my boss and would continue to make my life a living hell for the rest of my years.

After some time had passed, and I had calmed a bit, I clutched my golden elephant in my fist. I raised the edge of the pillow to let just a tiny bit of light spilling under the pillow to make his eyes glint. I rubbed the smooth red enamel blanket on his back. I lost track of time until the door opened. I peeked out to see my mother gently lowering herself onto my bed.

"Wanna talk?" she asked softly. I shook my head under my pillow.

After a pause, I asked, "Can I change bus stops?"

"Change bus stops?" she asked. I nodded under the pillow.

"How? You want them to drop you off in front of the house?" she asked.

I shrugged.

"I don't think that's an option," she patted my leg.

"Can I at least cancel my birthday party?" I pleaded.

"I think it would be good for you to have your classmates over. Give them some social interaction." I didn't care for her tone.

"No, it won't," I muttered in what I knew was pointless dread.

"Come down for dinner," she patted me on the back and slipped out of the room. I kicked my mattress, one single hard kick.

"When are we buying a house?"

"Soon," she poked her head back in the door.

"Not soon enough." I groaned.

"Well, we have to find the right house, in the right neighborhood." She tilted her head.

"Why? We didn't worry about this crap before? Why are we so worried about it now?" I demanded.

"Well, this is a different town, you have to be more careful about where you live and what school you go to."

"That's stupid," I protested.

"It's not that we want to live in a snooty neighborhood," she rolled her eyes in frustration, "but we want to make sure you boys have opportunities to do things."

"Like get my butt kicked? I hate my school. Buy a house where I don't have to go there. We pass another school on the bus every day. Just put me there."

"Well... That isn't really a school you would want to go to," Mother tried to reason with me. Little did she know, I couldn't be reasoned with.

"Why not? It looks like my old school," I shook my head.

"Well, I suppose it does, but *here* it is not the kind of school you want to go to."

"Why does that have anything to do with it?" It all made no sense to me. She was starting to sound like Grandmother.

"I don't expect you to understand, but someday you will see." She nodded, as if that would soothe my protest. "Dinner," she chimed as she left the room. I clutched the pillow to my face and screamed a not so quiet scream she surely heard from the hall.

15. Come one, Come all

The days went back to drifting mostly under the radar. Every day, I sprinted from the bus to home, and only most days did the Cougars try to catch me. Some days, they didn't bother, and some of those days even ended up in a row! I lived in dread every day, but none more so than my birthday.

My Grandmother and mother rarely agreed on the same issue, the same day, but when it came to inviting everyone in my class to my birthday party, they were tight knit. I hoped and prayed that every one of them would fail to show up, but I got the feeling no matter how much they resisted, their mothers would force them to go. Some of them might even plan on coming just for the chance to make my life further hell. I hoped for rain, but it was a perfectly beautiful Saturday. A guy couldn't even get a break on his birthday!

I hadn't heard anyone mention the party in class, so maybe I would get lucky. Except maybe the brown eyed girl! I would be ok if she were the only one to show. I kept her note in my sock drawer where I could take it out and read it if I was sure Joseph was outside. I hadn't been able to make eye contact with her in a while, and she had no doubt decided I hated her long ago. She and her blonde friend never did join in the frequent group of cool kids who gave me hell. I looked at her often and quickly darted my eyes if I even thought she might return the glance, or anyone else may have taken notice. I often thought about her smile and sparkling dark eyes while I fell asleep. Every time I took out the note, I felt that flighty butterfly feeling. I tried to hold onto that feeling, but all I felt was an icy lump of dread in the pit of my stomach.

"Jeffery!" I heard my name being yelled up the stairway. I dragged myself away from the note, and downstairs. "Grandmother want you at door, greet guest." Kim pushed me toward the other end of the house. Grandmother was waiting in the sitting room near the front door.

"Come along, we will greet your guests as they come," she nodded and moved to the door.

It didn't take too long before guests started showing up. Sure enough, as each guest made their way up the walk they wore disdainful looks of children who were being forced to eat soggy spinach. They shoved wrapped gifts at me, no doubt feeling the sting of being forced to give away something they would rather keep for themselves. Perhaps they bought me the ugliest, most useless gift they could think of. A couple of them grinned fake slick grins, and those were the gifts I was sure must have come from the girl's section.

When Grandmother had finally decided the appropriate window of timeliness had closed, I was dismissed from my post. I made my way through the house and tried to peer through the back door to the porch without being seen. It was obvious that kids were quickly assembling into their regular school yard clicks. My mother was trying to talk kids into playing games on the lawn near the garden. It was mostly girls.

"Go on," Grandmother urged, opening the door for me. I reluctantly slid onto the porch, trying to not be noticed, and sat down on the edge, dangling my feet down to the bushes below the edge of the porch.

Suddenly, my behind got a shot of pain, as Devin stomp kicked his toe sharply into my back side, pinching the skin at the ground. He stood looking around as if he didn't even see me. I turned back around and tried to ignore him.

"You know, *peanut*, the only reason we are here is because we have to be," Devin huffed.

"If your grandma wasn't Rose Alfrey, no one would be here." Jason said while smiling a smarmy smile.

"Well, then we are both miserable," I added.

"I'm going to punch you in the nads when no one is looking." Devin said in a sickly sweet voice with a fake grin.

"That's great, Devin," I nodded.

"Did he say *that's great*? He wants me to punch him in the nads... Sick!" Devin took a step back.

"Gross!" Jason was like a parrot that was obligated to add something in agreement after everything Devin said. I was feeling a bit lucky no one else from the Cougars came. At least there was pleasure in small favors.

"Can we just have cake already?" the two wandered off, which I was glad for. I rubbed the sore spot on my butt as soon as their backs were turned. I moved off the porch and to my mother's side. Not that I wanted to be a mama's boy, but I didn't feel like being the donkey Devin was constantly trying to pin a tail on all day on my own birthday party.

"Can we have cake yet?" I begged.

"Cake? No! We haven't even played duck-duck-goose." I rolled my eyes. She knew of the sufferance I endured... why did she insist on subjecting me to further punishment? I might as well have become my Grandfather. All I wanted for my birthday was to be left alone with a little cake.

"Come on!" she pulled me toward her and made me sit down. "Ok, everyone get around in a circle!"

The worst thing about duck-duck-goose was that as juvenile as it was, it was still a little fun. It didn't matter how cool and grown up I thought I was, as soon as I was tapped I became a greyhound off at the shot. I could run a circle like one of those daredevil dirt-bike riders. No one stood a chance against me. Of course, first, someone had to pick me as the goose. After several rounds, no one had picked me. Some of the girls giggled as they got close and then practically rolled their eyes and tossed their hair as they skipped on by.

"Let's make sure everyone gets a chance," my mother urged, to my horror. "Even the birthday boy," she faux whispered. I wished there was a hole to crawl into. Perhaps I could just dig one while I waited to be dubbed *goose*. I think it began dawning on my mother that all of my complaints about not having any friends may be manifesting itself at my own manufactured birthday *party*.

"Ok, I think it's time for presents, and everyone's favorite... cake and ice cream!" Mother clapped her hands together.

Kids ran to the porch with excitement. I was grateful for the reprieve. It would be nice to switch from one form of humiliation to another, it meant the end was somewhere in sight. I figured the kids who were forced to be there felt the comfort of the end coming as well, but for a much different reason.

I shuffled up to the porch where the presents had all been stacked and were waiting for me. Kids sat in a semi-circle, chatting and giggling, not paying attention. My mother smiled and handed me the first package.

"This one is from Cameron!" Mother smiled.

I didn't know who Cameron was. I thought he was the kid who had gold framed glasses and spiky hair, maybe. I slowly pulled the wrapping paper off and exposed a Ninja Turtle toy... Some kind of Mutant Moose? I loved Ninja Turtles, and I had plenty of them, but I had never even heard of this one! There was a certain group of Ninja Turtle toys that were directly from the cartoon, and then a line of them that were B-Side characters the manufacturers were testing out before they dared put them into a guest star role in the cartoon. This was one from the reject pile if I had ever seen one. Even the toys from The Island of Misfit Toys would have made fun of this guy, and exiled him to his own floating block of ice in hope he would soon drown.

"Oh, that's cool," I nodded. It was a trick I learned from Joseph when he got a gift he hated. You didn't need to say anything else, and it had an undercurrent of sarcasm that no one could prove. "Thanks," I set it down. Maybe I could make him a slave to the Ninja Turtles and pull the Turtle Van or something. I moved on.

"This one is from Jessica," Mother kept her smile in place. Now, the girls I knew every one by name, and could identify most of them by the back of their head, based on their hairstyle and adornments. Not that any of them spoke to me, but they were by far more worthy of learning names than the bunch of jerk guys I was in class with. Jessica wasn't making eye contact, she seemed to be pretending she was talking to Hollie, but Hollie didn't seem to be talking. I again forced myself to pull off the wrapping paper. This one was some kind of art project? Something you were supposed to paint and hang in a window?

"Oh... I remember something like that when I was in college," my mother mused. Maybe she would enjoy doing it, so I didn't have to.

"Cool," I nodded my head along, pursing my lips in feigned interest.

There was a string of lame gifts and things I had little interest in, other than ideas of how to destroy the gift, and turn it into something other than what it was. Still, nothing had prepared me sufficiently for my Grandmother's gift. I use the term "gift" very loosely. My Grandmother was a product of the great depression, and there was no object, scrap, or opportunity that went wasted. Birthday's and Christmas gifts became a Russian-Roulette of random artifacts or trinkets that could not possibly be accompanied by an explanation, so there was no use in asking for one. Generally, gifts from Grandmother came after a Sunday dinner, or family cake, not in front of people who were not part of the family. Inside the family, there was no explanation needed, but when an outsider was introduced into the situation...well, there was nothing you could do but shake your head and shrug.

When I heard my mother say, "This one is from your Grandmother," With raised eyebrows, I felt panic set in. *Why? Why, would they do this to me?* There was nothing to do. I couldn't save it for later, or shout 'Cake,' and empty the room before opening it. My stomach sank as I took a deep breath. Maybe if I didn't pull back the wrapping paper all the way. I tore the paper and peeked inside, I tried to pull up the sides like a box. In the bottom sat...something... A giant red wallet perhaps? It was big enough to put two wallets inside of. A wallet for your wallets? I hoped my face didn't show my confused disgust.

"Thanks, Grandmother! Are we done?" I shifted it to the table.

"What is it?" my mother smirked.

"It's like a...wallet," I explained and tried to put the box down. My mother reached for it. I tried to pull it back to my lap, but her hand was already on it, the paper came straight off. Didn't my mother know better than this? She knew of the horrific nature of my Grandmother's gifting! What gives? Why was she out to destroy my chances of recovering a normal life in this school? She furrowed her brow at the wallet thing as she pulled it out. It was worse than I thought. It zipped closed, and the zipper had a keychain attached that looked like it was supposed to be some kind of light bulb with a smiley face, but the strange, fleshy light yellow color made it look far more phallic than it should have to a child. My mother opened the

143

wallet and turned it over and over in her hands. There was a card inside that identified it.

"The Great Coupon Organizer," mother read. Why was this happening? "Maybe you can keep school note cards and assignments in it," my mother shrugged and opened a Velcro pocket.

Yes, just what every boy yearned for, a method of organizing their notes cards and coupons. I tried to not look at the faces of my confused, giggling peers. I knew it wasn't *my* fault I got the worst gift ever, but that didn't matter much to them. At least it wasn't sparkly or something. It couldn't get worse, and there was only one gift left. Remember when I said it couldn't get worse? I was wrong. If I have learned anything it is the universal governing principle that *It* can always get worse.

"There is something..." my mother fished something out of the Velcro pocket. It was a cassette tape of some kind. "Becoming a New You: A Childhood Journey of Discovery." Why did she keep reading things out loud? Seriously. I didn't know who to place more blame on, my Grandmother, who was old and couldn't be overly blamed, or my mother who should have closely monitored the gift giving and held that one for much later when there was no one around. Obviously, my mother was the one who should bear the most blame.

"Can we move on?" I begged.

"Ok. I think we have just a couple more," my mother set the tape, wallet, and keychain down on the table and handed me the next gift.

Finally, we had come to Devin's gift. I wished I could just shove it back at my mom and skip it. I didn't want anything from him, even on the off chance his mother took over and bought the gift for him and he had no clue he was going to give me something good, I didn't want anything. Still, I couldn't stare at the package all day either. The sooner we got things over the better.

I started to tear the wrapping and saw the black marker writing on the package, *"To PEANUT."* I expected a fruit cake, an old shoe, or a dead animal... I unwrapped it, I must have looked confused as I discovered the football inside.

"We can throw it around at the park," he said in a sickeningly sweet voice. He was staring right at me, taunting. My blood boiled. It was like he walked into my house and punched me in the face, which made my family all smile and say *Oh look a friend!* I couldn't believe the audacity.

"How nice!" my mother smiled. Nice? It wasn't nice! There was nothing nice about Devin! How was it that my mother could be so oblivious? If I had used that fake tone of voice with her, she would have seen through it like a freshly cleaned window.

"Are you done?" I sighed.

"Almost. Close your eyes," mother beamed. I almost didn't dare, but the sooner I did, the sooner this could all be over. I could hear something as someone getting closer. I wondered if it would be some kind of setup and Devin was going to throw a football at my face.

"Ok, open!"

I was taken back a little. My father was standing in front of me with a bright red dirt bike. Red. I hated red, but Joseph loved blue and was older so I always got red. It was one of my many double edged burdens to bare. But I had a new bike...

"Whoa!" I was stunned. "Gnarly!" I approached the bike as cautiously as if it were a puppy that was about to be taken away and given to someone else.

"You like it?" Mother asked.

"Yeah!" I nodded, wondering what it looked like in blue, but not wanting to look a newly gifted horse in the mouth.

"Bring on the cake!" my mother clapped, and cheers were heard from the other kids. They weren't cheers to celebrate me, they, like me, were celebrating the end drawing near. I shuffled at first, but then sped up, not wanting to end up last on the porch with Devin and Jason or anyone else who decided to troll behind them.

I stood by the cake with a heavy heart and kept my gaze fixed on the cake. Why wasn't grandpa here? At least I would have a like-minded person I could have groused with. If Grandfather were here, we could escape to the garage and work on something. He was like built-in protection from being bothered by anyone else, regardless of who they were, even Grandmother. Alas, if I escaped to the garage I was a sitting duck for Devin and Jason to zero in, like spy bombers with noogie and nad punching missile fists.

Everyone sang happy birthday, which was great. A bunch of people I hardly knew, most of which either hated me or were willing to throw hate in my direction for social status and approval of a miscreant juvenile dictator, all wished me a happy birthday through song. It didn't get much more backward or depressing than that. Each word of the song was like a sticky note that said *"We hate you, no seriously."* I drew a deep breath and blew out the candles quickly.

I furiously grabbed the first piece of cake and darted for the back door. If there was one chance I had to get out without anyone paying attention, or being preoccupied, cake was the opportunity. I zipped to the back corner of the house and up the walkway, down the back steps that ran along the side of the house, and to the back driveway. I slipped along bushes to the front of the property and across the street to another long drive that was covered with hedges. From there it was a series of careful sprints, not to drop my cake, and I was near the wood in two minutes time.

I finally felt free. I untucked my stupid shirt, or the parts that hadn't already untucked, and bounced from the path to logs and root, deeper into the woods. I finally found a familiar log and sat down. I sat the cake down on the stump the log had been cut from and closed my eyes, listening to the bird's sing. Now that was a happy birthday song I could deal with, not a hint of disdain or coercion.

"You, uh, eat cake in the woods very often?" the deep voice startled me. Bob was sitting in the weeds feet from me.

"Hey, Bob," I relaxed.

"I was just taking a nap," Bob took a sip from a small bottle and tucked it back in his jacket. "So... cake... fancy shirt and pants you will probably get in trouble for getting dirty..." Bob nodded knowingly. It was a riot how all grown-ups thought alike.

"It's my birthday," I dismissed his warning.

146

"Well, of course, it is," he shrugged.

"Yeah."

"I don't mean to rub salt in a wound..." Bob settled back into the grass a bit.

"What does that mean?" I asked.

"Salt in a wound? Have you ever put salt on a scratch?" he asked. I shook my head. "Oh, well it hurts like hell. Ya ever scratch a mosquito bite open and then push a finger on it and it burns?"

"Yeah," I shrugged. What kid didn't do that?

"Well, it burns because there is salt on your finger. Ya know? I guess it takes your mind off the itch by making things worse. So, why are you eating cake in the woods with a hobo on your birthday?" He nudged my knee with his foot.

"My Grandmother threw me a birthday party with my mother," I growled.

"Well, that's nice of them." Bob pursed his lips.

"No, it isn't! I have no friends here. Do you know who showed up at my party?" I exclaimed.

"I'm going to go ahead and guess one of those guys who put you in the trunk of that car the other day?" Bob reasoned out.

"Two of them! And they are the popular kids so everyone does whatever they say! So they both show up and twenty other kids who can't wait to hate me!"

"Why do they hate you, anyway? You just got here. Did you pee in his cheerios or somethin?" Bob winked.

"No. I like won a spelling bee and this girl one of them likes liked me."

"Oh! Yeah, it all makes sense now. That one will do it every time. I don't have much playground romance advice that would be real useful." He scratched at his beard. "You gonna eat that cake, by chance?" Bob narrowed his eyes at me.

"No, go ahead. There will be like three feet of cake still left all weekend."

"Thanks!" he popped up and snagged the plate and plopped down on the log next to me. "Oh man... That is ambrosia!" he closed his eyes.

"Ambrosia?" I asked.

"Yeah! The food of the God's," he took tiny bites, savoring each one. "I couldn't tell you the last time I had cake. Maybe my birthday, like fifteen years ago?"

"You haven't had cake in fifteen years?!" I exclaimed in surprise.

"No. I don't often find cake just sitting around the woods," Bob joked.

"I guess not."

"I had this friend in high school," Bob paused eating for a moment, "We liked the same girl. She liked me, though, so that was where our friendship stopped for a time. And then she liked someone else and broke my heart. I wish I could say we went right back to being friends. He told everyone she broke up with me because my cousin told her I peed the bed still. Kind of his revenge for his own broken heart. We kinda hated each other until our senior year after that."

"Is this suppose to make me feel better?" I asked.

"Probably doesn't, does it?" Bob twisted his mouth.

"Nope." I leaned forward on my knees.

"Hmmm... well, I guess what is important is to know for sure who your true friends are. They are the ones who will stand by you and be happy for you. If they don't, they aren't worth being friends with. Doesn't mean you should tell people they pee the bed or anything, you can still be friendly. That's part of the golden rule, right there," Bob nodded and took another bite.

"Yeah..."

"You'll know the true friend when you find them. I think I better not finish this cake all at once. You don't mind if I save it for later?"

"Ants will get it," I shrugged.

"Oh, don't worry about them. Set it on some of those mint leaves and they will keep their distance."

"Hey, Optimus," I asked.

"Hmm? Oh, right. Yes?"

"Wanna sword fight?" I smiled.

"I don't dare say no to the birthday boy. Not when he rules over all the wooded land," he motioned to the woods around us. I smiled, jumped up and set to finding a suitable stick.

16. Chutes and Ladders

I had expected the days after my birthday to be horrible, but I was somewhat off radar which I counted all to my keen efforts to stay there! I tried my best to emulate Bob's skills from the woods in the school. I blended into the background of every situation. Even teachers forgot I was in the room sometimes. All I had to do was keep that up until high school.

I dragged myself in the door of Grandmother's house after school in the usual way, ahead of everyone else getting off the bus. Whenever I saw cars in the driveway, I went into super sleuth spy mode. I crept in to see if I could locate who was there and what they were talking about without detection. I listened to many boring conversations. I often had no idea what grown-ups were talking about. The concepts were beyond my grasp, but I just liked to be a fly on the wall.

149

My Grandfather was the ultimate fly on the wall. Sometimes, you thought he was asleep and suddenly he would spring up from his chair and put everyone in their place, then settle himself back into the chair, eyes closed, as if nothing had happened. It often left a group of debaters slack-jawed and unable to continue their discourse, or unwilling to at the least. I was never sure if he was silently meditating, listening for the opportune moment to jump in, or if he just happened to wake up and hear them talking, aggravated they had interrupted his slumber. The mystery had given him the upper hand with the elements of mystery and surprise. I supposed that was where I drew my spy skills from.

I slipped into the hall and around the corner to the study where my father, uncle, and Grandmother were talking.

"It doesn't matter what I think about the government, and their role in anything," Uncle Russel's voice could be picked out easily, it had a certain whinny quality to it, "What they should or shouldn't do. Our family can't afford to get involved in anything controversial right now. With father passing away, we have one less voice on matters in the community, and people know it. I'm sorry mother, I am not trying to be disrespectful. I know you have long had a seat on the city council and committee boards, but father was a force. People are looking at us, trying to size up our position and how they can undercut us." Uncle Russell seemed quite worked up.

"I agree, father's presence is missing," father was always the calm collected one, but once he reached a boiling point, you better look out. "But when we are talking about losing the hill, we need something to help charge people and get them to pick a side. People want a reason to thumb their nose at government involvement. That is exactly the base of what is going on with The Hill. People just need to be reminded of it, they need to have a vested interest. They need something to compare against so they can realize what they are actually dealing with," father explained. I crept right up to and behind the open door, where I could properly peer through the crack and see them all.

"By getting people to join on to sue the government? That's insane," Uncle Russell threw himself back into his chair.

"No, they don't need to join the suit. All they need to do is hear the discussions, or be aware of the concept. If they want to join the suit, great.

If not, then at least it made them think about what is going on in their life and how it affects their own property line in this country. How can you get more real than that?" father contended.

"Yeah, that doesn't seem to be working so well for your wife," Uncle Russell smirked, folding his arms across his chest.

"Hey..." Father cocked his head toward Uncle Russell.

"What? Whose side do you think she's on? Really?" Uncle Russell leaned forward.

"She's on our side," my father shook his head in frustration.

"No, she is *not*. You are blind. She would starve orphans to displease mother," Uncle Russell waved a dismissive hand in the air.

"She has nothing to do with this. Why are you taking things there?" father threw his hands up. Grandmother sat behind her desk, her gaze trading between the two like a tennis match.

"You're talking about how to convince people? You can't even get your own wife under control. You saw her at that meeting!" Uncle Russell pointed a finger at my father.

"My wife isn't someone to be controlled. She is free to ask whatever questions she wants," father shook his head.

"No, she has freedom of speech, but she does not have a say. She married into this family. She's not blood," Uncle Russell shook his head back. I was even getting offended, and I barely understood what was going on.

"Mother married into this family to, or have you forgotten her maiden name?" father bit back at Uncle Russell. *Get him dad!* I thought to myself.

"Stop this," Grandmother finally spoke, waving her hand at the two men who looked like they might wrestle on the floor at any moment.

"She lives in mother's house, and she can't show enough respect for mother or any of us to keep quiet," Uncle Russell sank back in his chair. "Does she have any notion of what we are at stake of losing? Does she honestly think it's just about a dozen homes being built? We are talking about the Alfrey name being nullified, starting on the hill and moving across this town. Alfrey Windham Moore might as well have a fire sale!" Alfrey Windham Moore was the name of the corporation Grandfather had run, of which Grandmother and her children were majority shareholders.

"You think I don't know that?" my father slammed his hand on the desk between them. He wasn't usually one to lose his cool.

"I don't think she does," Grandmother cut in. "I think she is being short sighted and sees it as a chance for the two of you to have your own place on the hill, but can't see the cost of getting that without earning it."

"Excuse me? I *deserve* to live on the hill as much as anyone in this family. My wife is an Alfrey, and my children are Alfreys."

"Yes, but you haven't fought in this fight like we have. You left when things were falling apart," Uncle Russell glared.

"I provided for my family, without taking a dime or a handout, or a made up job." I knew that was a dig at my uncle! "And I did it before things started to get hard for the company, So sorry if I didn't come running back to save you all. I had no idea I had so much influence."

"I have put in more years of labor and toil for the company and community than you could ever catch up by some scam lawsuit!" Uncle Russell put his hands up.

"If you want to live in this house alone, mother, just say the word, and I will be happy to move me and my wife off the hill." Father sank back into his chair, leaving a hand up in the air, palm to the ceiling, like he had some kind of offering for Grandmother.

"The two of you can suspend with the dramatics. Neither of you has any idea what your father and I went through to get here. You think you know what hard work is, and what people deserve...you have a vague notion of it. You haven't the gift of wisdom of having fought that fight. Children fighting over cookies now, with no thought of spoiling their appetite for dinner. That is what this fight for the right for property is. Children who want their cookies now. Is that what either of you want your children to grow into? Of course not. The two of you are blood born Alfreys, that

152

affords you a certain rite of way that does not automatically extend to your wives. That is something they can earn with time, maybe not even in my lifetime, as short as it may be. Hopefully, it doesn't die with me. Which is where things for this family are headed at this rate!"

"Mother!" my uncle protested.

"I live on borrowed time," she continued, "just as your father did. We all do. My point is, I suffered a long, hard life. My brothers fought tooth and nail to establish this family, and your father was neck deep in the fight with them. And if they were neck deep in the mud, it was well over my head as a woman. We always have to fight twice as hard to get what our husbands come by easily. We wouldn't fully appreciate it otherwise. Maybe I will live to see a day when you boys can lead out, with your wives supporting you, by your side, not pulling you back at the belt simply because I have your hand.

We walk together in a line, or we all risk breaking apart and sliding off this hill." It was quiet for time. No one said anything.

"What are you doing?" Joseph crept up behind me.

"Shhh! Dad and Russell are talking to Grandmother about stuff. Dad and Russell are like getting into a fight."

"Really? Gnarly!" Joseph struggled to quietly peer through the crack in the door while I filled him in, in a whisper.

"Yeah, Russell said mom isn't an Alfrey, and that she hates Grandmother. And Grandmother said mom is ruining the family or something," I whispered excitedly.

"What?" Joseph couldn't believe what he was missing. "Did Dad punch him?"

"No. They are just sitting there now. Grandmother kinda told them to shut up."

"My brothers and I lived in a basement for several months during the great depression. My father was looking for work, or that's what our stepmother told us. We were sent ahead to California, where they were to follow after things were packed up and sold or some other. They sent us to stay with a friend of her family who had a house about this size. His name was Angus something. He wasn't much on children, but we were allowed to stay in a guest room at first, all of us in the one room. After a week or two, when our father and step-mother didn't show up, Angus decided he needed the room for a guest more important and we were. He asked to sleep on makeshift beds in the basement. We were instructed that this guest was important to the nation, and solving the depression of the economy was the mission. Too important to be bothered with loud children, so we were not to make a peep, and we were not to poke our heads out of the basement. Any failure to do as instructed would yield disciplinary action. We didn't make a sound for three weeks. Twice a day, someone came down with food and water and shook their heads with concern or sympathy, not so much that they were willing to do anything mind you. Maybe some of them thought we were simply a waste of food and water and couldn't believe he didn't simply sell us.

After maybe six weeks or so, Angus told us that my father had absconded to Mexico with our stepmother and wasn't coming back. He was just trying to figure out what orphanage to send us to.

We spent the day playing with tiny figurines your uncle Robert flinted out of the sandstone walls. He made tiny tigers, and camels, and elephants. I'm sure they were crude as they could be, but with the dim light and some imagination, they were finely crafted works of a master artist. We would pretend we were wealthy debutantes on safari, or we owned and ran a circus and traveled to all the biggest cities, Chicago, New York, Detroit.

Every day, we would wonder if it was nearing noon, or nearing dusk. Suddenly, it would become apparent that it was pitch black, and we knew it was night. We knew it was time to sleep when footsteps overhead became infrequent or stopped altogether. We weren't sure if we were not sleeping in the middle of a cloud day sometimes. But every night before bed, we would say our prayers and thank our heavenly father we were alive, warm, and had food - as horrible and meager as the scraps were. Every morning I would get up and greet the day ahead with a prayer of thanks. *I am alive and well today, I am alive and well. I am alive and well today because Jesus made me that way.*

Finally, after three or four more weeks, a woman showed up and sharply instructed us to come with her. We marched like sodden ducks. She took us outside of the town to a vineyard where we lived with a woman named Claire in a one room shack and picked grapes all day, every day for several more weeks before the woman came and instructed us to follow her again. She took us to the train station where we stood on the platform alone, not sure if we were waiting for someone, or waiting to be shipped off somewhere. Out of nowhere, father showed up. He patted us each on the head and lead us to a bus where we rode all night and woke up in a three-room cement house where we lived for years while father took work on machines. He was alone, and we never saw our step-mother again.

We all worked jobs. Back then, there were no child labor laws. We had a host of odd jobs. We all had an unspoken vow that we would never end up in a basement or a vineyard again. And we never did.

Your Grandfather never once asked about the conditions we endured, and we never once complained about them because we had family, and that was a gift from God.

This generation complains about not having things dropped in their laps. They wake up with a silver spoon in their mouths and complain that it isn't gold! They look at the hill and think, *we should live there,* without any notion of what the residents of this hill have done in their lives, the hard work that got them here. They look at fifty acres and demand one because they were born. They have no idea what it took to turn this wasteland of a hill into something respected.

This new generation is lazy and has no perspective. If you ever wondered why I worked you, kids... It was so you wouldn't end up like them, or so you and your children would never end up living in a basement."

"And we are better for it," Russell got up and kissed her on the cheek.

"And yet you fault your brother for having left to take care of his family," Grandmother saw through his attempt to cuddle up.

"Hmm," My father mused, never looking up from the floor.

"I'm an old woman, I'm not always able to toil in the vineyard as much as I would like. More and more it will come down to you boys and your ability to carry on and protect what this family has fought for since before you were even thought of."

155

"We will," my father finally looked up. Joseph and I didn't know what to make of the situation. We reverently backed away from the door and quietly retreated.

17. Beat Down

If there was a day I didn't hate so much, art day was it. We had a three-hour block of time where we were split up into areas of the room to work on projects, and Devin was nowhere near me.

Today, we were painting. We were set into groups and each group had a table with an object on it. We were all wearing white smocks so as to not get anything on our clean uniforms. I would have rather painted in the uniform.

"Very lightly, sketch the object onto your canvas first. Just so you can barely see the lines, and then we will start filling in the middle with color. When you draw, you start with the edges first, but in painting, we like to do what is furthest away, and then the middle of objects, and the outlines and edges last," Ms. Beck was our art teacher. She was a tiny blonde woman with massively curly hair. She reminded me of Dolly Parton but with a big nose.

While sketching, I noticed the edge of a head kept popping out from a canvas. Sure enough, it was Aaron. I couldn't have been lucky enough to have NONE of The Cougars in my group, but if I had to be stuck with one, at least it was Aaron. He was quieter with his dislike for me than the rest were. Sometimes, I actually wondered if he disliked me at all.

I set to work on my sketch. After some time, Ms. Beck came around to help give us pointers. It seemed like most of the time, she was trying to not laugh at our work product. I was sure after she left she went to some teachers' bar where they all told stories about the stupid kids they work with, and she would hold up our drawings so they could all make fun of them - like a bit from The Tonight Show with Johnny Carson or something.

She bent at the waist like no one I had ever seen. It was like a Barbie doll. She simply kept her back straight and bent right over. It was odd to notice at that age, but she seemed to be hiding the body of one of those girls on swimsuit calendars under her somewhat puffy, boxy shouldered shirts, and high-wasted pants. Her pants were often bright colors, or just straight up black, and she for sure had one of those tiny waists and rounded hips and butt that Joseph locked onto in determining if a woman was a *Babe* or not.

The shapely figure was something that seemed to start in high school girls, or at least teenaged girls, and follow right up to grown-ups. I could see the merits in a teenage girl having those assets, but it felt wrong to notice it in a teacher! *Ew!* But there it was, right next to me. I tried to not notice... If it weren't for that hair!

For a second, Aaron looked at me with a furrowed brow, he had seen me staring! I covered up my quest to resolve my ambivalent interest in Ms. Beck's curves making a face like I was grossed out, then I took my paint brush and waved it like a magic wand over her rear end. I quickly snapped back to my canvas before anyone noticed. Aaron smirked and let out a giggle. Hopefully, I was in the clear. It was a bonus that Aaron laughed. I would take any positive interactions I could get, no matter who it was with. I was most thankful that he didn't discover my stare and out me to the entire class! I couldn't imagine trying to recover from the mocking that would follow something like looking at a teacher like they were a swimsuit model!

"Jeffery! Wow..." Ms. Beck marveled at my painting, putting her fingers on her chin. Of course, she bent over my shoulder to get a look at it. Her hair filled the space, and I had to lean away to keep the fly-a-ways from touching my face and tickling my cheek. She smelled like some kind of fruit bowl that managed to get hairspray all over it. "That is impressive. The proportions and ratios are just great. I think you're ready to fill it in with color. I am excited to see how that ends up!" She placed a hand on my shoulder with a smile and moved to the next group. I secretly wanted her hand to stay there for just a bit. *Ew! Why?!*

"That's sooo good, my little teacher's pet," Jason mocked from behind me. He was carrying a cup of water and paint brushes over to the sink with Devin behind me. The sink was in the back of the room and around a corner near the entrance door. The alcove was blocked from the view of most of the room, which made it the perfect place to horse around. Unfortunately, my position that day was quite close to the corner.

"Teacher's pet. Teacher's peanut!" Devin chimed in a sing-song voice and his usual evil elf laugh.

"I was done like two minutes ago," Devin shrugged. I was sure his painting looked like a finger painting of a kindergarten chimpanzee. Devin never spent any more time than he had to so he could say *done*. I was just sure he would get held back a year, and then oh how the tables would turn then!

"You're so stupid, Alfrey. That looks like you drew a butt." Devin whispered from the sink. I just hoped he didn't say *Ms. Beck's butt*!

"That's worse than a butt! It looks like a turd." Jason said in a not quiet voice. Ms. Beck didn't seem to notice, or if she did she wasn't concerned.

"He's as stupid as his mom," Devin said to Jason. "My mom says she brings the IQ of the entire hill down."

"My mom says she is going to ruin the entire city council because she doesn't understand anything. She's a hippy Mormon."

"Mormon?" Tyson asked in confusion, joining them at the sink. "What's a Mormon?

"I don't know. That's what my mom said."

"I think you mean moron," I added with a blank expression, standing up and stepping to the corner.

"Shut up!" Devin shoved me. "Your mom is a stupid whore!" That started a slow boil deep inside, I stepped around the corner. I was now out of the line of sight for most of the room, except some kids on the back row who all smiled quietly, like kids who were eager, waiting for thanksgiving pie to approach the table, with glee.

"Peanut's mom's a who-ore!" a kid named David chimed in. Devin laughed and pushed me again. I doubled my fist and swung for his face. I must have been further away from him that I had thought because I didn't even come close, and all my weight, which had been expecting to make contact with a solid object, shifted and pulled me to the ground before my feet could keep up. I wasn't sure which was first; laughter, or the kicks to my ribs, but I found myself wondering which it was while I gasped for air.

They quickly disappeared and the back row of kids all snapped their attention back to their painting as I limped back to my chair. I wiped spit from my chin. I could hear Devin and Jason and others laughing and sneaking high-fives.

"Ok, ok. Settle down," Ms. Beck peaked over a painting easel, and then ducked back behind it.

I favored my aching ribs the rest of the day and all the way home. It was lucky for me they didn't chase me, as I was not in any shape to run. When I got home Kim was waiting at the door.

"Where Joseph at?" she asked.

"He's coming," Kim never waited for us. "What up?"

"Your parents no home. Your Grandmother fall on stairs. They take her to hospital."

"What?" I shook my head, deciphering the detailed explanation.

"You do homework." She pointed inside. I slowly went. I was strangely calm. I felt like Grandmother falling was an important trauma, but I had nothing to measure that assumption by. Still, Grandmother falling down stairs and being taken to the hospital so close to Grandfather's death was not something easily reconciled, and it seemed I should be somewhat upset.

I shuffled papers out of my bag onto the table and worked on math. Math multiple choice was my gig. I loved those worksheets almost as much as cookies. Joseph joined me soon enough. Kim brought us fancy dessert glasses with leftover birthday cake. Joseph and I exchanged glances of suspicion. Maybe it was because Kim was the only one home that we were getting the fancy snack. She did seem to like us more than any of the blood relations adults in the family, and with none of them home she seemed inclined to show us a little favoritism.

"What does it mean if Grandmother fell down the stairs?" I asked Joseph, quietly.

"I don't know. It could mean anything," Joseph shrugged.

"Like a heart attack?" I asked.

"Maybe. A stroke. Maybe she slipped on the carpet or something." It became harder to work on homework the longer we sat alone. The longer we sat the more intense and looming the situation seemed. My thoughts ran away with questions. What if she had died already, and she was there in the house at that very moment? What if she was in the house, in her office, and Grandfather was out in the garage. What if ghosts couldn't see each other, and they were both alone and just haunted the house for the next hundred years that way? That would probably be just the way they wanted it. It was probably how they lived when the rest of the family wasn't around.

What if they were ghosts who could see each other, would they still choose to sit in their respective corners? Maybe exchange a phrase or two in passing once or twice a year? What if they couldn't see each other, but they could see living people? Would they even know they were dead?

"Do you think ghosts can eat?" I asked, poking at my cake.

"What?" Joseph looked up with raised eyebrows.

"Do you think ghosts can eat? Like could Grandfather eat this birthday cake if we left it out?"

"That's ridiculous. Like Santa Claus and cookies? No," he shook his head.

"The cake was made out of grain, which was a living thing right? And eggs are baby chickens... so maybe the cake has a ghost because those things had ghosts. So like Grandfather can eat the cake's ghost," I inspected my cake closely. Joseph looked at me like I had grown a horn in the middle of my face.

"You are an idiot," he said, closing his book, and walked away from the table. I thought it was a pretty good question. I left a corner of my cake untouched and slipped outside and into the garage.

The garage was an interesting place. It had moods. Sometimes it was hot when it wasn't hot outside. Sometimes it was cool when it wasn't cool outside. Sometimes it seemed dark and felt scary. Other times, it felt like home. I crept inside. It felt cold and scary that particular day. I glanced around, half expecting to find someone or something lurking in the pantry storage room. I edged up to Grandfather's workbench and set the glass with the cake down.

"Here you go," I whispered, and dashed back out. I felt like something was standing behind me, and I shut the door as quick as I could.

After dinner, mom and dad showed up with aunts and uncles, who all quietly slipped in and talked in corners of the house in hushed tones. Some were tearful or looked like they had been crying. We stayed in the family room with the TV, watching some documentary about Tigers.

"What do you think is going on?" I asked Joseph, who was laying sprawled out on the couch, while I was laying on a small pillow on the floor.

"They'll tell us when they want us to know," Joseph shrugged me off. I started to get up. "Don't!" he urged.

I ignored him and slipped out of the room. I found my parents lying on their bed next to each other. I slipped in quietly.

"We can't think negative," my father said plainly, without a hint of emotion.

"I know. It's just, timing. Poor timing. She has been under such a load, and she hasn't even had time to grieve."

"She doesn't grieve," my father almost laughed.

"She has to! Everyone grieves," my mother insisted.

"Not my mother. She's the rock of the family. When Aunt Marla died...Rock," my father planted his fist in the palm of his hand.

"Well, that isn't losing your husband," mother put a hand on father's arm. Both of them were still staring at the ceiling, my presence unnoticed.

"Still," father frowned.

"Well, I'm sure it had something to do with her collapse. She's under enormous strain with your father passing, and all of this council business with the hill," Mother said with concern. That wasn't something I often saw between my mother and Grandmother.

"Well, that's how she deals with things, she gets to work and stays busy," father explained.

"Hi," I squeaked.

"Hey, Pal," my dad raised his head just enough to see which one I was.

"What are you guys doing?" I asked.

"Just talking, Honey," my mother waved me over to the bed. They had barely said anything more than grandmother fell and got hurt and was in the hospital. We were not a family of sharing details. If you weren't in the know, too bad, there was a reason.

"Is Grandmother coming home?" I asked, sitting on the edge of the bed.

"Maybe in a day or two," my mother said.

"She is going to be fine. She just slipped is all. Let's get going to bed," my father got up.

"I can get them to bed," mother didn't move a muscle.

"No, I'll round them up," he pulled me toward the door with his hand steering me by placing his large hand on my head.

"Night, Mom," I said as I was pulled out the door.

"Good night!" she called.

"Is that my Jeffery?" Aunt Bessie called as we reached the hall outside the kitchen.

"Hey, Aunt Bessie," I smiled.

"Twice in as many months. It must be my birthday! Come give me a hug, child," I complied. "Ought you be getting to bed?" she nodded at my father.

"I guess so." I said in a half questioning tone.

"Well, run along. You can tell me all about your new school tomorrow."
We crossed into the dining room on the way to the back stairs.

"So, there's twelve pieces in that set, and then twenty in the set with the
inlay," Uncle Russell was writing down something in a notebook.

"What's going on?" father asked.

"We're just staying busy with some estate stuff," Uncle Russell dismissed
father.

"Why would *you* be doing ... estate stuff?" father stepped toward them.

"Well, whatever we can take care of now, we can avoid having to deal with
later," Uncle Russell didn't even look up.

"I'm not following you. I'm sorry, are you taking inventory of the silver?
Oh, for saint sake! She's in the hospital, Russell!" father exclaimed
without caution of who was in the room, or within ear shot for that
matter.

"Yes, and let us not be naive about the situation, she's in her 80's with a
bruised hip and a blood clot! These things don't often go well. You heard
her the other day. Those were the words of a woman who is familiar with
her mortality. We are not to sit idly by. We were raised to work and keep
busy," Uncle Russell might as well have been talking about the weather,
what with the flat tone of his voice. Even I thought it was odd and what
did I know?

"Do you hear yourself? I'm not doing this... *You* are not doing this, not
while she's in the hospital trying to recover," father closed the dark
wooden box that was on the table.

"I am trying to save us all from dealing with things... later," Uncle Russell
shook his head. "Whether that's this week or years from now. There needs
to be a ledger of inventory of everything in this house. It only makes
sense."

"Later? You aren't welcome here right now little brother," father's tone was deep and firm. "Please leave, and when mother comes home I'll be sure to leave out this part of the explanation when she asks why you thought you would be more comfortable in a hotel, or back home."

"I'm not leaving. This is my house too," Uncle Russell laughed.

"No, it's mom's house. Not only am I the oldest, but I happen to live here. And she isn't coming home to find the silver inventoried," father set a pointing finger down on the wooden silver box.

"Yeah you do live here," he said smugly, "and I am the Power of Attorney." He pulled a letter from a folder on the table and slid it toward Father.

"You're what?" father looked at the paper. "Since when are you?" There was a pause. "This was signed the week father died," he said cold and flat, with a sternness I wasn't accustomed to hearing from him. It was scary!

"That's right. With everything going on, we thought it best if someone rational held the POA."

"Get out," father instructed.

"Not going to happen, brother," Uncle Russell said with a smug folding of his arms.

"You want me to paint a picture for the entire family about how you swooped in on our grieving mother with legal documents days after our father died? So you can circle the estate at the first sign of her ailing health like a vulture? Get out," father nudged his head toward the door.

"You'll thank me for being a rational thinker. You'll see," uncle Russell sighed.

"Will I?" my father raised his voice a tad.

"Boys." Aunt Bessie stepped into the room, "Oh for heaven's sake, Russell, what in the world are you doing?" she demanded.

"It needs doing. I'm keeping busy," Uncle Russell pressed a hand flat on the table.

"You are not counting your mother's silver at nearly ten pm the night she falls down the stairs, child. That is the definition of bad form! Gain your propriety and get yourself some sleep. And the two of you get some distance and get your heads on straight. Your mother needs her family united and supportive. Now get, unless you honestly think you are too old to be punished by me." I loved Aunt Bessie. Even as old and frail as she seemed, she was like lightning when she spoke. When she spoke, you jumped, it didn't matter how, or how big and important you thought you were.

Father pulled me close and crossed the room with me in tow, he paused looking back from the doorway to ensure Russell was putting things back into the buffet. Aunt Bessie stood watch at the doorway, her eyes fixed on Uncle Russell. Uncle Russell looked like a dog who had his nose put a damp spot on the carpet.

I smiled all the way to bed.

18. The Catwalk

The garage was warm and scary. I was climbing the stairs to the loft, which usually seemed much smaller. For some reason, I had never noticed it being a huge expansive place. I followed a black metal walkway that went over the middle of the garage to the other side. The walkway continued down the far wall. I stood at the rail of the catwalk and looked into the garage below, it seemed like a hundred feet down. The light below was green cast and interrupted by bursts of bright blue. I knew that light, it was the bright glow of welding. Grandfather and father were expert welders. I was sure the man in the welding apron was too thin to be Father. It couldn't have been Grandfather, but it just seemed natural for it to be him.

"Grandfather!" I yelled. The crackling buzzing sound of the welder was so loud it drowned me out, even from my height. "Grandfather!" I kept trying. I was certain it was him. I was desperate to get his attention. I continued down the walkway trying to get in his line of sight. He was standing in the middle of several rows of huge aquariums, welding stands for them to sit on, or fixing the stands, I couldn't tell.

I crossed the garage, which was actually more of a warehouse the more I looked around at the huge building. I couldn't even see Grandfather's workbench anywhere in sight! The catwalk was blocked by a huge cardboard box. I tried to move it aside but there was no budging it. I opened the top and found it was full of picture frames. The pictures on top were from our old house. Easter morning, riding bikes in the drive, first day of school, Halloween costumes. I ached for the now unfamiliar feeling of being comfortable in my environment. I longed so much, I felt anger rather than ennui. It was stupid that we had to move. It was stupid that I had to leave behind friends, and a school that wasn't full of students and teachers who were completely stuck up.

I took a picture of me in front of my old school and threw it straight down into the warehouse below. It flew like a guided missile and practically exploded on the floor. I dug out another and threw it the same way. It was a visceral release the moment I threw a picture, and the feeling echoed the moment that picture exploded on the ground. It might have been the first time in months I had smiled, genuinely smiled. I grabbed an armload of pictures from the box and started throwing them like a mechanical skeet trap, flinging them in rapid fire, in groups of three or four. I waited to see where they would crash and explode. I was practically giddy.

"What on earth are you doing, Jeff?" A familiar voice came from behind me. I spun to find Grandfather, standing in a heavy leather welding apron, and massive gloves.

"Breaking pictures," I continued to smile, still on my picture breaking high, but also because I was happy to see Grandfather. I missed him. I wanted to hug him, but I wasn't sure if I had ever hugged him before.

"Why?" Grandfather cocked his head, questioning.

"Because I hate the pictures. They're stupid," I grumbled.

"And what good does breaking them do?"

"I don't have to look at them anymore. It just makes me feel better."

"Does it fix anything?" He paused. "No, it doesn't, does it?"

"I guess not."

"Some of those pictures you destroyed were family pictures. That one...that is one of my favorites. That's at the family reunion." He picked up a shattered picture frame off the walkway. I must have dropped it. He shook the glass off, it tinkled as it fell into the warehouse below, sounding like fairy wings as the glass met the concrete. "Look at that fine looking group of kids. I love every one of them." I had never heard Grandfather say he loved us. It was something you assumed... but I had never heard it before. It was nice, and strange at the same time. "Why are you so angry?"

"Because... I hate living here in this stupid town, at a stupid school."

"Oh, I see," Grandfather nodded, knowing.

"I hate it," I groused, near tears.

"Rough time making friends?" he nodded and pursed his lips.

"I don't have any friends. I don't even have a home. And you, you aren't here anymore." I looked down at the mess of broken pictures on the floor below us.

"But I am," Grandfather stood next to me.

"You are right now. But you aren't in the garage, or in the house." I was only vaguely confused at how I was aware Grandfather was dead, but standing in front of me. I knew he wasn't a ghost... *I half woke up, stuck between standing on the catwalk, and turning over in bed.*

"But I am," he put his hand on my shoulder. I looked down at the picture I was holding. I must have been no more than two years old in the picture, sitting on Grandfather's lap. His arms were wrapped around me, sitting in his big old chair. I felt the tears welling up with a bubble of emotion. Tears of frustration, of loneliness, of loss. I looked up, determined to breach protocol and throw my arms around the gruff old man, but he wasn't there.

I stood alone on the catwalk.

The large dark building was silent.

The only sound was a stifled tearful whimper of me trying to keep it together. I sniffed as my nose began to run. The sound of my feet on the metal catwalk carried in a loop back and forth across the warehouse. I looked below into the darkness. The only thing I could make out below was Grandfather's workbench on the far wall as if a spotlight shown down on it.

I found a ladder off the catwalk and climbed down into the darkness. I was in the middle of rows and rows of dark aquariums. The tops of each aquarium was covered with black plastic, like what Grandfather used to protect plants in the garden.

I strained my eyes but couldn't make out any details of what was in the aquariums. There seemed to be movement in the black behind the glass of each one. It stirred anxiety in me. I tried to stand in the center of the isle so as not to be too close to any one aquarium. I walked quickly, trying to see the end of the row, but each row ran into another row running another direction. The building seemed to be so large that it had no walls. I couldn't see anything but darkness beyond the aquariums. I ran, my feet getting wet from the water that was all over the concrete floor. I stepped on and nearly tripped on garden hoses running all over the place. Some hoses pumped water into aquariums, other hoses seemed to siphon water from aquariums and drain onto the ground.

Blue and green light spilled down from above us. I searched the dark for another ladder, so I might climb back up to the catwalk, at least then I could maybe see my way out. There was nothing but dark. I kept running, pausing now and then to look around but only found more of the same. I kept running.

Eventually, I noticed some rows had men working. They had metal push carts of some kind, with buckets and tools. They seemed to me moving things from the buckets into the aquariums, and from the aquariums into the buckets. They were all wearing long dirty lab coats and welding goggles, which masked most of their plain facial features. I didn't want to get too close to any of them to see if I recognized any of them. I wondered how they could see what they were doing. My heart raced, and I kept moving quickly down the rows. They all looked the same. I was sure I was running in a circle, a never ending circle. I felt lost, hopeless, and above all, alone. There were any number of strange people working in the rows that I could have asked for assistance, maybe I would have been pointed toward a way out, but I wasn't about to say a word. For all my anxiety and fear of this place, I was comfortable being alone.

I opened my eyes to find myself in bed with early morning light just starting to glow in the dark sky. I jumped from my bed and looked out the window at the garage. It seemed to be its normal size.

19. Mr. Chatterly

"Jeffery Alfrey. To the office." A voice came over the speaker in the classroom. Everyone in the room, "Ooooed," as if they all knew I was in some kind of trouble. I slowly got up and left the room. I walked painfully slow down the hall, stepping on each and every title of the floor in a straight row, not skipping one. I tried to step in the exact middle of each one. It must have taken me ten minutes to reach the office.

"Jeff," a man with a mustache and a brown tweed jacket with patches on the elbows stood up. He had blondish pale hair that was thinning on top. If Tom Selleck had a wussy brother with thinning hair and an iron deficiency, he would look like this guy.

"Yeah?" I replied with reservation. I had never seen this guy before.

"I'm Mr. Chatterly. Why don't you come to my office, and we can have a talk." He held a hand out toward the door I had just come through. I followed him out of the office and down the hall. I didn't like anything that came after a grown-up telling me *we* needed to talk. Grown-ups never wanted to talk about Transformers, of GI Joes, or helped you with your plans to build a fort. They only wanted to talk about something you were in trouble for. And *talking* meant that you were basically going to tell them whatever they wanted to know, and then they would tell you what they wanted you to do. There was no discourse or exchange of ideas involved.

I started racking my brain to think of anything I had done they could get me for. I kept coming up empty. My old school I had a collection of friends that I was a regular instigator for getting into trouble. We use to drink our chocolate milk and then carefully fold the carton back closed, slip them under the lunch table and stomp on them as hard as we could. If it was done correctly they would pop like a paper bag, only much louder! Quite startling, especially if you were an unsuspecting lunch lady who was bent on having a silent lunch room. I had been at a serious lack of opportunity to get into any trouble at this school. It was saddening really. I just added it to the list of reasons to be morose with my situation in life.

Mr. Chatterly opened his office door. Inside was a desk on one side of the room and a table on the other, next to a bookshelf full of games and puzzles.

"Have a seat," he pointed behind the door where two orange bean bags sat in front of a short table with an orange top. I carefully sat down and sank into the bean bag. When Mr. Chatterly sat down at the table, his knees were above the table top. He was holding a folder. "How are you, Jeff?" he asked with a disturbingly friendly tone. I didn't recall telling him he could call me Jeff. No one called me Jeff.

"Good," I stared at him.

"Are you adjusting to school ok?" he asked, his face full of concern. It was strange for someone who didn't know me, who I had never met, to have that much concern right off the bat.

I shrugged.

"Making friends?" he asked in the same manner.

I shrugged again. I knew what all the grown-ups wanted to hear. I wasn't going to pretend things were fine, but neither was I going to whine and cry about things sucking.

"I noticed you are quite the artist," he nodded.

"Yeah," I narrowed my eyes a bit. When had he seen anything I had done?

"Does that run in the family? I know we have a painting your Grandmother did in the library," he smiled.

"Yeah, I guess?" I nodded.

"It's amazing. The trees look like you could reach in and pick leaves off of them. She's very talented," he beamed, talking about it the way everyone did whenever they spoke of Grandmother. It's as though they thought I would run right home and report on how gushing they were with her praises and it would somehow endear them to her.

"Yep," I pursed my lips.

"Let's look at a couple of your drawings," he opened the folder in front of him. Why did he have a folder of my drawings? He started laying them out on the table. I felt my stomach flip. I didn't like anyone looking at my drawings. I knew Ms. Beck saw them, but I didn't really want anyone else seeing them. I didn't even want her seeing them. I kept my sketchbook at home hidden, and I freaked out if anyone ever touched it.

"I like this one. Can you tell me about it?" he pointed to a picture of a hill, there were cougars, actual cougars, with blood dripping from their fangs and chins, creeping over the top of the hill while a single turtle sat on the top of the hill, perched on a rock, barely poking his head out enough to keep an eye on them. In the distance was a blue and black dirt bike leaning on a tree.

"It's cougars and a turtle." If he thought for a second I was going to explain or even discuss any of my drawings with him, he was crazy. He was not my buddy. He wasn't even someone I knew. He was probably just a janitor who stole things from classrooms and put them in his closet. He was probably some kind of pervert!

"Are you the turtle?" he asked and cocked his head to the side.

"If I were a turtle, I would be a Ninja Turtle," I stared at him flatly. I don't think he picked up on my dislike for him.

"What about this one? I like this one," he pointed to a picture I drew of an old man at a workbench.

The old man in the picture was fixing a doll house. I knew it was Grandfather, but Mr. Chatterly didn't *know* that, not for certain. "What can you tell me about this one?"

"We were asked to draw something with contrast. The workbench is dark, and the man is standing in light. That's called contrast," I said with a very sarcastic and condescending tone.

"Is this your Grandfather?" he raised eyebrows, questioning.

"Is what my Grandfather?"

"The man in the picture. Is it your Grandfather? He died recently, right?" Mr. Chatterly tried to not be obvious about studying my expression, but I had one heck of a poker face. My other grandfather had taught me to play poker starting when I was six.

"Yeah. I don't know, it's just a guy under a light," I shook my head. How was this jerk figuring out my drawings?!

"How about, this one? I like this one," he seemed to be my biggest fan. He liked my drawing more than my own mother, and she couldn't prevent herself from telling total strangers that her son was an artist. Was he going to like everything?

I rolled my eyes and looked at what he was pointing at. It was Bob and I playing transformers in the woods. Bob had an Optimus Prime head, but a camo jacket, a traditional hobo pack made from a red handkerchief tied to a stick was propped on a log. I was in my school uniform.

"Who are these people?" he asked, staring at the picture. I stared at the picture.

"I don't know," I shook my head. "Just a kid, and Optimus Prime."

"No? They look like they are two friends having fun. Hey, that guy looks like Hobo-Bob, doesn't he? Do you *know* Bob?" What the heck was going on? I knew better than to answer that! I knew when a grown-up was fishing for information, and this guy was a fisherman if I ever saw one!

"Who?" I asked.

"Hobo-Bob. He lives somewhere near you, I believe."

"If he's a Hobo, wouldn't he live in the train yard?" I combatted.

"Well..." Mr. Chatterly wasn't ready for that. "I don't know. Do you know any Hobo's?" He tried to do the thing where he didn't want to seem like he was studying my face too intently.

"No, do you?" I asked back.

"I know who Bob is."

"Then why are you asking me?" I picked up a game off the table that seemed to be a tiny golf course, with a tiny white ball that you had to roll around and get to drop in the hole. Mr. Chatterly sat and thought long and hard while I casually played with the game. I wasn't shaken. I wasn't being forced to sit in class, I could have done this all day long!

"Kids sometimes want to protect their friends, or people they think are their friends. Sometimes there are dangerous people who make you think they are friends with you so they can hurt you later," Mr. Chatterly tried to explain.

"Oh..." I pondered for a moment, not looking up from the game. "Are you one of those people?" I whispered back.

"What? No! My job is to help kids."

"That sounds like what someone would say if they were trying to trick a kid so they could hurt them later." It was quiet for a bit, just the sound of the tiny ball rolling against the plastic game. "I know all about stranger danger. I've never met you before, so you're a stranger. Oh, dang it! Almost got it." I cursed the tiny golf ball.

Mr. Chatterly twisted in his chair, unsure how to handle me. I had amazing mentors when it came to putting someone on the defensive. I had a slew of grown-ups who took every chance at every family function to verbally combat one another. I was born for this little game, the mental game with Mr. Chatterly, not the tiny metal box in the plastic maze game, though I was good at that one too.

Mr. Chatterly sat quietly and scratched his head for a while watching me. After a time, he stood up.

"Well, let's get you back to class," he finally said with an element of defeat in his voice. That was fine with me. I lived out the day with a smirk. I loved when adults thought they could out smart kids. Like we were weak-minded simpletons or wind-up toys that adults could simply open the back and inspect at their leisure. Of course, if that were true we would always do exactly what they had expected and they could never get frustrated with our behavior. I loved when they realized we were smart people who had our own lives, and couldn't be manipulated.

I was still smirking by the end of the day. Until I walked out the door and my mother was waiting across the hall with her arms folded. I almost stopped walking.

"Hey," she said with one of those looks and tones of voice that gave her away. Something was going on.

"Hi?" I carefully approached.
"How was school?" she asked.

"Good?" I raised my eyebrows.

"Well, we got called to come have a talk." *Argh!* "So, let's go." I rolled my eyes and dragged my feet. I felt like every passing student had a snicker for the boy being escorted by his mother. I knew where we were going.

"Why do we have to do this?" I begged.

"Well, the teachers have a concern, so we need to hear them out," Mother nodded.

"This is stupid," I protested as we made way into Mr. Chatterly's closet. My father was there, as was the principal.

"Ok. Well, welcome." Mr. Chatterly had taken off his jacket and was wearing a checked plaid button up shirt, rolled at the sleeves. "Well, Jeff and I had a talk earlier, and Jeff, since then I had a talk with your parents and some other teachers, ok?" Why was he asking me if it was ok? Of course, it wasn't ok. "So I noticed some things in your art that got me curious. Now, I love your art, it is amazing. I want you to feel comfortable expressing yourself in your art just the way you are doing." Yeah, I was never going put any of my own thought into art again, ever. Maybe once I was a grown-up, but not in school. I was going to draw bowls of fruit and puppies from now on, like the other jerks in my class. None of them were being harassed for drawing pictures of race cars, and jet planes!

"So I asked around the school and it would seem that there is a character known as Hobo Bob. I think you know that name?" He nodded at me, like I was going to nod back?

"An urban legend," my father rolled his eyes quietly.

"Well, we hear all kinds of urban legends around the school. The haunted bathrooms and ghost of Mr. Pickler's room, and such..." Mr. Chatterly folded his hands together. "Some of them are based on actual events. Not the haunted bathroom room, obviously, but things taken out of context. Now one of the things that brought this to our attention was another student told their parents you had made friends with Hobo Bob and paid him to be a bodyguard."

"That's ridiculous," my mother folded her arms with a laugh. "How would he even be able to do that? On a five dollar allowance?"

"Well... I try to never make an assumption, I just try to get to the bottom of things and let the truth prevail." Mr. Chatterly held up a hand. "I asked you if you knew this Bob, and I don't think you were quite truthful with me, now were you?" he raised his eye brows.

"You told me you knew Hobo Bob. Were you being truthful?" I asked him.

"Jeffery," my mother sharply gave me a glance that was like an urgent hand over the mouth.

"I think you misunderstood," Mr. Chatterly was taken back. "I said that I knew of this Hobo-Bob character. I think it is important for all of us to be truthful with each other. So, here is what I know. I know a lot of kids have told parents and teachers about this Bob, and how he lives in the woods near your house. So let's be honest, is that something you've heard?" He tilted his head forward at me.

"Sure. Every kid knows that story," I said flatly.

"Have you ever played in those woods?" Mr. Chatterly asked in the same head tilted way.

"Sure. We all play in The Orchard field and the trees." I was leading them to what they wanted to hear, but being ultra-careful about my disclosures. "That's where the Cougars have their hideout." Everyone in the room exchanged immediate looks of concern. Mr. Chatterly wore a sense of triumph at getting me to admit what I had. I threw the bait out and they picked it right up. I knew I could shift their *concerns*.

"Cougars?" my mother asked.

177

"Yeah... They have a gang. Devin, and Jason, and those guys..."

"What do you mean?" Mr. Chatterly asked.

"Their gang is called the Cougars," I nodded matter-of-factly.

"Oh!" My mother sighed in relief.

"I use to play with them. We built the fort in the woods, but no one goes in there anymore. It's boring." I shrugged.

"Is that where they say Bob lives? They say he lives in a fort or a shack," Mr. Chatterley asked.

I shook my head with furrowed eyebrows.

"I mean kids fit in the fort to play, but no way a grown-up fits in there. I mean it's like just made out of a few sticks. It's probably fallen down by now, or broken to pieces like all the weapons they made."

"Weapons?" they all asked at the same time.

"Yeah, like fighting staffs and spears made out of branches and things," I nodded plainly.

"Is that in the woods?" Mr. Chatterly asked, looking through a notebook.

"The weapons? The Cougars put them in the woods. The fort isn't in the woods, it's kinda in the field near the stream, by the Orchard."

"Ah," father nodded, knowing where I was talking about.

"The woods on the other side of the road?" my mother asked.

"You mean the trees that go off the hill?" I asked back.

"Yeah," she nodded.

"No, it's on the other side of the hill." I shrugged. I knew what she meant.

"I mean, do you ever play in those woods off the hill? Do you know of someone living in those woods?" She had a genuine concern in her voice. I

178

knew it was a genuine, and frankly a reasonable, concern but I also had an interest in protecting my woods, and my friend, if I could call him that. I was mostly vested in my safe haven, and I wasn't above selling out the Cougars along the way. After all, who would have told a parent I had a hobo guardian?

"We aren't allowed in there," I shook my head.

"What about someone living there? Have you ever seen someone in there?" Mr. Chatterly leaned forward. I think he was picking up on my omission tactic. I also didn't think he believed my implication that I hadn't been in the woods simply because we weren't allowed.

"How would I know? I'm not allowed in there?" I stared back.

"Now Jeffery, we agreed, to be honest with each other." Mr. Chatterly reminded me. Actually, I had made no such agreement. "So I want you to believe me when I tell you if there is someone living anywhere around your neighborhood, in the fields, in the trees, woods, forts, or shacks. That is not a person who would be safe for kids to be around. That is a person who has made bad choices with their life and can't be trusted." It was an interesting conflict. From my perspective, it was the students I associated with and by extension the grown-ups who allowed their behavior to go unchecked that were not to be trusted, who made bad choices. Bob was the only one who seemed to not have it in for me, or tried to set me up to fail. Bob was ignored by the same people who ignored me.

"It's an urban legend. There isn't an actual Hobo-Bob living in those woods." My father shrugged off the idea. "Kids have been playing in those woods since I was a kid, and even back then we were telling stories about how it was haunted by ghosts and Hobo's," my father was clearly not entertained with our conversation. I couldn't disagree with him. "You even said these urban legends take root from prior events. Well, go back to 1965 and there are your roots," father sat back in his chair.

"Well, we would hope that is the case, but when we hear that this person has been seen by other kids, and been seen with Jeff," If Chatterly called me Jeff just one more time I might have screamed, "we have to take it seriously. I think you should as well." Mr. Chatterly folded his arms on the table. My father sat up straight. My father wasn't one to accept someone else implying he wasn't doing his duty in any regard, especially if they were implying he wasn't doing something proper with his own children.

"If I think there is a credible concern I will investigate it and resolve it." My father stared through Chatterly, making me feel quite vindicated. My mother put her hand on my father's arm. "And I think we have quelled your curiosity, and wasted our valuable time doing so."

"Jeffery, tell the truth," my mother looked at me, deep into me in that human lie detector way mother's did sometimes. "Have you talked to any strangers anywhere around the neighborhood?"

Strangers? "No." I shook my head with an honest expression. Strangers were people I didn't know. I could honestly say I didn't know any strangers on the hill.

"Thank you, Mr. Chatterly. We will let you know if we think there are any further concerns." My mother stood. My father and I followed suit quickly. Mr. Chatterly jumped up, looking for something that would keep us there. He wasn't finished.

"I think we need to spend some time..." Mr. Chatterly protested.

"Thank you," my father stepped out, pulling me with him. "Next time you want to know if there is a Hobo in the woods or a ghost in a bathroom, why don't you inspect it for yourself before calling us at work. Thank you. Perhaps Superintendent Myers can help you navigate these tricky situations. Marcus is very level headed, we've enjoyed working with him for many years." Father said and turned down the hallway. I smiled inside. I did *not* like Mr. Chatterly at all. "I love *shrinks*," my father said as soon as we were around the corner.

"He's just doing his job," my mother defended, though she didn't seem inclined to let him do whatever job he was trying to do.

"I'm not sure why I had to leave work for *that*! He could have told us his concerns on the phone, and left it up to us to ferret out."

"Jeffery, we will talk about this more at home." Mother raised her eyebrows at me.

"I need to get back to work and finish some things. I'll be home late," father kissed mother good-bye, and gave me a raise of his eyebrows as he walked away.

"Can we go?" Joseph whined, sitting on the trunk of my mother's car as we approached.

"Yes. Get in." She nudged me with annoyance saturating her voice. I was not looking forward to a follow-up conversation without a third party there to keep my parents in calm collected, concerned about public appearance. I was sure I would have to stay in the yard, even if I wasn't grounded, I would have to avoid suspicion or Joseph being a watchdog. It was all just as well, whatever kept me from The Orchard was fine by me.

20. Disappointment

No one said anything more about the meeting at the school the whole night. It was like it hadn't even happened. I woke the next morning wondering if it had been some kind of strange dream. Grandmother had come home while we were busy having my art analyzed, which accounted for some of my parent's annoyance, and no doubt played to my benefit when my father wouldn't tolerate the meeting any longer. It all suited me perfectly fine.

I made my way down stairs like any other morning. It was a tad too early to find breakfast made, so I decided to creep around and see what kind of figurine I could find to sneak with me to school, forgetting Grandmother was now home. I crept too close to her bedroom.

"Hello?" I heard her call. I dodged out of the line of sight from the cracked open door. I didn't move a muscle. "Is that Jeffery?" she called. I sank. I knew not to test her. Out of fear, she was in some kind of condition to come after me, I poked my head through the door.

"Good morning," I chirped. "Welcome home."

"Come in," she motioned. She looked something of a wreck. I wasn't used to seeing her first thing in the morning, still sitting in bed, without her hair coiffed, or blush and lipstick. I guess she looked about like you would expect an elderly woman to on her first morning out of the hospital. I had kind of built up the expectation that old people checked into hospitals, but they didn't check out, so she had my chagrin already. Then again if the grim reaper showed up, my Grandmother would likely have chastised him and sent him on his way. I stepped next to the bed.

"Yes?" I asked.

"Imagine my frustration and concern, coming home from the hospital to find my son and your mother not here to welcome me with my grandchildren." SHE KNEW? Of course, she knew. Someone from the school probably phoned her at the hospital and she was revived, making a miraculous recovery, fueled by the need to redeem the family name I was burning down.

"What is this I hear about you consorting with a vagrant?" I didn't know what those words meant, but I assumed it meant Hobo-Bob. I shrugged.

"Children ought not be involved in welfare service. I hear you have made acquaintance with this person," I shrugged again. "Friends?" she asked. I shrugged in some vague way. "Why on earth would you want to spend time with anyone so far beneath you? To make friends with some homeless transient?" I shrugged yet again.

"I'm an old lady, Jeffery, I don't have time for shrugs and head bobbles. Speak up," she instructed. "Why would you talk to someone like that?"

"I don't know...he was friendly?" I might have played games with Mr. Chatterly, but my Grandmother commanded like the Queen of England herself.

"Serial killers and perverts seem friendly too," she shook her head in frustration.

"I just talked to him."

"And what of your friends? Were they with you?"
"I don't have any friends," I furrowed my brow.

"Well, that is ridiculous. What about all the children from your party?" she questioned.

"I didn't know any of them really."

"Well, they go to the school, don't they?" she protested.

"Yeah. I don't have any friends at school though," I shifted.

"Well, I would rather be alone than consort with anyone so far beneath me, be it socially or intellectually. Joseph doesn't have your issues. He is a model student."

"I'm sorry, Rose, I really don't see where this is any of your business." Suddenly my mother was standing in the doorway. I would have described what my mother had said as bristling, but then my Grandmother's reaction fit the description much better.

183

"None of my business? My own grandchild, who lives under my roof I might add, who I put my reputation as philanthropists on the line to get into the best school possible, a school I have dedicated years to establishing and shaping into the institution it is."

"Spare me," my mother rolled her eyes, interrupting Grandmother, and pulled me toward the door.

"Rose, we are appreciative of your support, but we need to handle the parenting part on our own," my mother nodded.

"If you were handling these children, they wouldn't be running around like disobedient hooligans, dragging us all into the mud with them!" Grandmother practically yelled to get the words out before mother left the room.

I was shocked that she lumped Joseph in with me. Moments ago, her little Joseph was a model student. I saw Joseph's face twist to scorn from his hiding spot in the hall. Suddenly, I didn't want to go out the door, or stay in the room.

"None of you even care, so why is this a big deal?" I piped up. Me...I spoke up! No one talked over my Grandmother, other than my mother now and then. I guess I had just joined the list with mother.

"Jeffery," mother squeezed my shoulder.

"I don't care?" Grandmother sounded shocked. "Here I am flat in bed, fresh from the hospital taking an interest in the behavior and safety of my grandchildren, and I don't care? I really don't know where this lack of gratitude comes from. It certainly isn't a character trait in my bloodline." Grandmother shook her head with exasperation.

"None of you care that I don't have any friends, or that everyone in my class hates me," I shook my head.

"When I was a child, my brothers and sister had no friends. We didn't see the inside of the school most our lives. We had only each other to befriend. I have given you much more than I ever had, and you haven't had to do a thing to get the access. I really don't know why I try! I need my rest! Please don't come in here upsetting me, and attacking me while I am recovering, or any time after, for that matter!" I heard her as my mother dragged me down the hall.

"We won't," my mother called over her shoulder.

"The disrespect..." Grandmother's words faded as we turned the corner. Joseph ran off ahead as soon as we turned his direction.

"Why did you have to go in there?" mother asked me.

"She called for me," I protested.

"Well, try to just stay away. She is not in a good mood... not that she ever is. Go eat breakfast," mother sighed.

I scurried into the breakfast nook where Father had just sat down with his coffee and newspaper.

"Morning," father said without looking up

"Hi," I settled into my seat as Kim brought me a plate with scrambled eggs and toast.

"Your mother seems back to her old self," my mother huffed as she sat down, Kim poured her a glass of grapefruit juice with her eggs over easy. "Thank you, Kim."

"You are welcome," Kim smiled and hurried away.

"Mother isn't up, is she?" father asked.

"Oh, she isn't out of bed, but she can wield her mighty sword of vicious rhetoric from her bed just fine," mother said in a warning tone. "It's like she didn't miss a day. She knows all about our meeting at the school."

"She does?" father lowered his paper. The topic of conversation inspired me to hurry along with my breakfast. At the very least, I couldn't be expected to participate if my mouth was full, and once I was done eating, I would have to go get ready for school.

"Oh yes," mother explained. "I'm shocked she didn't drag herself up to the school yesterday with an IV in her arm and force herself into the meeting as a special consultant to the school board." My mother was agitated.

"Hmm," father sat, looking as if he were figuring a math problem out in his head. "Well, I'm sure it's common knowledge then." Father picked his paper back up.

"It wasn't before? Nothing can happen on this hill without it being the dinner table gossip that night. Did you know I was given a seat on the PTA? Do you recall me ever saying anything about wanting to be on the PTA?" mother picked up a bit of egg on her fork and continued to talk, waving the fork around with hand gestures. "I mean, don't get me wrong, our children's education is important, and I surely have an interest in them doing well. I would at least like to have gotten in the PTA because I actually put forth an effort, or was asked because they saw something in my conduct or background. Not because of who I'm married to, no offense." She stopped waving around the bite of egg and put it in her mouth.

"None, taken," father shrugged. "I'm sure Russell knows too then. He's probably who told her about it. He probably stopped on the way home yesterday just to tell her."

"It is ridiculous how that school works! Issues involving a student, and their possible safety shouldn't involve anyone but the teacher and the parents. No one else in that school should know about it, and people outside the school?!

I'm probably going to hear about this at work... but it will be overheard and behind my back," mother glowered. "As soon as that zoning ordinance passes. We are building a house near The Orchard, slightly uphill so she can see it every time she comes home," mother smirked an evil smirk. Build a house on the hill? That sounded horrible.

"Yeah, that will solve all of our problems," father rolled his eyes.

"It will solve a load of them," mother nodded.

Not for me, it wouldn't! That would be the most horrible thing to happen to me since, well since moving to the hill in the first place! Were they paying any attention whatsoever to what was going on in my life?!

"We could look for something on the east bench," father pondered.

"No... I don't want to live that far away. I mean I would be ok closer to the school. I think that is as far as I would want to move." Mother took a second bite. *A moment ago, mother loathed the school and the people, now she was wanting to move closer?* "I mean... it is unfortunate that this damn hill just happens to be in the right part of town!" She said sourly. I must have been forgotten about, even more than I had been moments ago.

"Well... We'll just have to try and live as far back as we can get on the hill," my father sipped his coffee.

"Well, not so far that we are like some tiny place that seems like we're an afterthought, you know? Like we couldn't really afford to be here, so we just took whatever was left over so we could say we live on the hill," mother argued.

"No, I know," father nodded.

I shook my head in disbelief. My mother hated nearly everything about the hill and made no secret of the fact that she thought my Grandmother was a pretentious busybody snob. I couldn't see how it was different if we were trying to live here. Why would we actually lobby to live somewhere I knew they hated. Grown-ups drove me crazy! I cleaned the last bit of egg off my plate and quietly slipped away from the table, before it made me completely insane.

"I'm going to stop and check into that *thing* we talked about," I heard my father say as I scooted around the doorway. I had a feeling whatever this *thing* was, it had to do with me.

21. Sneaking in the Long Way!

"Hey, freak." I had gone almost the entire day without anyone bothering me and then Jason plopped himself into the seat next to me on the bus. I kept looking out the window. "I said *Hey freak!*" He shoved my head, I managed to stiffen my neck just enough to keep me from banging into the window hard. I glanced at him and returned to looking out the window, keeping my entire body tensed, to resist anything he might do.

"I heard you're Mr. Chatterly's new boyfriend! Or are you Hobo-Bob's boyfriend?" I glared, but not at him of course. I wasn't about to make more eye contact. "Hey, freak! I'm talking to you!" he shoved my shoulder. Frustrated that I didn't run into the window again, or budge more than a few inches, he punched me hard in the shoulder, probably his hardest given we were sitting next to each other. "He flinched!" Jason smiled. I hated his smile, maybe more than Devin's. It was greasy.

"Flinch!" He pretended to throw a punch that stopped before his fist made contact with my face, and then he laughed his cackling donkey of a laugh. "Don't flinch, freak!" He did it again, but this time, he lightly tapped me in the cheek. *In a flood of rage, I turned and lunged a punch at him. I could practically see the flames trailing off my fist as it cut through the air. I could see him sailing across the bus and knocking over my idiot classmates who had been laughing at his stupid flinch jokes. Everyone falling silent, fearful of who I might attack next. Jason would of course cower and tenderly try to touch his new wound, but it would be too painful. He would try to look for help, blinded by the blood dripping into his eye. . . Of course.*

I didn't know the first thing about punching someone, so I slowly raised my fist while Jason had turned to laugh over the seat, and quickly lowered it again.

"Leave me alone," I said, and regretted the choice of words as they left my lips. Before I knew what was happening, he punched me square in the cheek. My eye felt like it had broken, and then the second blow came when my head met the window. The window didn't crack, it simply bounced my head right back. My ears rang and my vision blurred. There were, "woos" and "awes" followed by laughter. Jason laughed back to his seat.

I tried to sit casually and hide the tears that were pooling up. I tried to blink them away and block anyone from seeing me by holding my hand over the side of my face as I looked out the window.

By the time they got off the bus, they were all laughing and high-fiving each other. Jason was busy boasting his third or fourth retelling, as if they weren't all there and hadn't witnessed the event.

At our bus stop, Joseph was otherwise engaged, as usual. I stumbled all the way home. For some reason, only seeing out of one eye threw everything off on the whole left side of my body. It was like sympathetic paralysis. I didn't bother much trying to sneak into the house in any covert fashion. I was just about fed up with all of that. I didn't care who knew what was going on, maybe they would all finally realize I was a bit out of my element at school, and not just being sensitive to my new surroundings.

"What you do?" Kim seemed to come out of nowhere, but she was probably standing next to the door in plain sight, I was just not able to see that half of the house in my condition.

"I got punched," I said in a blunt, *isn't it obvious,* tone.

"In the eye?" she asked.

"Duh," I pointed to my eye.

"You kicked in the rib too?" she raised an eyebrow.

"Not today."

"Why you walk funny?" she pointed at me.

I shrugged.

"Come," she motioned me to follow her. She pulled a stool to the counter in the kitchen and set to work. She pulled out random things and mixed them in a bowl. Some kind of oil, and herbs. I thought maybe she was going to marinade a steak before putting it on my eye. Which didn't seem like a sanitary thing to do. Everyone freaked out if a kid touched raw meat. They would make you wash your hands like fifty times, but put raw meat on your optical orifice after an injury? Go ahead. It never made any sense to me.

In a moment, Kim came at me with the small bowl and pasted the concoction on my eye. It didn't sting, but it did tingle on the tender skin.

"Why you no fight back, huh?" Kim asked.

"I tried," I said with a sigh.

"You hit him too?" she said, carefully dabbing the paste.

"No," I shrugged.

"Your father never teach you?"

"No," I nearly laughed at the idea of my father teaching anyone to fight.

"Father must teach son to fight," Kim nodded.

"Do you know karate?" I asked, hopefully.

"I look Chinese to you?" she stopped dabbing the goo on my face and gave me a look. "No?" she muttered something in her native Korean.

"You talk to Father. He teach you to fight white boys like a white boy. Go do school work. Out of kitchen, I hit you other eye!" she swatted me as I jumped off the stool.

My eye felt a bit better, but it smelled like some kind of Asian stir fry meat.

I stopped at the English wall shelf in the study, collected a couple of figurines, and headed upstairs.

I pulled my favorite gold elephant from under my dresser and dangled off the edge of the bed, setting up a scene below. Sometimes, I arranged toys so perfectly I could hardly move them, I just created a dialog in my head for what they were saying. To anyone else, I was just staring at them. It was tough being the younger one, everyone wanted you to act like the older kids, stop playing make believe, stop talking to your toys.... I was a

191

kid. I supposed someday I would put the toys away and stop playing pretend, but then again, maybe I would be my father's age and lock my office door and pull open my desk drawer to set up my toys into a perfect battle scene. Or maybe I would keep them on my desk and tell people they were for decoration. Perhaps that was all any adult did when they arranged figurines on a shelf or bookcase.

"I am an elephant, I could crush anyone of you."

"Well, I am a panther, and I can kill an elephant, easily."

"Try it. Run at me, I will beat you with my trunk," the elephant taunted.

"I will rip your trunk to shreds," the panther growled a deep guttural growl of frustration as he knew the elephant was right.

"I don't think so. And if you do, I will squash you with my foot. You go do whatever panthers do in the jungle, and I will stay here and eat," the elephant grabbed a bunch of grass with his trunk.

"I am a natural killer," the panther smirked, as much as a panther could smirk.

"Well, I was taught to defend myself," the elephant said with a full mouth. The panther and elephant continued to square off, reasoning back and forth how they could both damage the other. The other animals on looked and watched carefully, swaying their support back and forth as the argument continued. Eventually, the whole thing was exhausting, and I fell asleep.

When I woke, there was a puddle of drool on the floor below me. I scooped up the figurines and jumped off the bed. I had all but forgotten about my eye until I was upright and the pain kicked in and reminded me. I tucked the elephant back under the dresser and put the others under my pillow. I hurried downstairs.

I carefully looked around downstairs. My father was sitting at Grandmother's desk in her office going through a notebook.

"Dad," I decided to try Kim's... advice was it?

"I don't have time Jeffery!" father waved me away.

"Ok... can you maybe teach me to fight after dinner?" My father dropped his notebook and squinted at me. He lowered his glasses and blinked at me, looking at my eye.

"What is that?" father pointed at my eye.

"I got hit on the bus." My father came alive. He promptly pulled me along as he headed to the backyard.

"Listen, first of all... you can't ever go picking a fight, ok? But if a fight comes to you, you should be prepared.

Walk away from trouble if you can. It doesn't mean you're weak if you turn the other cheek." I thought this all sounded like a song I had heard before, but I wasn't sure. "But if they won't let you leave, or they go too far... Well, first of all, you don't ever punch with your fist. That is the natural reaction. You need to hit with the palm of your hand. If you land a punch, you hurt your fist and then what? You can't punch again? But you can hit over and over with the palm of your hand."

"Like this?" I held out my hand like a slap.

"No, like this. It's like a punch, but with the part of the palm before your wrist. It's not a slap from the side, it's a hit straight at them. Try it, here at my hand." I tried it, kind of soft at first, making sure I hit his hand at all. I couldn't suffer another humiliating miss!

"Good. Harder." I was more than a little surprised that my father was teaching me anything about fighting! It seemed quite contrary to the passive nature of my parents. I couldn't imagine what Grandmother would say if she saw us! It might have been one of the only times my father dropped whatever he was doing for me as well.

We practiced moving around and trying to block or dodge the other person's blows. I felt like the karate kid by the time we were done.

"Good. Now I don't want to hear about you going to school tomorrow and beating up half your class, ok?" father winked as we walked back inside.

"Ok," I smiled.

"Good," he patted me on the head.

I felt better about the situation right up until my mother walked in. She was looking at something in a book.

"Gerald showed me the preliminary zoning charts for how they are going to parcel properties if this thing gets passed," my mother whispered with excitement.

"Really?" father put his hands on his hips, his shirt untucked from our exercise.

"Yeah, there are a couple of properties that would be perfect for us to build on... he thinks we could probably get an accepted bid the same day the new zoning goes into effect. You know if it gets voted through," she winked. "So how long do you think it would take to build?"

"We're building a house on the hill?" I suddenly wanted to throw up.

"Well, it would depend on how things work out. But if they open the hill up for building smaller houses, I think we might," she beamed. But she hated people on the hill, just like I did. She glanced at me and then did a double take.

"What on earth?!" she slammed the book shut and set it on the curio.

"Oh, he just got into a little tiff," my father said, ruffling my hair.

"A little tiff? That black eye is no tiff!" She reached for my eye, I swatted her away.

"Oh, it's fine. It's what boys do. You should see the other guy," my father joked.

"You hit someone back?!" mother seemed more upset by the idea that I would fight back than me having been hit.

I shook my head. She gave me that look that demanded the entire story.

"Devin. He was at my party. Remember I said they hate me?"

"Well, I'm calling Devin's mother!" mother said with intensity.

"No, mom!" I protested immediately.

"Sharon...don't do that," father shook his head.

"Why? He attacked another child!" mother put her hands on her hips.

"And you think you will magically make things better?" my father seemed to get it.

"They will tease me forever if you call his mom! Please... It will be so bad!" I pleaded.

"I don't like this! He should be suspended," she reached for my eye again. I darted my head to the side.

"Next time, I'm going to drop him!" I grinned.

"You will not! There better not be a next time! You tell him if he does this again you will go to the principal," she nodded.

"No!" I protested. "Dad taught me to fight back!" Things got quiet. My father shifted.

"What?" father mounted a defense without mother having even said anything. "He should be able to defend himself."

"No," she said in a dark serious tone.

"If they come after him, and there are no teachers around, he has to be able to defend himself. He isn't going to just sit there and take a beating," father reasoned very plainly. Made sense to me!

"He isn't going to strike another child!" mother folded her arms.

"He isn't going to be a punching bag either," father folded his arms in kind.

"What do I know? I'm just his mother. I suppose this is your mother's idea?" mother raised her eyebrows.

"As far as I know, she doesn't even know about it," father cocked his head.

"She knows everything that happens in that school," my mother rolled her eyes in frustration.

"It was on the bus," I piped in.

"This should have been discussed," mother huffed.

"Well, I thought..." father didn't finish the statement.

"Did you?" she picked up her book. My father watched her leave and then looked at me.

"Why do you smell like hibachi?" he asked.

22. Stuffed

I went to school with a new found confidence. I walked with a swagger that came from *knowing* I could defend myself against any bully that came my way. I went all day not caring that I hadn't a friend in the world. I beat people to answers in class, I made comments without fear of my peers giving me scornful looks of disapproval. I simply stopped caring. I actually hadn't realized how much I had cared previous to that moment. If you had asked me if I cared, I would have said no, which clearly hadn't been the case.

Even with my new found confidence, I wasn't overly eager to run to recess, but that was more out of caution than fear. The only real concern I had that day was waiting for Mr. Chatterly to call me down to the office so we could talk about what happened on the bus. I was pretty sure my parents wouldn't call the school, but you never knew what Grandmother would do, or why.

As soon as we were dismissed to recess I bolted for the upperclassmen bathroom, with the secret passage. I made sure that there was no one following me. As soon as I got into the bathroom I froze, staring at the vent to the underground hideout. As much swagger as I came into the bathroom with, I didn't have enough to dive back into there. I checked into the last stall and sat on the toilet, fishing two G.I. Joe's from my pocket.

"I stashed the money in here," one Joe said, quietly scooting down the metal handrail toward the toilet paper holder.

He carefully jumped down to the toilet paper holder and slid down to the underside hanging on like a monkey. Just then, the bathroom door opened. My G.I. Joe's would have to be extra careful and stealthy. I heard laughter and voices of several people.

"We have visitors," the Joe still above whispered as he quietly swung down to meet the other. The Joe's kept looking for the money stash. The voices in the bathroom belonged to Devin, Jason, Jacob, Brock, and Aaron.

"My parents won't be home until like six, so if we hurry... we can get my Nintendo hooked up to the big TV and we can probably find that hidden level."

"I got to level six on Saturday, but my mom turned it off!" I was certain it was Jason, Devin, and probably Jacob.

"Mine is on pause. I'm like level five right now."

Hmmm... they were going to be indoors today. I smiled to myself. I probably couldn't get onto the playground at the Orchard. That was too visible, but I could probably at least get up toward the Turtle lair. I would head there right after I got off the bus. I knew I still couldn't head to the forest, but I would take any chance I could to get outside of Grandmother's yard. I had a good hour before my mother would be home.

"I might need cover. There are Cobra all over this station," the GI Joe radioed in a near silent whisper. He was losing his grip quickly. He carefully repositioned and found his stash of bills. He "spider-monkeyed" back up the side of the structure he was dangling from moments before.

"Hey check this out!" Devin said with excitement.

197

"Dude!" Jacob replied.

"No, it's like this!" Jason said, crossing the bathroom. They were all in front of the mirrors, which were on the wall parallel to the bathroom stalls I was hiding in. I froze, the GI Joe froze as well. I tried to position myself so I could see through the crack in the stall door, but I couldn't tell what was going on.

In a moment they all three broke out in laughter. They kept on whispering about whatever they were doing, and then trying to control their laughter.

"Hey, who's in here?" Jason asked loudly. I didn't move a muscle.

In a second, I jumped when a hard knock came on the stall door.

"Who's in there?" Devin asked, pressing an eye up to the crack. I tilted my head down and pulled my pants as far up as I could while keeping my butt on the toilet seat. What kind of pervert kid peeked into the bathroom stall?

"Is that Jeffery?" Devin exclaimed. "Peanut!" He rattled the door. "What are you doing in there, Peanut? Are you spying on us?"

"Sick!" Jason yelled out.

"You hang out in the bathroom, Peanut?" Jacob knocked on the door. "He's a bathroom boy!"

"Yeah he is!" Jason laughed. *A bathroom boy?* Could they try to be less original? Their insults weren't even insults anymore, they were just vague yet obvious observations of what was going on. I was in a bathroom, and I was in fact a boy. Bathroom boy? It was like some kind of failed super hero sidekick. As stupid as it was, it seemed worse than Peanut, and I hoped it did not stick!

"Come out and play, Peanut! I want to show you something!" Devin rattled the door.

"Wait, wait!" Jason called out. I hear whispers, followed by giggling. In a moment a sopping wet ball of paper towel came flying over the stall door. It struck the wall and splashed on the back of my shoulder as it hit the floor. They erupted in laughter. Yet another paper towel wad came flying over the stall, and another, both which narrowly missed me, but managed to still get me wet. I waited for the next one with a hand held up. Sure enough, in a moment, another wad came sailing over. I swatted it away, to the wall, and onto the floor. I was admiring my ability to adapt what my father had caught me and apply it to wet wads of paper products when two more came over. One hit me square in the face and the other in the shoulder. The one that hit me in the face plopped into my lap, caught by my pants - which I had hiked way up. Had I not hiked my pants up so far, the paper towel wad would have fallen into the toilet, with minimal contact. But no, in my infinite wisdom, I had created a ledge of the wet mess to fall into, cradled and caught by my zipper and fly. It was the ultimate worst place a grade school boy could get any kind of moisture.

I picked up the wad and threw it against the stall door, with quite a loud bang. Of course this made my audience burst out in laughter, but at least they started to exit.

"Bye, bathroom boy!" they chimed musically as they left.

Just as I was surveying the wet spot on the front of my pants, the lights went out. As the door closed, I was now in absolute and total darkness. My only hope now was that someone else would come in to turn the light on, or my eyes adjusted to the fraction of light coming under the door.

I sighed heavily. I was pretty sure I could hear them still laughing in the hall, close to the bathroom door. So much for my confidence. I should have flown out the door and beaten the crap out of all of them! In the darkness, I closed my eyes, which seemed silly to do when it was already pitch black, but it seemed to help me find my pocket to put away my GI Joe.

I kept my eyes shut for a time, still hoping someone would turn the lights on. I needed the lights so I could start figuring out how to dry my pants before recess was over!

I sat still in the silent black. I thought about the brown eyed girl. I pictured her shy smile. I imagined her sitting next to me during art, smiling at me whenever I looked at her. Maybe sitting together on the playground after school, trying to hold her hand, and finally kissing her!

I opened my eyes and tried to strain them in the dark to see if I could focus them on my GI Joe, but it was of no use. I was going to have to figure out how to get out of the stall and bathroom, in the dark. Of course, when I got back to class, it was going to be pointed out that my pants were wet, and the Cougars would no doubt use the opportunity to try out my new nickname in public. But if I didn't get a light on, I had a pretty good excuse for never going back to class. Shoot, I wouldn't even have to explain anything other than the light got turned off, and I was totally disabled, unable to get out of the stall, unable to find the door. Maybe if I weren't new to the school, I would have been able to get out of the situation, but as unfamiliar as I was with the facilities, I doubted if anyone could blame me for missing the rest of the day!

I leaned forward and folded my arms across my legs, laying my head on them. I waited. The quiet darkness was soothing. Peace wasn't something I often had during the school day.

I had no concept of how long I sat there, but I figured out a rough estimate when the bell rang.

I raised my head and opened my eyes. It was still dark. The door opened. I was both hopeful that the light would turn on, but also fearful that it would, and I would lose my reason for not going to class.

"Bathroom boy! Come out, come out!" Devin yelled mockingly.

"No, no! Bathroom-boy is in there!" I heard Jason say to someone. I heard giggles as the door swung closed again.

"Bye, Bathroom-boy!" I heard from the hall as voices faded. I sat, in the dark still. I didn't care. I laid my head back down and thought about movies, cars, and video games. I tried visioning playing Mario Brothers in my head. I could see the screens in perfect boxy clarity that our TV didn't have. I executed every move perfectly, sailing through the levels. I lost track of time. Finally the door opened and the light turned on.

"Hello?" the voice of a teacher echoed.

"Yes," I replied.

"Who is in here?" the teacher demanded.

"Jeffery Alfrey, Sir. The light got turned off," I explained.

"Well, it's on now, get out here," the teacher instructed. I was pretty sure he was holding the door open, waiting on me.

I got off the toilet and inspected my pant as I did them up. They seemed to be mostly dry. I exited slowly.

"How long have you been in here?" the teacher asked. He was a sixth grade teacher.

"Since recess. I don't know how long that is," I shrugged.

"Since recess?" the teacher exclaimed. "Follow me." He pointed down the hall. I slowly complied. He marched me right down to the office, and held the door open for me.

"This young man was hiding in a bathroom with the lights off since recess." The teacher was only telling part of the story! I furrowed my brows.

"Have a seat," the office lady pointed at a chair as the teacher left the door to close. I was furious at how unfairly I was being treated. There was no due process in this school! There didn't seem to be a lot of due process for kids in general. Adults just assumed they were correct about everything and who cared about the truth, or the whole story?

I slumped into the chair. But I did have at least one silver lining. The Cougars were going to be leaving the Orchard unattended after school. Playing on the Cougar's turf was like licking desserts at one of Grandmother's meetings, it was a secret thrill. I hoped they would leave something of their unattended, so I could mess with it.

Mr. Chatterly came to the office in a few minutes.

"Jeffery," he smiled. "Why don't I walk you to class." He held the door open. I would have rather stayed sitting in the office.

I gathered myself and begrudgingly followed.

"So, didn't want to go to class this afternoon?" he asked. I was half inclined to not respond, since grown-ups just made up their mind before they asked questions anyway.

"I was in the bathroom and some guys turned the light off. I was stuck," I was sure he wouldn't believe me, so what did I have to lose?

"Oh. You don't think you maybe could have found your way?" he raised an eyebrow.

"I don't know that bathroom very well," I frowned.

"Maybe you could have felt your way in the dark?" he asked.

"I have a thing about the dark," I shook my head. It was pretty much a lie, but he didn't know that. A pitch black bathroom was nothing compared to a pitch black basement at Grandmother's, or a pitch black trunk of a car, or any other places I had been stuffed, tricked into, or chose to hide.

"I see. Well, maybe there was a little bit of not wanting to rejoin your class, though?" he tried to carefully eye me from the corner of his vision.

"It was dark," I muttered.

"Ok, well then. Here we are, ready to go back to class." He stood outside the door and folded his arms.

"Ok," I shrugged. At least my pants had dried! And I had gotten to miss a chunk of class. It wasn't all bad. Although I had likely picked up another unfortunate nickname. We would have to wait and see how that played out.

"Ok, then," Mr. Chatterley seemed a little surprised when I moved for the door. Like I would suddenly decide I wanted to spill my life story to him in the hall, and beg him to not make me go back to class. He obviously didn't understand me at all. While grown-ups did provide a certain safety from the Cougars in most situations, they were not endeared to me. I would happily trade a supervised classroom over a one on one chat with Mr. Weirdo, or most grown-ups for that matter.

I raised my eyebrows, to express my lack of interest in whatever he was trying to pull over on me, and slipped through the door.

"Mr. Alfrey," Mrs. Potts turned from the board and looked over her glasses.

"Jeffery was with me," Mr. Chatterly said from the door way.

"Very well then," Mrs. Potts turned back to the board.

Did Mr. Chatterly think he was going to brownie point into my graces? That guy was really starting to bug me.

"Welcome back Bathroom-boy," I heard whispered as I passed Devin and Jacob. I wasn't sure which one it was, but I heard plenty of snickers join in.

I continued on the rest of the afternoon uneasy, yet aloof. I milled about when the bell rang for the day. I kept a watchful eye as I walked to and onto the bus, waiting for any Cougar to change seats. Luckily they seemed to not be paying any attention to me. I heard more than a few Bathroom-boy references behind me, but no one was close enough to the front of the bus to give me any real grief.

The Cougars got off the bus at their stop without so much as a glance behind them. I watched as they ran off, with purpose, as expected. I smiled down the block to our stop, finally resting with some ease. I hopped off the bus and headed home in a beeline. I grabbed my bike from the side of the house and took off toward the Orchard. I kept a cautious eye surveilling the park as I approached.

I was one of the craftiest spies in the business. I scanned the oil rig station. No one in sight. I acted casual so no one would have a reason to suspect me of anything.

I easily scaled the rig and found the control tower where the enemy usually was posted century. They left no traces of what they were up to. I fished a computer board from my backpack and wired it into their computer system. They would have no clue. I dangled off the edge and swung under the platform. I tucked the computer board into a slot on the

underside of the platform, so they wouldn't stumble upon it. I climbed
back to another part of the rig and slid down a pole.

I was too exposed. I could be seen. I quickly darted to the taller grass at
the edge of the compound. I took to the edge of the stream and worked
through the grass on hands and knees. I checked my map. There was a
bridge along the stream that I could use as a temporary base. I made
good time reaching it. I pulled out a few computer boards and fake ID's
and stashed them in a new hiding spot.

I had a narrow window before the agents would return to the oil rig to
continue their mission. I just needed to find a few supplies before I got
myself back out of their turf and back across the border. When I was
dropped into the country, I had seen a plane crash or wrecked car from
the air. It shouldn't have been far away from me. I set off through the
grass. I was sure there were some parts inside the plane or car I could
use. I found what I was sure must have been the spot. It was a car. It
looked like it had been a nice car once upon a time. It reminded me of a
car I had been trapped in once upon a time, on a previous mission.

I quickly slipped through the grass and into the car. I took a good look
around, making sure there was no one, or nothing moving through the
grass.

Bingo! There was a weapons cache in the car! I couldn't imagine what was
being planned, but the car was full of bow staffs (long and short), wooden
nunchucks, rocks tied to twine, etc.

I loaded the weapons in my backpack. I must have found the agent's
secret stash. They must have been using the oil rig platform as a scout
location to keep the weapons cache a safe secret. I cleaned it out in a
hurry! I darted back into the grass, my heart pounding in my chest. I
could practically feel their eyes on me. If I could make it out alive, I could
disable whatever they were planning. Maybe not forever, but for some
time. Once I was into the grass, I moved across the stream and started
taking apart and disassembling weapons. Some, by untying, some I had
stomped on and cracked into short pieces. I started throwing weapon
pieces in random directions. I kept a few of the nicer pieces intact, I
would take those with me.

When I was done with the work, I reached the bridge. I paused and used the location to scout around. I heard voices.

"What the hell! He's been here already!" I smirked.

"No, it couldn't have been him. We would have seen him."

"Someone has been here! It's all gone! My staff is gone! My...everything!"

"He's right, it had to be him!"

I flattened myself to the bank of the stream. I knew they would be coming to the bridge... I scooted down the bank and behind a bush. Sure enough, they came right to the bridge. I didn't move a muscle. I could see their faces, but it was ok. I was a trained professional.

They were beyond angry! It set in that I had a whole hour of self-defense training and my new found confidence was waning quickly.

"I'm going to kick his butt into next week!"

"I'm going to actually kill him! That is the second time that weasel has stolen a staff from me!" Jason yelled, his fists clinched. "I even had a cougar carved into the handle!" I smirked. Is that what that had been?

"He has to be around still," Devin said scanning around. I prayed he didn't see me. I was tucked in pretty well. He seemed to be looking more toward the Orchard. *I mean the oil rig.*

They headed out of the grass. I kept moving down the stream once I couldn't see or hear them. Suddenly the quiet was broken by battle cries and flying rocks. I was caught between wanting to duck and cover and run... so I did both, not particularly well.

Once I heard the splash of their boots in the stream, I knew I would be done for if I didn't step it up. I took off at a full sprint down the bank, but as I did so, I was caught in the middle of my back by a rock. It wasn't a particularly heavy rock, or thrown that hard, but it was enough to offset my balance mid-sprint. I tumbled to the ground. Quickly, they were on me as I tried to get back up.

"You don't know when to stay down! Where are our weapons?" a foot in my chest pushed me to the ground.

"Gone." The staff I was running with had landed in the grass ahead of me, I could see it still. Maybe if I could get to the staff I could fight them back.

"Where are the mustard bombs?" one of them asked.   "Go get them!" a few ran off toward the car, leaving only three of them.

"I'm going to enjoy this." The one with crazy eyebrows smiled. While they were laughing, I jerked the leg on my chest to the side, dumping the owner of the leg onto the ground. I jumped up and swung a wild punch at the person closest to me, knocking him off balance. I took off in a sprint, scooping up the staff as I ran. No one else was even close to me. I quickly reached the end of the tall grass and jumped out into the open. I had to get some major distance between us, and some kind of cover. If I kept running straight, they would probably be able to take aim at me. I was caught between running for the forest border or trying to make it back to my home base. I ran for *the oil rig* to get some obstruction between us. I darted through the hardware. The battle cries faded and turned into beating feet against the ground, chasing after me. I ran as hard as I could toward the border, and was gaining ground quickly.

"He's going into the woods!" Some of them changed their direction and ran straight toward the border of the woods. They were running for the flattest, easiest part of the border, but I was heading for the more difficult part, the part I knew they would struggle to follow me into. The problem was going to be, if they got far enough into the woods, they could cut off my path. I didn't really have many other options. I changed my path a bit, I knew I could get into the edge of the woods and tuck into a drainage ditch opening that lead downhill. Maybe they wouldn't notice, and think I made it all the way ahead of them. I had the benefit of knowing where I was once I was across the border, they were likely unfamiliar with the terrain.

I made it over the guardrail and into the edge of the tree line. I was sure I was clear. I tucked into the pipe head and pulled grass and leaves in on myself. It was a nice tight fit, but that just meant I was protected. I was poised to defend myself with the bow staff. I tried to quiet my breath and catch it at the same time, waiting like a treed cat.

"I know you're here! You didn't run that way, we would have seen you." That's right, yell louder, alert my friend in the forest that you are hunting me. They made all sorts of sounds as they combed through the edge of the woods, as deep as they dared. Suddenly, the grass moved outside my hole. I wiggled deeper into the pipe.

"Found him!" Suddenly, their laughter and footsteps echoed into the pipe. In the dark, I felt a sharp stab in my ribs. It struck me repeatedly. The gathering outside the pipe had sticks they were jabbing in the hole. I tried to block them with the staff I had, but it was too long to do any good from inside the hole. I tried grabbing the sticks and breaking them. After a minute, they stopped.

"How do we get him out?" a voice questioned.

"Burn him out!" someone yelled. Certainly my ally could hear them.

"Do we have matches?"

Suddenly, I heard yelling. Maybe they had awoken Optimus! I heard scrambling commotion outside the pipe. Soon it was quiet. I didn't move for a while. When I was pretty sure there was no one there, I jabbed my staff outside the grass. Nothing. I slowly peeked out. I didn't see or hear anyone... I darted from the pipe and ran into the woods. I heard a familiar voice yell something. It sounded like my brother. That was impossible. He was a long ways away. I found my usual clearing, checkpoint. I looked around for Optimus. He could have been hiding right next to me in his camouflage and I would never know it.

"Are you there Optimus?" I asked. "Thanks for the rescue, big guy!" I danced across the roots. "Where are you?"

"You have a knack for getting into trouble, human," Optimus growled. He was holding his head and squinting at the light. I wasn't sure what kind of damage he had taken.

"I found their weapons," I shrugged.

"And you took them of course?" Optimus rubbed his forehead.

"Yep," I held up the staff I kept.

"What will you do when I don't show up?"

"I was hidden well. I thought I could fight back, but … there are too many of them even if I try. I need a better defense."

"Perhaps you should talk to your father about that," he grumped. I heard rustling from behind me. I looked toward the road. It was Joseph!

"Jeff!" he demanded.

"What?" I ran toward him.

"Who were you talking to?"

"No one," I shook my head.

"Was it Hobo-Bob?" he glared at me.

"No one! I was hiding from Devin and his goons. They chased me from the playground into here," I explained.

"Get home! I just saved your butt!" he smirked, self-importantly.

"You did not," I challenged. Had he? Joseph wouldn't have come to my aid.

"Oh really? Who was up here with your little friends? I've had to watch them ever since I got off the bus, because mom told me I better not let anything happen to you," he glared, his head cocked, arms folded. She had sent Joseph to protect me? Oh, the shame! That was almost worse than being beaten up. I begrudgingly climbed out of the woods and stormed off ahead of Joseph.

I was furious that I had been issued a keeper, Joseph of all people. Joseph jumped on his bike and slowly pedaled, following me back home. I hurried into the house and tried to slip away, but my mother caught me coming through the door, she must have been waiting for us.

"Where were you?" Mother demanded.

"Nowhere," I shrugged.

"Well, it sure took you a long time to get home from nowhere."

"He was talking to Hobo-Bob in the woods," Joseph said coming through the door.

"I was not!" I rolled my eyes.

"You were so!" Joseph smirked.

"Jeffery?" My mother questioned.

"What? I wasn't."

"I can't deal with this right now. Your Grandmother is hosting the zoning board meeting in an hour and she's going to have an utter fit if this gets brought up. Do you understand me? You stay in your rooms, and we will get to the bottom of this later. Don't talk to anyone," she ordered.

"What?" I maintained my innocence.

"We will talk about it later!" she glared.

"Fine," I rolled my eyes. What did Joseph know, anyway? Nothing!

I tried to shrug off my aggravation. If Grandmother was having a meeting, that meant snacks! My mood changed in a flash. The only snacks being prepared seemed to be chocolate chip cookies and lemonade, but there were dozens and dozens of the cookies, and gallons of lemonade, enough to fill the bathtub. I casually walked passed the table of cookies and cups of pre-poured lemonade, as adults milled about the back patio. No one paid any attention to me, as I carefully reached a hand out from my folded arms and quickly snatched a cookie and tucked my hand back, hiding the cookie in my palm. I then continued to the other end of the house where I could eat the cookie. I waited a bit, and then proceeded with the same maneuver again, this time being extra careful as I took a cup of lemonade. I was pretty sure I had two cups, and five or six cookies before I hid on the outside porch staircase to the second story patio. I belly crawled to the edge.

"Excuse me, ladies and gentlemen," Uncle Russell said loudly, tapping a tiny wooden hammer on the table as people took a seat. There was a sea of folding chairs all over the patio and lawn. There had to be two hundred people. "We are going to get started. My mother has asked that councilman Russell Alfrey take over directing our meeting and vote tonight. We thank her for the use of her home for this very important meeting for our community.

This is how the meeting will go. First, the floor will be open to anyone who wishes to say something about the rezoning of the North and North West sections of the Hill neighborhood. Following that, we will be addressed by my mother, Chairwoman Rose Alfrey, immediately followed by the vote for the zoning ordinance. After the vote has been taken and the motion for the zoning ordinance is closed, this meeting will be concluded and participants will disburse. If anyone wishes to make comments or address concerns with the council, they will wait for the next regularly scheduled meeting, or they can write and send correspondence to the council in the appropriate manner. This is not, and will not be the venue for anyone to complain about our democratic process. This meeting will now come to order," he tapped the tiny hammer again.

I had my face pressed up against the railing around the upper patio. I slowly drew spit in my mouth and let it drip out, falling on the walkway of the lower patio. I counted as it fell, every second it fell was ten feet, or that was what Joseph had told me, so we were about twenty feet up.

"My family has lived on this Hill since before the Orchard was an actual orchard." An old man stood in the middle of the chairs, "There were less than a dozen estates here back then. Your property was something you could be proud of, take pride in turning into something of beauty. Now, people have a right to do what they want with their own land... but I recall a meeting, like this one, in which we set out the covenants of the Hill and created a document that would protect all residents from any other resident doing something extreme to their property that would negatively impact anyone else's property values, or view. I don't see how the city can step in and override that.

That covenant should remain in effect. The residents of the Hill agreed to those covenants when they bought their land, and they should stand by that covenant. Selling off your back yard so someone else can build a tiny house back there to make a buck, or an apartment building. They would rent it out to a bunch of people who couldn't afford a house south of the tracks, let alone on the Hill is exactly the kind of extreme the covenant was put in place to protect against.

This is not just some piece of paper that can be redrafted or disregarded to suit whoever has the next wild hare. It was thoughtfully created by the residents and agreed to by the same residents who are trying to bypass it now to suit their desire. Even worse are the people who are petitioning to build on The Hill who are not residents of The Hill. If you don't like the terms of the homeowner's covenant, that's fine, don't move here, and they won't apply to you! If you are a resident and you don't like them, fine, move off of the Hill and they won't apply to you. But the covenant exists, so too bad." He sat down to a good half of the people applauding. A middle-aged woman took the center of the crowd next.

"We live in a free country, where people get to live wherever they want to live, without being told by someone else what to do with their own property because of some crazy document a bunch of old fuddies made up years ago," she promptly sat down. Again, half the crowd applauded.

The meeting carried on like that for some time. I waited for mother or father to jump in, but mother just sat still with her arms folded. I sat in my perch and giggled every time someone went to the refreshment table and stepped in one of my dozen spit patches.

"If there is no one else who wishes to address the body, we will now take the vote," Uncle Russell had such a fake important air about him, as if he were conducting the affairs of a grand kingdom. It bothered me, and I was only a kid. I couldn't imagine what grown-ups thought of the guy.

"The official vote for the motion of zoning ordinance thirty-two twenty-three to prohibit housing community covenants that reach beyond zoning commission rulings will now commence." He looked up from the paper he was reading from and tapped his tiny hammer. "All of those in favor of passing the motion may now make it manifest." It seemed every other person in the crowd raised their hand. Two men with notepads started moving down the center row, counting every raised hand. When they had finished they returned to the front. My mother voted for the motion to pass... I hoped my Grandmother hadn't seen her hand up. Mother probably hoped that as well, but we all knew Grandmother had her eagle eye fixed on her.

"All of those opposed may now make it manifest." Again it seemed every other hand went up, including Uncle Russell's, and Grandmother's. You couldn't have strapped the woman to a hospital bed and made her miss this meeting. It was probably why she came home from the hospital in the first place. She was probably on her deathbed but refused to not be counted in this vote, and sent the reaper away!

My father abstained from voting, which seemed like a good neutral position, but I wondered if both Grandmother and Mother would be angry that he didn't cast a vote in their corner. It might have been wiser to only make one of them angry.

Again, the two men went through counting everyone and returned forward. They both handed a piece of paper to Uncle Russell, who stared at the papers over the rim of his glasses, like a librarian.

"It would seem we have a consistent tally from our clerks. The motion has been carried, the '*I's*' have it." There was an eruptive buzz in the crowd, both people on the edge of cheering, and others on the verge of revolt. "This meeting is adjourned," Uncle Russell tapped the tiny hammer on the table. He looked like he might spit, or vomit flames. I was poised to watch a good hockey-style fight break out. Some people happily whispered to each other, unable to suppress smiles, they seemed to be the younger crowd. The others rolled their eyes and stalked off in bitter haste. They seemed to be the older crowd.

I hurried down the stairs and asserted myself behind the cookie table as if I were somehow officially bidding people farewell. I swiped a couple more cookies and found my parents, who were keeping a buffered radius away from Grandmother and Uncle Russell. Grandmother looked as though she may be loaded into an ambulance at any moment, in a fit of despair. Mother and father were heading for the house.

"Go put your bikes away and get ready for bed," my mother said, with urgency as she headed for the house, keeping an eye out for Grandmother and Uncle Russell.

My bike! I had left my bike at the Orchard!

23. Defensive Actions

I waited until it was deadly dark. There was hardly a sound in the house, just a couple of people milling about with final clean up items after the meeting. I slipped out the back and into the carriage house. I knew right where to go to find a flashlight. I knew every inch of the carriage house, eyes closed. I slipped down the side of the carriage house and crossed the fence in the back of Grandmother's property. I darted through the property behind Grandmother's and out onto the street, which was a dangerous move as Jason's family lived one house over.

I hurried to the Orchard and crept through the playground, looking around for my bike. I left it in the grass, but you never knew. I headed toward the grass. I clicked the flashlight on, and kept my hand over the lens, letting just a bit of light spill through my fingers. I searched through the grass, but found nothing. I combed through every inch. It was gone.

I took a deep breath and headed toward Devin's house. I sneaked past each of the Cougars houses, looking down their driveways, on the sides of their houses, their front porches. There was no sign of my bike. Nothing. My heart sank. I slowly dragged back toward home. I put the flashlight away and quietly slipped back into the house. I darted up stairs silently and threw myself onto my bed. I let out a long ragged huff. Oh, how I hated that whole group of boys.

I stewed all morning over my bike. When I got on the bus, they were all smirking and snickering, whispering to each other. I grumbled to my seat.

"Wanna ride bikes after school?" Devin laughed as I passed his seat getting off the bus. I paused for a moment.

"Sounds like fun."

"Shut up freak!" his smile turned into a sneer. I snapped.

I jumped on him, rapidly punching him in the chest and stomach. He fell backward, cowering, unable to do anything but get pummeled. I landed several blows to his head. Everything my father had tried to teach me weren't even tertiary thoughts. It was only a matter of seconds before I was pulled off by Mr. Speaker.

"Would the lot of you knock it off! This isn't a zoo! You want to work out your differences, do it somewhere else, but not on my bus! Now sit down!" he ordered. Devin was fuming. I glared right back. He didn't look injured, but he was for sure frazzled by the attack. At least I had made contact this time!

People whispered and giggled the whole bus ride to school.

"Hey, Jeff," some kid I didn't know nudged me from the seat behind me. "Are you gonna fight Devin after school?"

"What?" I asked. I was pretty sure my attack wasn't the end of things. Nothing ever seemed to be the end of things. Every event was simply a gateway into the next hostile situation. We seemed destined for this pattern the rest of our lives.

"I don't know," I shrugged.

"Yeah, he said he's going to fight you after you get off the bus," the kid seemed quite excited. Everyone was always primed for a good fight, no matter what school you were in, public or private. The same was true from kindergarten to college, if there was a good fight brewing - there would be people to see it go down.

I started thinking of ways I could end up in Mr. Chatterly's office, or get sent home. I had attacked another student, after all. When we pulled up to the school, Mr. Speaker grabbed me out of the crowd of kids getting off the bus and held me while everyone else got off, and then did the same to Devin as he passed. Mr. Speaker dragged the two of us off the bus and handed us off to a teacher who monitored the front walk as the buses arrived.

"This one attacked this one. Other than that, I don't care what is going on," Mr. Speaker shoved me at the teacher. I was pretty sure she taught sixth grade. She didn't look like a kind woman.

"Follow me," she dragged the two of us off to the office by our arms. "These two were fighting on the bus," she said, hauling us through the office door.

This was ridiculous. Devin deserved anything he got and probably more, as long as it was negative.

"Take seats," the office lady pointed at chairs.

"I'm going to kick your butt," Devin whispered.

"Yeah? Cause I think I just kicked yours," I smirked. My right hand was throbbing.

"Shut up. You got us sent to the principal, you idiot," Devin narrowed his eyes at me.

"No, you got us sent here. Give me back my bike." I said slightly above a whisper. Devin laughed and settled into the chair.

"Jeff. Why don't you come with me?" Mr. Chatterley popped his head into the office. At least he didn't ask Devin to come along. I took a long breath and followed him back to his office.

"How's it going, Jeff?" he asked, shutting the office door. He was wearing a blue shirt and brown sport coat that looked like it was made out of a couch.

"Good," I sank into the bean bag.

"Good, huh? I heard you got into a fight with... uhh, Devin is it?" he asked, sitting down with his fingers intertwined and locked.

"Yeah," I bit my lip.

"What was that about, hmm?" he raised his eyebrows.

I shrugged. I wasn't telling him anything! Not after having to sit there with my parents and have them all drone on about my affairs like I wasn't even there! "No?" Mr. Chatterly asked. "I'm going to level with you here, Jeff. Anything you tell me stays in this room. I'm not allowed to repeat anything you say, not to anyone," he leaned in. He probably thought I was going to start pouring out my secrets now that he fed me that line. I looked at him and tried to stop the words, *"What are you serious?"* from coming out of my mouth, if not simply worn on my face.

"We just don't get along," I said plainly.

"Why don't you get along?" he tilted his head. He probably thought he was getting somewhere.

"I don't know. He hates me," I started messing with a puzzle on the desk. It was all geometric shapes that interlocked to be completed. I had done them before at my other school, but hadn't seen once since.

"I wouldn't like getting punched. That might make me feel negative feelings toward someone. But hate is a strong word," Mr. Chatterly leaned on one arm, watching me do the puzzle.

"Yup," I nodded. Wait... I couldn't tell if he thought I was the one who didn't like someone because I was getting punched, or if Devin was...

"What I would like to do is bring Devin in here and we can all talk about how to improve the situation."

"No," I said flatly.

"No? We can have a civil conversation," he nodded. "I think you and Devin might even come away friends," he shrugged.

"I don't think so," I plainly. I knew better. Grown-ups always thought they were going to solve your problems and everyone would have some graham crackers and sing Kumbaya together and hug.

"Well, before we bring him in here, why don't you tell me your side of things, ok? And then he will tell me his side, and then we can come together."

"He's a jerk. The end."

"Well..." Mr. Chatterly tried to stifle a laugh. "There is always more to the story than that. Why do you say he's a jerk?"

217

"Because he is one. He's been a jerk to me since I got here," I shook my head. I was just restating a message I had been trying to convey all along.

"Well... you did just punch him. Repeatedly, I might add. I know Devin, and he is a star student, so maybe he just feels a little threatened by a new student, and you are misunderstanding how he is feeling." I couldn't believe this crap! Was this one of those hidden camera shows? This guy thought I was the bully! I paused my puzzle and stared a flat stare at Mr. Chatterly. I was just the kid who was fighting back from being bullied. I kind of hoped my parents would be called in, so my father could put this guy in his place!

"What about me? I'm the new kid, I get dropped into your stupid school and instantly like my whole class hates me, are you talking to them about misunderstanding my feelings?" I shot him a stare. He had no idea what to do, and it showed.

"Ok. Well... I think we all need some time to think about this situation. So I'm going to go ahead and have someone pick you up for the day, ok? You go home and think about things, and I will do some more detective work and we will talk tomorrow. And Devin will be here when we talk, so just be ready to have a calm grown-up conversation together. Ok, I want you to think about that." I wanted to punch Mr. Chatterly now. I was in shock.

I turned my gaze down to the puzzle and put the last two pieces in place. Mr. Chatterly stared at the puzzle for a moment.

"You did that while we were talking?" he asked with some kind of interest. I had no interest in fielding any more questions. I got up and went into the hall and waited. Mr. Chatterly lead me back to the office.

"You can wait here," he pointed at a bench outside the office. "I believe your Grandmother is picking you up shortly." Mr. Chatterly raised his eyebrows in a way that said 'Take that'.

"What?!" I exclaimed. "What about my mom?"

"Shhh... We called and your Grandmother picked up and insisted on picking you up herself," he nodded.

"That isn't legal! She's not my mom or dad!"

218

"Well, she is your Grandmother, though."

"So?" I shook my head. What did that have to do with anything?

"Jeff... just wait here," Mr. Chatterly instructed, and he stepped into the office. This was getting more ridiculous all the time! In a moment he came back out with Devin, who looked quite chipper, though he was holding an ice pack on his face. An ice pack? Where was the ice pack for my aching hand?

I sat, boiling angry, waiting for Grandmother. When her big white Oldsmobile pulled up, I could tell Kim was driving with Grandmother in the back seat and a scarf on her head, sunglasses on. I climbed up front. We drove away in silence. Kim wouldn't even make eye contact.

"You are not the only one in this family!" Grandmother finally broke the silence as we turned the corner, the school out of sight. "Your thoughtless actions affect other people! I have spent a lifetime building a reputation and all you and your mother seem to be capable of doing is torpedoing my years of work!" Torpedo... I wasn't sure what that meant, but it sounded like war stuff.

She didn't say another word on the way home, so I sat quietly. When the car pulled up to the house and stopped I slowly opened the car door. I wasn't sure what happened next. Did I go to my room and play? Did I sit on a chair? As I was walking up the walk I saw mother's car down the drive, she was home. Now I was in trouble! At least I knew Grandmother couldn't really do anything to me, but my mother...

I slunk inside the house. Mother was waiting, arms folded.

"Are you trying to make my life difficult? It's bad enough living in your Grandmother's house, but couldn't you just...not cause problems?" she said in what could only be described as yelling in a whisper. "You punched another child?" I nodded. "I suppose this was foreseeable." She shook her head. "Did he punch you first?" she asked, somewhat hopeful.

"He stole my bike." I replied.

"He what?" She exclaimed, dropping her folded arms.

"He stole my bike. Then he joked that I should ride bikes with him after school and laughed at me, so I punched him," I explained.

"When did he steal your bike?" she narrowed her eyes, assessing the validity of my story.

"Yesterday, at the Orchard."

"Who is he?" she asked.

"Devin!" I couldn't believe she wouldn't just know who my nemesis was.

"Devin, who gave you the football at your party?" she asked confused.
"Yeah," I said in a condescending tone.

"Maybe you are wrong," she implied.

"I'm not wrong! He stole it with the rest of his friends right after they threw rocks at me and knocked me over. They all hate me! Why doesn't anyone listen to me!" I grumbled.

"The boys from up here?" she motioned to the streets behind ours.

"Yes! They all hate me, I have no friends!"

"I thought you had a group of friends by the park..."

"No, they all joined Devin's gang."

"Gang?!" she questioned with concern.

"Yes," I plopped down in a chair. It was exhausting trying to explain things you had been explaining for so long.

"Good," Grandmother came in the door. "Someone who can whip him properly.

"Rose, no one is going to whip anyone," mother rolled her eyes.

"Well, someone had ought to! You are raising a bully!" she said pulling her scarf off.

"He's the one being bullied, Rose," my mother folded her arms again.

"If he were my son, I would whip him until he can't stand upright. I would punish him so bad for this behavior!"

"If I were your son, that would be punishment enough!" I folded my arms, to match my mother.

"Wha!" Grandmother gasped. "I don't know where they learn this kind of disrespect, but I can guess it isn't from their father's family."

"Excuse me, woman?" my mother turned and faced down my Grandmother. I froze. I knew exactly where the battle lines existed, and when they were crossed. Both of them were standing on the crossing!

"Bullied. He has been going around disrespecting teachers, bullying other kids, fraternizing with some homeless vagrant in the woods."

"What on earth are you talking about?" my mother shook her head.

"When you move into this house, you act a certain way, with a level of propriety."

"Propriety! The kind that lends license to overstepping a parent's right to parent?" mother cocked her head. I wished to hide under a pillow where I could safely watch them both explode.

"Meaning you are the parent?" Grandmother smirked. "No child of mine would spit in the face of hospitality, after being taken in off the streets, and torpedo the legacy they have worked to build their whole life."

"Off the streets?!" my mother laughed. "We moved in to do you a favor during a difficult time of grief, Rose. If you even recall! Though I'm kind of wondering what on earth we were thinking, wanting to live close to you!"

"Excuse me! This is still my house, is it not?" Grandmother questioned, shaking her head.

"Yes. It is. And make no mistake, I wouldn't want you holding that over me a moment longer than needs be!" my mother stormed out of the room.

I wasn't sure if I should move and draw attention to myself, but then I figured it was safer to be with mother. I hurried after her once I realized I would be alone with Grandmother.

"Sit in your room and read until your brother gets home. I have work to do. I'll be in my room," mother instructed as we walked. I complied without a word.

24. No Ducks Were Harmed in the Writing of This Book

My mother took us to dinner at a drive-in while my father was busy doing something at Grandmother's. It was a treat. I was all confused. I think Mother was upset at what I had done but was secretly rewarding me for being a bigger upset to Grandmother than I was to her. It was an odd situation to navigate. We took our takeout dinner to the park to eat. Mother also had brought a loaf of bread to feed it to the ducks.

Maybe thirty or forty ducks clamored around our bench. All fighting to be closest to us, yet none coming within three feet. They wanted what we had, but they weren't about to risk being in arms reach of us.

There was an odd pecking order to the ducks. For the most part, it was the big white ducks that were first in line. They simply shoved other ducks out of the way, giving little notice to the smaller ducks, or quieter ducks the same size. They were quite plump and practically barked at other ducks to get out of the way as they dove for pieces of bread thrown into the midst of the flock.

The front row of white ducks were broken up by some of the smaller brown ducks, but only the ones who were quite feisty. They opened their bills and hissed, spreading their wings out to look more intimidating. There were other ducks that seemed more docile, and shy, grouped in the back. In the middle of the flock were ducks that seemed to be happy with whatever was going on, regardless of their size, color, ranking, or attitude problems. We tried to throw pieces right in front of ducks that we thought seemed to be the most deserving.

"You know, these ducks were once wild. They have been domesticated though, almost to the point where they can no longer survive without people feeding them so they can fatten up for winter," mother explained, tearing off pieces of bread.

"Really?" I asked.

"Yup. When I was a kid, you maybe got a duck or two, one of the brave ducks, but the more people started feeding them, the more the ducks have gotten used to it. It's like evolution, they have an easy means of food, so they adapt to it. The ones that are willing to come close are the ones that benefit. The ones who fly away and won't come close still have to try to find their own food."

"When it gets colder and fewer people come to feed them, don't they just starve?" I asked.

"Well, that is the tricky thing, isn't it? The wild ducks have a greater struggle all the time, but they know how to hunt for themselves. The tame ducks have a feast given to them, and only risk starving for a few months or so. But if they get all fattened up, like that one," she motioned to a large white duck. "Well, I think he will be just fine in February. He's figured out how to play the game right."

"I heard you went crazy on some kid," Joseph inquired casually, tossing a piece of bread.

"Joseph," Mother warned.

"Yeah... Devin. Stole my bike," I said plainly.

"Guess I should have stayed on the bus. I heard it was pretty good," he laughed. Wait... was Joseph being nice to me? Was this some kind of bonding moment? I didn't know what to make of the situation.

"It's not cool to hit someone else," my mother interjected.

"I heard it was pretty rad!" Joseph laughed.

I smiled.

"Well, whatever your father may have told you, violence isn't the answer," mother shook her head and tossed another piece of bread into the swell of ducks. They clamored and squawked.

When we got home, mother drove us through the back door and upstairs, like cattle. Father was in the upstairs parlor with a drink in hand, looking through a file folder, barely paying attention to the noise we made as we got ready for bed. I climbed into my bed and laid quietly, straining to hear them.

Finally, I decided to creep to the bedroom door, joined by Joseph. I leaned as close to the doorway as I could without being seen.

"I've been all over those woods. I couldn't find anyone. That shack looks like raccoons live there," father sounded tired. What was he doing in the woods?

"Are you sure?" my mother asked.

"Yeah. It doesn't matter. Part of the zoning ordinance calls for cutting down most of that woods away."

"What?" I blurted out in shock. Joseph darted backward as if he had encountered a snake. He slipped back into bed silently. My father looked at me down the hall in limited surprise.

"The zoning ordinance... the woods will be part of the housing expansion in the spring. They are going to start cutting down wood next week. Give any vagrants a chance to leave," his tone was thinly veiled. "Did I hear something about you getting into a fight today?" father asked.

I nodded.

"You better remember what I said about not starting a fight, only defending yourself," he nodded toward me.

"I didn't use what you taught me," I defended my actions.

"Well... then why did I teach you any of it?" he drained his drink dry, standing up. "Go to bed," he pushed the parlor door shut.

I dragged myself away and slipped back into bed.

They were going to cut down the woods? Where would I go to play? We just needed to move off the hill!

"Hey," Joseph rolled over, "Did you really make friends with Hobo Bob?" he said with a good amount of doubt in his voice but just a tinge of hopeful curiosity.

"Why does anyone suddenly care what I do? I get beat up, no one cares. Someone says I talked to a hobo in the woods and suddenly everyone wants to know all about stuff?" I pulled my covers tight.

"I dunno, just curious," Joseph shrugged. "Most people don't even think he's real. It's kind of weird that people even care. If we lived in California, and he lived under a tree on the beach, we would just call him Surfer Bob or something. And everyone would give him high-fives and stuff.

Come on, did you really see him, in there?"

"Hobo Bob?" I asked.

"Duh!" Joseph had very little patience.

"I don't know," I darted his inquiry.

"But like you play in there a lot. Have you seen him, or like people near the shack?" he had never so interested in anything I did before this. While I frequently wished for that kind of attention from him, I was also weary of it because once he had information, he could use it against me and often did.

"I see people walking through there and stuff," I shrugged.

"Yeah, I bet he is an urban legend. You know what that is, right?"

"Yeah, I guess," I was loosely familiar with the term.

So much interest over something so trivial as to where a person lived, or rather what they lived in. We *all* lived on the hill, he simply lived a hundred feet to the right, and instead of a huge house with a massively well maintained yard and gardens, he resided in a one room shack and had a tangle of wildly overgrown woods. It wasn't right how people with silver spoons and crystal with gold rims to drink wine from, looked down on someone else just because he lived on the other side of the road and pooped in a coffee can.

I could come up with all kinds of differences between Bob and people who lived on the hill, but it kept coming down to barely any difference between them at a minutely human level. Simply put, we all lived on the Hill.

I wrestled with thoughts of fairness, and what Bob was to do now as I drifted off to sleep.

All day during school, I watched my back. I heard whispers and snickers constantly. Every time I turned around and looked to my left or right, I seemed to catch someone pointing at me, then suddenly break eye contact and pretend to pay attention to whatever was going on. I went to the bathroom four or five times, easily, partly so I could get a break from them, but also because my stomach was not interested in retaining food. My stomach was a ball of nervous nausea waiting for Cougars to attack me from behind at any moment. I envisioned them grabbing me in the hall and dragging me into a classroom or a closet.

I skipped lunch altogether and hid in the bathroom. No one seemed to notice I was gone. My stomach grumbled with hunger and nervousness, which actually seemed to cancel each other out and resolve my need to frequent the bathroom the rest of the afternoon.

I kept my head down and ignored everyone around me while doing math. Suddenly, there was a buzz in the classroom. Mrs. Potts stepped out the door, quietly closing it behind her. A kid ran to the small window in the solid door and peeked out.

"She's gone!" the kids grinned. Devin stood and slowly pulled a glass out of his desk. He walked to my desk, careful to not spill it. I kept my eyes down and kept working. It seemed as though everyone in the class was forming a giant circle around me. Devin set the glass down on my desk. A strange brown watery milky liquid sloshed over the edge and spotted my math sheet.

"Drink it, bathroom-boy," he instructed, leaning on my desk.

"Nope," I kept trying to figure out my problem, though I had lost my ability to focus, so I faked it.

"You have what's coming to you. Drink it freak!" he slammed his hand down on my desk, causing the liquid to slosh and spill a little more on my desk. I slowly looked up. His face had various bruises and scrapes. It was the first I had looked at him.

"Nice face," I smirked.

"Yeah, you're going to get into a ton of trouble for that too! Now drink this, or I will pound your face in! And I'm not alone this time!" he nodded toward pretty much the entire class. Their faces were either intense and trying to look as menacing as a child can, or alight with glee that I might be forced to drink the concoction.

"You weren't alone on the bus either," I turned back to the paper and scratched some random numbers down.

"Drink it!" he picked it up and shoved it at my face. The liquid spilled down the front of my desk and onto my pants. I jumped up. "Oh look! Bathroom-boy peed his pants! Waaaa!" he mocked me with a baby cry. "You want your bike back? Drink it." I stared at him, a dark intense gaze. I wasn't going to be baited into attacking him again, not in class where he had a dozen kids on his side, who would gladly testify for him. "We made it special for you. It took all day to make!" He smiled. "I had lots of help."

I didn't move a muscle.

"He doesn't want to drink it," Aaron shrugged.

"He's drinking it," Devin growled.

"Shut up!" Jacob pushed Aaron.

"What?" Aaron recovered his footing. "Mrs. Potts will be back soon. He isn't going to drink it, and we're all gonna get busted." Aaron shifted and sat back down in his seat.

"Maybe *you* should drink it!" Jacob got in Aaron's face.

"What's your problem?" Aaron waved him off.

"You're defending your boyfriend?" Jacob mocked. "Are you a Cougar or what?"

"Yeah, but..." Aaron looked around with a deep breath.

"But what?!" Jacob demanded. Devin was now watching Jacob and Aaron.

"Whatever," Aaron leaned back in his chair. I wasn't so sure Aaron was defending me, but he was distracting Devin, which I was happy for. I reached over and knocked the bottom of the glass. Devin jumped and almost all of the liquid dumped out, splashing on Devin's pant leg and shoes. Devin flung the remaining content at me in a fit of rage. I wiped it off my face, it didn't smell particularly horrible, but I wasn't about to taste it either.

"What the hell, Aaron!" Devin shouted. Aaron smirked.

"She's coming!" the lookout yelled. People scrambled back to their seats.

"I want my bike back," I said calmly, wiping the spot from my math sheet onto my pants, and sitting back down.

"Screw you!" Devin gruffed as Mrs. Potts came back in the room.

"What was that, Devin?" she questioned.

"Nothing," he stared at me. I didn't look up the rest of the afternoon.

The day was getting close to ending, there was only about an hour left when the door opened. "Mrs. Potts, I need Devin and Jeff for a minute," the office lady pursed her lips.

"Boys," Mrs. Potts motioned us to go.

"Grab your backpacks." The office lady added. I had been waiting for it to come all day, but half hoped they had forgotten.

"You're gonna get it now," Devin whispered as we headed out the door. We silently walked down the hall to Mr. Chatterly's office. My mother was just coming out of the door as we arrived. My stomach sank.

"I appreciate it, Mr. Chatterly. Hopefully it will work," she was saying, her back to us.

"Sometimes you just have to think like a child," Mr. Chatterly smirked and then noticed us walking up. "Ah, boys. Come on in," he welcomed us.

"Sweetie," my mother raised her eyebrows. She walked down the hall and sat on a bench. What on earth had then been discussing? I forced myself to follow Devin and Mr. Chatterly inside the office, sparing an inquisitive glance to my mother.

"Ok, boys. I've talked to Mrs. Potts, and Devin, your mother on the phone, and Jeff, your mother just now," Mr. Chatterly started, as he shut the door. "Mrs. Potts says you have no problem with each other. Devin's mother doesn't know who Jeff even is, and Jeff's mother says Devin has been picking on Jeff for weeks. So it seems the two of you are the only two who really knows what is going on. So, what's shakin'? Come on, let's get it out. Why are the two of you fighting?" Mr. Chatterly interlocked his fingers on the desk in front of us.

"He just attacked me on the bus!" Devin feigned a shocked expression.

"Yeah, because he bullies me. He ruined my birthday party by being there, and he stole my bike!" I sank back in my chair.

"He sent his brother to beat me up!" Devin threw his hands up.

"After you chased me into the woods, and I hid in a drain pipe while you poked me with sticks!" I glared.

"You mean where you play with Hobo Bob?" Devin made a face, raising his eyebrows.

"Boys! Calm down..." Mr. Chatterly shushed.

"I'm tired of it. They locked me in a car trunk."

"I didn't even take your bike, you left it on the playground, so we put it by the car for you," Devin looked so innocent, I wanted to jump on him and punch his face, again.

"Bull!" I objected.

"Jeff!" Mr. Chatterly tried to get in between us from across the desk. "I don't even know who to believe in all of this. Devin, do you pick on Jeff? Or do anything he might be confusing for picking on him?"

"No! We've tried to play with him, but he just like shoves us and runs away and stuff. I gave him a football for his birthday. Ask his mom, I offered to play football with him."

I rolled my eyes. I was going to vomit in rage!

"Jeff, have you looked for your bike there?"

"It's not there," I insisted.

"Oh, it's there," Devin smiled a sickening smile that gave me pause and concern.

"Jeff, maybe you should go back and look where Devin said they left it and thank him for putting it somewhere safe." I wanted to laugh like a maniac, this was ridiculous! How could anyone buy the act Devin put on?

"Is that the car where you threw rocks at me? The car you locked me in the trunk of?" I challenged Devin.

"What are you talking about?" Devin shook his head.

"Well... this isn't the first time your names have come down to my office, so I just don't know what to believe. Since this school has a zero tolerance for fighting, I'm going to have to suspend you both." Mr. Chatterly threw his hands up.

"What?!" Devin exclaimed. I shrugged. It was time I wouldn't have to put up with the Cougars? I was sold.

"This isn't fair!" Devin continued. "I didn't do anything!"

"Oh please," I rolled my eyes. He shot me a look of disgust and mouthed something at me silently.

"Enough, both of you. Devin, you wait here and you will ride the bus home, Jeff you can leave with your mom. You are both suspended until Monday, and I will be meeting with each of you on progress reports when you get back." Progress reports were like the elementary version of probation. You went on progress report for like two or three months and if you repeated your sin, something else happened. Eventually, it would all lead up to getting kicked out of the school. I casually strolled out of the office. My mother and I didn't speak. We just got in the car and drove. We were blocks away before she broke the silence.

"I talked to Bob today." What did she just say? What did she mean she talked to Bob?! "I met him in the woods. He's nice enough. I can see why you would be friends." I was confused. She didn't actually go to the woods and meet Bob. That was insane. "He agreed that he shouldn't be hanging out with children anymore, and he was going to pack up and go away. Living in the woods isn't a good place to live for, well, for anyone. He's gotten sick. So he needs to go be with his family and rest. We agreed its good timing since they are cutting the woods down anyway." Bob didn't have a family to go to! That's why he lived in the woods. She was lying. I knew she was.

I needed to look for my bike and swing by the woods before the bus came. I shook my head and stared out the window. My mother kept glancing at me. She probably thought I didn't notice her efforts to evaluate me, but I knew she was lying.

25. Desperate Times

I spent the entire weekend grounded to the house. I wasn't allowed to leave even for a moment without being accounted for. Mother made remarks to father about having talked to Bob and that he had left the woods to return to his family. The whole thing seemed like a production for my benefit. Grown-ups thought they were so clever. They thought tricks that worked when you were four still worked when you were much older!

I was still sure she was lying, but being grounded meant I couldn't go to the woods to find out anything for myself. I was confident I would find Bob there, first chance I got to go. In addition to being grounded, mother wouldn't even let Joseph go look for my bike, not that he would have, but I was dying to prove Devin a liar. Monday morning, I had a plan.

I set out for the bus like every morning. Halfway there, Joseph had stopped paying attention to me. I started walking slower until there was a distance between us. I slipped behind a set of hedges and let other kids continue. I waited patiently. I shifted my backpack and pretended to look through it as if I had forgotten something, just in case anyone was watching. I checked and rechecked every pocket multiple times. When I heard the bus pull up, I made sure I was concealed from sight. I carefully held my spot until I heard the door close and the bus roar off into the distance.

I came out from behind the hedge and headed toward the Orchard. The Cougars were all on that bus, and the hill would be empty. It was a liberating feeling to walk my own streets without *any* fear of being chased down and attacked! However, there was still an edge of alert that a grown-up might see me. Hey, I was just a kid who missed the bus and would have to walk to school now, which was why I needed to look around the Orchard for my bike. I wondered just how late I might be able to get away with. I would have to stay away from our street of course. I climbed the playground and carefully looked around. I might just be a kid who missed the bus, but if an adult saw me on the playground it might be another thing!

I decided to seek the cover of the tall grass. I headed toward the old Turtle Lair, kicking a rather perfectly round rock along the way. It was perfect for kicking. Some rocks were so flat, they just tumbled to a stop within a few feet. This thing really bounced as it rolled. I could get it a good fifty feet per kick!

I looked through the grass looking for my bike. It wasn't where I had concealed it! I kept looking, and my anxiety piqued. I made a sweeping circle through the edge of the grass, along the ditch, and around the car. Then suddenly I saw a junked up bike. It looked like something that had been run over by a train and then decorated by graffiti artists... female graffiti artists, as it was mostly spray painted pink. As I got closer, I confirmed to myself that it was, in fact, my bike, or what was left of it! My heart sank. My blood boiled and tears welled up. My frustrations came running. Fury surged through me! A deafening primal scream filled the air, it was seconds before I recognized it as my own. I kicked the wretched bike over. I refused to acknowledge it. I stalked off back to the playground. I sat on the edge of the slide tower. I didn't care if adults saw me now. I hated every last Cougar. I couldn't let this go unanswered. I had to take revenge. I had to exact justice, and soon. *How*, was the question. I looked around the playground, their playground, their grass, their turtle lair.

I leaped from the playground and headed back toward Grandmother's. I slipped through the property behind Grandmother's and sneaked up on the carriage house. I surveyed the back of the house. It seemed mother and father had already left. It was quiet. The lawn smelled of freshly watered grass. I quickly darted up the side of the building. I prayed the door was unlocked, and luckily, it was. I hurried inside, quietly closing the door behind me. The front part of the carriage house was a finished room, kind of like an office, sitting area. I needed supplies. I crept to grandfather's work bench and began looking for anything that might help me. I found a hammer and pry bar... I put them into my backpack. I wondered how long I had before the school would report me as missing. There was a torch and sparker. I had seen Grandfather use them before. I stuffed them into my backpack too. I moved to the front door and cautiously peeked out the window. I turned back and looked at the room. I picked up the phone, the dial tone buzzed at me. If anyone from the school called, they would have a tough time getting through with the phone off the hook. I set the handset down with a smile.

I slipped back out and headed back the way I had come. The jog back was impossible with the added weight. My backpack looked like it had bricks in the bottom, the way it weighed down, struggling to fall to the ground. I had to slow down. I crept around each corner, making sure no one was walking or driving my way. I sneaked into the grass and sat on the edge of the lair. I pulled my supplies out and set to work. I forced the pry bar into the edge of a board and started throwing my weight against it. It creaked and groaned before the nails let out a rusty yell as the board popped up. I worked on the other end, going back and forth until the board finally flopped off. I set to work repeating the process.

A few boards in, I could see sticks were under the edge of the lair. It was curious. I studied the edge of the old wood and found loose dirt and rocks. I cleared it away and pulled out a few sharpened sticks, short like daggers, as long as small spears. Their tips looked green still. They must have been made last night. I smiled. I had plans for them too. Time flew by, it must have been two hours since the bus left by the time I had the lair taken apart.

I piled the boards together in the tall grass and stamped the grass flat all around it. I took out the torch and sparker. I turned the torch on and clicked the sparker. The torch burst into a long feathered flame, making a loud rushing sound. I held the flame on the boards. Within a minute, the board was keeping its own flame that slowly danced up the side of it. I moved the torch to another board. In a few minutes, the board was slowly roasting away. The torch was hot! I dipped the end in the water in the ditch, it hissed and sizzled with a plume of vapor. I put it into my backpack and took the small bundle of weapons. I headed off to the playground.

I snapped the weapons in half, which was becoming a second nature task, and placed them on the slide tower in a pile. I took out the torch and looked around. The neighborhood was still nice and quiet. I sparked up the torch and set the weapons ablaze. I smiled as I watched the flame slowly consuming the pieces. Then I picked them up one by one and shook them until the flame died. I placed them back in the pile of ashes with the ends sticking out so they would be easily identifiable. Hopefully, the Cougars would see them and then immediately run to the lair to check on things.

With that thought, I looked up at the lair. There was smoke pouring from the grass. It was like a pillar into the sky! I ran back.

The fire was raging, and worse. It was spreading into the grass! I tried to stomp it out, but it didn't seem to be doing any good. I looked around for some idea, something I could do. I ran to the ditch and tried to throw water from the stream to the blaze with my hands, to no avail. Maybe it would just die out on its own. I didn't suppose that was very likely.

I looked around for a bucket, or a bottle, or anything I could put water in. It was just then I heard yelling. I looked through the grass and saw two women, out for a walk, running toward the smoke. I slipped into the grass and headed down the ditch! I didn't think they had seen me. I was well hidden. I managed to get well downstream, I dropped the torch as I worked my way up the hill's edge and to the main road. I could see the commotion in the distance as I hurried down the road, toward the school. My heart was pounding. I was sure someone had seen me. I tried to remain calm as I tossed the tools out of my backpack and into the bushes.

Somewhere along the way, I got control of myself. I was in a hurry to get distance from the Hill, but I wasn't in any hurry to get to school. Maybe I could give the Cougars some hints or clues about what I had been doing all morning. I approached the school slowly. I could hear kids at recess. It must have been first recess. It would be easy to sneak into the school that way. I hurried down the sidewalk. A teacher blew a whistle and signaled me toward the playground. I held up a hand a nodded in compliance. I made it! With soot on my fingers and a smile on my face, I made it. Devin was going to freak.

Mrs. Potts didn't seem to notice that I hadn't been in class all morning, but had suddenly appeared. Maybe she thought she was having an off day. I kept waiting for someone to rush into the classroom and order me down to Mr. Chatterly's office where the police and fire department would be waiting, but it never happened. No one could prove anything now. Devin could suspect and insist it was me all he wanted, I would just sit in that chair and play dumb, just the way he had done.

The day finally ended without much of a chance to make any hints that any Cougars would have picked up on. Devin seemed to be avoiding eye contact with me. Maybe suspension had gotten to him after all, but then what was up with the weapons cache?

The bus ride home was as uneventful as the day at school had been. I couldn't believe the insane luck I was having! Surely this was all about to come crashing down on me at any moment.

After dinner was far too long to have pushed my luck when the knock on the door came. I beat Kim to the door and reluctantly opened it. I wasn't overly shocked to find the fire marshal, a sheriff's deputy, and a couple of neighbors.

"That's him!" One of the neighbors, a woman will curly bluish silver hair pointed at me. "He's the one who burned down the playground, nearly set fire to the entire neighborhood!"

"Son, I'm going to need you to put you hands up and come with us." The Deputy said pulling out his handcuffs.

Or at least, that was how I saw the evening going down. Much to my chagrin there were no knocks at the door, no phone calls, nothing. I seemed to have somehow gotten away with the whole thing. The whole horrible thing. I had a lump of guilt sitting square in my stomach. I tried to rid myself of it through several breath sighs. I told myself I didn't need to worry because I hadn't really damaged anything but the Cougars makeshift weapons, and hide-out. They practically deserved it. Of course they would be looking for someone to blame, but my absence had seemed to go unnoticed, so they might start looking to blame a menacing hobo whose home was about to be destroyed.

I laid in bed that night wondering if what I had done was genius or a horrific mistake. I played out various scenarios in my head of Devin coming to the playground, surveying the smoking wreckage like a battlefield, and then bringing that battle to the playground the next day. Maybe he would wait until I was alone in the bathroom and the Cougars would attack me together. Maybe he would see the damage and back-off, thinking he had awoken a warrior inside of me.

I somehow shoved all of my fears into a ball and managed to fall asleep.

26. All Things...

"Rose, I know this will come as a shock to you, however you actually don't own this hill. Maybe once upon a time you owned a chunk of it, but that has been *decades!* We have every right to be here," I could hear mother as I came down the back stairs. I could hear the muffled raised voice all the way upstairs. As I came into the dining room, I found Joseph sitting at the table, nibbling French toast, kicking his feet with a huge smile.

"How dare you! How dare you live in my house and speak to me this way!" Grandmother practically spat the words back at my mother.

"What's going on?" I asked Joseph.

"Huh? Oh, Grandmother found out that we are building a house on the Hill. I guess the zoning thing came this morning because Grandmother is on the council thing." Joseph kept his eyes fixed on the scene through the doorway. I sat down at my place, my plate already waiting for me. I watched the commotion.

"How dare you try to control where other people live. Where your grandchildren live!" mother shot back, "and what schools they go to."

"Oh, come now. That hellian of yours is bound for public schooling. You might as well have the address to match it," Grandmother huffed.

"Wow, you really think you are this much better than everyone, don't you?" mother put her hands on her hips.

"Oh, Dear, you are confusing my assessment of your lack of parenting for snobbery," Grandmother said in a composed tone.

"Excuse me? You want to talk about parenting? With the lot of ego maniacs and money grubbers you've raised? And the horde of miscreant grandchildren they are raising?" Mother nearly laughed. "You are all perfect for each other!"

"You ought not throw stones, Dear," Grandmother waved her off.

"Oh, I'm living in your glass house, don't worry I can't forget it, not even for a second. You would never allow me to!" Mother bobbed her head.

"You needn't worry about it. You are so eager to not live under my roof, you throw my hospitality on the fire every chance you get. Don't feel the need to do me any favors for having lived here. You can move out on your own, and live wherever you desire," Grandmother shook her head.

"Oh, wouldn't *that* be nice!" Mother giggled, putting a hand on cheek.

"Where's Father?" I asked Joseph.

"Don't know," Joseph shrugged.

"Wonderful, you can leave at once," Grandmother clapped her hands together. "Kim will help you gather the boys' things while they are at school."

"Why wait?" mother stormed out of the room and down the hall, away from us. We assumed she was heading up stairs.

"School," Kim entered the room to hurry us along.

I quickly started stuffing my face with French toast while Joseph put his jacket and backpack on. We hurried out the door with me still chewing, and pulling my backpack on.

"So you think we are moving while we are at school?" I asked.

"Probably. We'll probably stay in a hotel or something while they build a house. I don't know." Joseph hurried along.

A hotel, that would be a nice break. Maybe my parents would not like being homeless and living in a hotel and they would decide to buy a house that was already built, one that was not on the hill. Maybe I would have to change schools again, and the next one I could start with a blank slate and do it right this time. I could find the cool kids and survey who they liked the least and make sure I was on the side of the playground that was the least likely to get me into a cycle of troubles.

Devin kept his eyes low as we got on the bus. He and the other Cougars sat quietly. They whispered still, but the tone seemed much more reverent, rather than malicious. As they got off the bus, Devin walked slowly, cautiously, like a cat on a wet sidewalk. The entire morning felt different.

During library, we filed down the hall quietly. I expected the Cougars to advance forward in the group of kids and surround me from all sides, pushing me into the wall, or shoving me into every girl's restroom we passed, but it never came.

"Hey," Aaron nodded and sat down at the reading table I was sitting at.

"Hey," I replied. It was the first real communication since he joined the Cougars.

"Check this out." He slid an open book across the table. It was opened to a page about how to make a survival tent out of an animal carcass. It had a crude pencil illustration and everything.

"Gnarly!" I nodded in approval.

"This thing is full of cool survival stuff. I check it out like once a month," he grinned.

"Awesome." I looked around to see if I was about to be ambushed.

"It has something in here about using a coffee can to filter your own piss into drinking water." He turned some pages, searching.

"Grodie!" I smirked, but with interest.

"I know, huh?" he smiled. It was like we didn't miss a beat. I felt like my friend had simply left the table for a moment, but had come back after some distraction. There wasn't anything really to say about it. Sure it was complex, but simple at the same time. It was like how a boomerang came back.

It was a simple enough concept, you couldn't really explain it, and trying to would just take the fun out of it anyway.

The rest of the day was pretty laid back. It was almost as if the Cougars had disbanded. Devin and Jacob seemed to only be hanging out with each other, Jacob and Nick were hanging out with some other boys, and Jason was playing soccer with kids in his own class at recesses. Even though I seemed to regain my friend, I wasn't going to run out and meet him on the playground after school just yet.

After I got home from school I grabbed a snack and set out for the woods. *I was being chased by a bear.*

It smelled the extra food I had stashed in my pockets before I made my escape from the prison. I darted quickly through the trees, trying to get upwind. There was a mountain man I had made friends with years ago in these hills. He taught me all about surviving on your own. It didn't matter what was chasing me, I had the advantage of being aware, and being well prepared. I could use the situation to make that bear into a feast that would last a month. His bones and teeth would make weapons and jewelry, his fur would make a blanket. All I needed was to lure him toward my friend, and he would help me take care of everything.

The wind whipping through the woods was cold and bitter. My fingertips were growing numb as I scaled the rocky slopes. I flattened myself against the rocky face to keep from being blown off the dangerous terrain by a rogue gust of wind. I hoped the bear hadn't changed position and was picking up my scent, but I was pretty sure I had a fix on him. As long as I kept the bear in my sight, I was in control.

Suddenly, I slipped! I strained and threw myself forward, trying to regain traction. I felt like a bat dangling from a branch. I inched my toes to better foothold on the slope, my fingers in a death grip on the ledge above. I pulled myself up with a heave and crested the ridge. A gnarled hook clanked against the rock next to my hand. It was my friend, the Mountain man! I grabbed the hook and he helped pull me up to safety.

"What in the world?" he grumped.

"Boy am I glad to see you!" I dusted off my clothes.

"Yeah, well..." he turned with a shrug.

"I'm being chased by a bear," I explained.

"I thought I smelled something foul."

"Well, he smelled the jerky I swiped from the prison pantry when I broke out. Oh, yeah, I kind of escaped from the prison this morning."

"Is that where you've been?" he inquired.

"Well, I ran into a bit of trouble," I smirked.

"A bit, you say?"

"A bit," I smiled wider. "I made friends with one of the guards."

"Always good to make a friend." He sat down holding his chest, trying to catch his breath.

"You ok?" I asked.

"Me? Oh, sure. Just a little winded."

"I heard you weren't feeling well and might leave the hills..."

"These hills, have been my home..." he smiled looking around at the trees. "Help me back to my shack, would you?" He strained to get to his feet. I went right to his aid. It seemed like a struggle to get back.

"Are you doing ok, boy?" Bob asked.

"I'm fine! Are *you* ok?" I inquired.

"I mean, have you stopped running away? Are you safe now?" he tightened his hand's grip on my shoulder.

"I think so. You taught me how to take on the mountain," I assured my friend. We reached the shack. He laid down and closed his eyes, wincing quietly.

"Bob?" I asked.

"Hmm?" he replied, without opening his eyes.

"Are you ok, Bob?"

"I'll be just fine," his breathing slowed down and there was a touch of pain with each breath.

"I can get help," I said with concern.

"I don't think there is time for help, Jeffery. I don't think it would come for me anyway. It's ok, I'm an old man. I've lived here on this hill a long time. It's about time I go. You can take it from here, can't you?" he winked at me.

"What?" I challenged.

"You'll be ok. You are a strong one. Lots of fight in ya." He reached up and flopped his arm back onto his chest and continued breathing slow and heavy, fading.

"Bob?" I said with urgency. "Bob..." He didn't open his eyes. I didn't know what to do, I burst out of the shack door and looked around wildly. I took off running down the hill, dodging trees and bushes like a forest animal dancing.

At the bottom of the hill was an apartment building with a pool and a pay phone. I ran across the grass of lawns and skipped over sidewalks with ease until I reached the phone. I nearly slammed into the metal structure. I grabbed the black handset and dialed nine-one-one.

"Nine-one-one, what is your emergency?"

"Yeah! My friend, I think he is... umm... having a heart attack maybe!" I blurted out, trying to catch my breath.

"Ok, where is your friend?" the operator asked.

"He's in the woods below Carterville Hill!"

"Ok, and what is your name?" she asked.

I froze. "Just get here fast! It's right below the Orchard! I have to get back to him!" I hung up and took a breath before taking off running again. I ran back to the shack, struggling to get back up the hill. I had never gone all the way down through the woods before. It was a twisted root filled rocky mess at the far end. I fought my way through the tangle and crossed back over the hill. I ran back into the shack.

"Bob?! I got help! They are coming!" I yelled, sliding into the doorway.

"Hmm?" he opened his eyes a bit.

"Just don't go!" I pleaded.

"Ok... help is coming?" he wrinkled his forehead at me.

"Yeah!" I assured him. "You have to hang on, ok? You have to teach me about the woods in the snow! And I can bring my Grandfather's axe and help chop wood to keep the shack warm," I explained.

"Well, that sounds good and all. Do me a favor, Jeffery," he tilted his head.

"Yeah?"

"I need you to get back up that hill when they come. You have to hide away, and stay safe. They will take care of me, ok?"

"What?" I asked in confusion.

"You have to head before they get here so you don't get into any more trouble," Bob explained.

"Ok," I said reluctantly.

"You are quite the kid. You know that?" he winked.

"Sure," the sirens were getting louder. I leaned out the door, it sounded like they were getting really close.

"Ok, time to go," he nodded.

"Ok..." I hesitated, looking at my fading friend. I was pretty sure this would be my last moment with him.

"Jeffery...thank you for being a friend," he said with his eyes closed.

"Uh huh..." I choked up. "Thank you too, Bob..."

"Don't be afraid anymore, Jeffery." I was torn between staying and running. When I heard a large truck door shut and boots hit the ground, the decision was made for me. I stepped through the door. Bob's eyes were closed tightly. I took off running. I darted through the woods like running on freshly trimmed lawn. Those woods were mine for as long as they existed!

I climbed up the hill to the edge of the road and tucked myself into brush. I watched as the EMT's disappeared below the descending tree line. My heart pounded in my ears. I moved from bush to bush to get a better view but could still see nothing through the thick trees. I could barely make out men darting back and forth, weaving through the trees, searching for Bob's shack. Neighbors stood at the top of the hill and tried to point out the shack to police and firemen, who relayed directions into their radios. Soon, one of them seemed to locate the tiny building and called the rest to his position. They seemed to be carrying gear into Bob's shack. I felt sudden relief, he would be safe now, taken care of, probably in the best care of his life.

I sat down and caught my breath and pulled the gold elephant out of my pocket, rubbing his red lacquered blanket. I would have sworn the elephant winked at me. I turned my gaze back to the shack. Soon the EMT's could be seen making their way directly downhill in a blurry line. I couldn't tell what was going on. I could hear the back door of an ambulance slam shut, followed by the roar of the large engine as it headed off. In a moment, the ambulances emerged from the tree line and traveled in a pack down the road, the sirens off.

A homeless man probably wasn't a high priority, accounting for the siren's being off, I hoped. Of course, when they had taken my Grandfather away they didn't have the sirens on either.

I was left with nothing but uncertainty. I once again felt like a stranger, visiting a place I didn't belong. I looked around the woods. They seemed colder suddenly. Empty. He wasn't there. I was alone in the woods. It was a strange feeling.

I had no desire to run to the woods after school anymore.

Aaron and I became best friends, and Jacob joined us the next year with a few other students who moved in. I put the gold elephant back on Grandmother's shelf, where I would always know where it was. My family moved into a house already built down the street, and I rode my bike to visit Grandmother nearly every day, if not just to say hi and sneak a few treats. Grandfather stopped visiting my dreams, but I frequently visited the hallowed carriage house and work bench.

I sometimes wondered how Bob was. I had no way of finding out anything. Either he lived or died. If he lived, he was loving room-service in the hospital, or a care center, giving the nurses a hard time. He probably insisted on eating his dinner from a can in his hospital bed. Maybe they would get him cleaned up and give him a job fixing things. Maybe they would put him on a bus to LA where he could live on the warm sandy beaches.

If he died, which I felt might be the more likely, he was surely an angel. Within weeks, kids at school had forgotten all about him, and his legend. In a year or two, I found a collection of friends who barely recalled there being a shack in the woods at all, let alone the hobo who dwelt there.

I alone had known him, and I alone remembered.

I would always spare a glance into those woods when we rode by on bikes for years after.

By high school, the woods were gone and houses stood there. Often times on my way home from a friend's house, I would stop my bike and spare a moment to look at the place the shack had stood, replaced by landscaped trees and bushes. Sometimes, I thought I could see Optimus hiding in the trees, between the houses.

If Bob were an angel, I bet he could be anything we wanted to be, a bird, a giant auto-bot that turned into a diesel... Maybe he followed the bus to and from school, maybe he followed me as a spirit of courage, as a mental concept of strength. Maybe... that was all he had ever been.

The End

I want my gold elephant back...

Made in the USA
Columbia, SC
08 November 2024

46011885R00150